THE EXTRADIMENSIONAL
REAPPEARANCE OF
MARS
PATEL

SHEELA CHARI

Based on the podcast series created by
BENJAMIN STROUSE
CHRIS TARRY
DAVID KREIZMAN
& JENNY TURNER HALL

WALKER BOOKS

FOR SURESH

FROM THE PODCAST

Hello, podcast listeners. Oliver Pruitt here.

Greetings from space!

I hope you're still tuned in.

Because if I know you listeners,

you're the kind who don't give up.

We haven't given up on you, either.

Or on returning to Earth.

There's just one pesky problem to solve:

Where IS Earth?

At least I have my son on board with me—

although Mars made me swear not to reveal that secret.

Oh dear. Did I just do that? SHHH.

To the stars!

---

30 Comments ⊗

staryoda   41 min ago
Mars is ur son???????

allie_j   33 min ago
I knew it

galaxygenius   26 min ago
fake news Mars is fake OP is fake

staryoda   19 min ago
not fake news check the IP address

neptunebaby   15 min ago
I don't get it why can't he find us

andromeda   12 min ago
maybe he doesn't know what's going on

allie_j   9 min ago
u mean he doesn't know about earth : (

LOST IN SPACE

■■■■■ he problem with your voice cracking was that it was
hard to call dibs on the last spaghetti taco.

Which was why Mars and Toothpick lost and Aurora
scored the win.

"No fair, our voices cracked," Mars said. "And I called it
first."

"According to Droney, Mars and I tied," Toothpick said,
referring to the Pruitt drone he had single-handedly captured
and reprogrammed. "But Droney only counts seconds to the
hundredth decimal. If we went further, I edged you out, Mars."

"Who cares what your drone says? No one could hear either
of you," Aurora said gleefully. She tore off the wrapper, and
a lone strand of spaghetti drifted away before she caught it
and put the dish in the microwave. One of the joys of space
travel—floaty food.

It had been close to six months since Mars and his friends

had boarded the *Manu 1* and left the Martian Colony in a state of impending doom. At first it was just a matter of survival on the spaceship. Like having enough food for everyone. But there were other problems, too. JP was spooked by the space toilet. Toothpick wanted to learn how *everything* operated and left training manuals floating around the crew cabin. And Aurora bossed everyone around while Oliver Pruitt holed himself in the flight room with his podcast equipment. He was technically the only one who knew how to fly, but it didn't exactly help since they'd lost Earth's signal right after leaving Mars.

Aurora was furious when she found out. "What do you mean, Earth's *gone*?"

No one was sure. A few moments after takeoff, the signal to Earth had disappeared, leaving the *Manu 1* stranded in space and all contact with Earth and the Colony dead. After consulting the manuals, Toothpick decided there was a malfunction in the shuttle's communication system. "Earth is probably still there. Or not."

"Thanks, Sherlock," Aurora said.

Toothpick said the best thing was to keep track of the months. "Our coordinates have been entered for Earth, and it takes six months to get there. So after six months, maybe we'll be home."

Right now, that was their best plan. Meanwhile, they were left to bicker over the food.

Not everybody joined in.

"Gross," JP said. "I can't believe you guys would fight over a spaghetti taco, two words in my opinion that should never belong in the same sentence."

"If we were on Earth, I'd totally agree," Aurora said. "But since we're stuck in this nightmare called Lost in Space, we have to settle for gross."

"Well, count me out," said JP, who had been repurposing Swedish meatballs and dried vegetables by microwaving them and eating them between pieces of toast. "Right now, sandwiches are about the closest thing to a religious experience I can get here."

"Until you run out of bread," Aurora said. "It's pathetic. We were never supposed to be on board for what, five billion years?"

"Actually, six months," Toothpick corrected, "according to Droney's extrapolation data."

"Affirmative," Droney chirped. "The *Manu 1* has been in flight 178.4 days."

"Does that mean we're close to Earth?" JP asked. "Shouldn't we see something by now?"

"It would appear so," Toothpick said. "But so far, nada."

"I miss training outside," JP said wistfully. "We've been on this ship for so long. Lifting weights is not the same as running down a soccer field."

"And I need a haircut, people," Aurora said, glowering. "I'm not Heidi." She was wearing her hair in braids, but she'd managed to weave colorful plastic strips in them and cut her bangs jagged across her forehead so she still looked like the rebel she was.

"*You* need a haircut?" Mars said, pushing back the black locks curling around his ears. He had taken to cutting his hair himself, but it was still growing at a furious rate.

"The joys of becoming a teenager," Toothpick observed. He didn't seem to mind too much. He had pulled his hair into a small bun while he did experiments in the service module.

They were all changing. Mars had grown taller. Toothpick, too. But Mars was changing in ways he hadn't expected. In the mirror, the face staring back at him had become leaner, his jawline more distinct, until it seemed he was starting to resemble . . . but *that* couldn't be happening. The news he'd found out right before leaving the Colony had been so shocking, he no longer could bring himself to accept it. Besides, wasn't Oliver Pruitt a pathological liar? Which was why Mars had made him swear to keep it secret. The only other person on board who knew was JP, who had been in the room when Oliver Pruitt had told Mars.

"But Mars, why keep it a secret?" JP had asked. "Don't you want Pick and Aurora to know? She'll freak. It'll be entertainment!"

"That's just it," Mars said. "Aurora hates Oliver Pruitt, and Pick isn't exactly a fan. And just wait until we get back to Earth. If word gets out that I might be related to the most hated man in the universe, everyone will be hating on me, too."

JP was skeptical. "It doesn't work that way. Pick and Aurora wouldn't hate on you. I don't."

But Mars was adamant. "We don't have proof. So let's keep it secret for now. When we get back to Earth, I'll talk to my mom." He swallowed. "If she's OK, that is." He hadn't heard from her since the day at the Colony when she had managed to call in for a few seconds before being cut off. There had been no way to contact her after that. It was an unknown that haunted Mars.

"I'm sure your mom is fine," JP said quickly. "She has to be. And listen, bro, your secret is safe with me. Can't speak for Pruitt, though. Liars keep lying, ya know."

Liars *did* keep lying. And Oliver Pruitt surely would keep hatching plans. Which was why Mars was obsessed with keeping an eye on him whenever he could. For all he knew, Oliver Pruitt was lying about Earth disappearing, too.

"There are two enchiladas left if you want one," Toothpick informed Mars.

"Thanks, Pick. Maybe later." Mars floated out of the crew cabin to go check on Oliver Pruitt. He was about to open the hatch to the flight cabin when he was struck by a hurtling shape that nearly sent him into a tailspin. "Cupcake!" Mars yelped. "Watch out!"

Cupcake was young, but she was still the size of a small elephant, with boundless energy. No one even knew when the tardigrade had snuck on board. In fact, no one even knew much about tardigrades, period. The first time Mars and his friends had seen one was at Pruitt Prep. That one was named Muffin, and she was huge and terrifying. When they got to the Colony, they discovered more of these creatures that were equally huge and terrifying. But by then Mars was able to befriend them, and he became conscious of their intelligence and personality. They weren't just immense animals that could live and breathe comfortably on Martian soil; they seemed to have a mysterious acceptance of Mars that he could never quite explain.

Cupcake was no exception. She was bright-eyed (all ten of her eyes) and smart, and her clear favorite was Mars, whom she made a point of charging into at every turn. In space, these leaps of affection became twirls in zero-gravity air.

"Cupcake, you goof," he said, rubbing her back in the spot that she loved. Cupcake responded with a sound halfway between a woof and a grunt.

In the midst of this boisterous greeting, the hatch to the flight deck opened to reveal Oliver Pruitt. While everyone else had seemed to change, Oliver had remained essentially the same. He was the world's most illustrious, brilliant inventor, with a huge cache of money to fund his advanced school, Pruitt Prep, on Earth. He'd launched his most daring experiment: a fully functioning colony on Mars, designed and run entirely by kids. It was a success—until of course the volcano erupted and spewed molten lava, the tunnels collapsed, and a dangerous ash cloud blew over everything. At that point,

Oliver had abandoned the Colony and its inhabitants with an ease that shocked Mars. How could Oliver leave all those kids behind—including Daisy, Julia, Orion, Axel, and . . . Caddie? If they were to survive, they would need to get more oxygen, fix the tunnels, and find enough to eat.

The worst part was that Mars had left them, too. He had boarded the same spacecraft, never dreaming that Caddie wasn't inside with him until it was too late. And now here he was, millions of miles away with no way of knowing whether the Colony had survived all that destruction. It would take a miracle to rebuild. And Caddie—was she OK? It was the other fear that gripped him, along with the absence of his mom. The only way to know for sure was to return some day to Mars. For Caddie.

"The prodigal son," Oliver Pruitt announced dryly, floating calmly outside the flight deck.

"Stop calling me that," Mars said.

"It's just an expression," Oliver said. "It means a person who repents and asks for forgiveness."

"Shouldn't that be you? Shouldn't you be the one who's sorry for what he's done?"

"I've never heard of a prodigal father," Oliver said. "Dads have to make do, I fear."

"Stop saying that, too," Mars said. "I don't want anyone to hear you."

"Mars, it's like I was saying on my podcast; I think we should—"

"First of all, I don't even know who you're reaching if we don't have a signal," Mars said. "And second, you better not be telling anyone on your podcast about me. I don't want anyone to think what you're saying is true because—" He was interrupted by an alarm blaring overhead.

"WARNING—NAVIGATION SYSTEM FAILURE."

Mars and Oliver looked at each other.

"What does that mean?"

"I'm not sure," Oliver said.

The spaceship suddenly lurched. Then inexplicably, it began to pick up speed.

Mars felt himself get pushed to the wall. "Did you just make us go faster? How can you control the throttle from here?"

"I can't," Oliver gasped.

The door behind Mars opened, and Toothpick, JP, and Aurora tumbled in.

"What's going on?" JP asked. "Stop it, I'm getting carsick."

Oliver disappeared into the cockpit.

"According to Droney, we're accelerating," Toothpick said.

"Isn't that a good thing?" Aurora asked, bracing herself against a wall.

"WARNING—NAVIGATION SYSTEM FAILURE."

"But I thought we didn't know where Earth is," JP said. "Or is it nearby? Maybe the spaceship is heading there on, like, autopilot."

"I'm afraid not," Oliver Pruitt said. He had returned to the door of the flight deck, looking pale. "There's something I didn't tell you before. We ran out of fuel. A long time ago."

"What do you mean we ran out of fuel?" Aurora said slowly. "You mean we've been . . . ?"

"Drifting, yes," Oliver Pruitt said. "Our initial thrust has been keeping us going in the same direction since the fuel ran out. There's just been enough to keep the lights on. I thought we would manage until we found a solution, but now we're picking up incredible speed. Only it's not us."

"If it's not us, then what's making us accelerate?" Mars asked. "Who would know?"

Everyone looked at Toothpick.

"Do you want the good news or the bad news?" he asked.

"Both," JP said. "Tell us the bad first."

"The bad news is that it's probably a wormhole," Toothpick said. "That's the only force capable of pulling us this way. And we can't control it."

"Oh my god, we're getting sucked in, aren't we?" Aurora said.

"Pick, what's the good news?" yelled JP.

Toothpick pushed up his glasses. "The good news is that at least we don't need fuel now."

"That's *not* good news!" Aurora said. "Why are we talking? Shouldn't we do something?"

Around them, an alarm bell started to sound as Oliver Pruitt clicked a control pad on the wall of the compartment they were in.

"There are five of us and five launch pods," he told everyone. "Each of us jumps in one, and we're off. I've already entered the coordinates. Who's in launch pod 1?"

"Me!" Aurora said immediately. Within seconds, she was outfitted and grabbed a helmet from one of the racks. Oliver Pruitt removed a panel from the floor to reveal a small, dark cavity with a padded interior, swivel seat, and a fully automated computer dashboard.

"Jump in and strap yourself up," he told her.

Aurora peered in and swallowed. "You mean in there?" She took a breath. "OK, anything is better than a wormhole." Then she climbed in, and Oliver sealed the pod shut.

"Three, two, one," Oliver counted down, giving her time to buckle up, and then he pressed a button. "Launch pod 2? JP?"

"We're going to die, aren't we?" JP wailed. "OK then, what do I have to lose?"

They grabbed their space helmet and jumped into the second unit.

Toothpick was next. "Mars, ad astra," he said. Moments later he was sealed in with Droney.

"Mars, you're the last one, so you will have to eject yourself, son," Oliver said somberly.

"Why am I last?" Mars sputtered. "Aren't you the captain?"

"That's only in the movies, son," Oliver said. "When you get inside, press the blue button, then the green one."

"But, wait, what if I mess up?" Mars had watched his friends scampering into their pods with barely any hesitation. Were they really that brave? Or was there no time to have second thoughts? "And why won't the wormhole suck the launch pods in, too?"

"The ship has no power," Oliver told him. "But the launch pods do. Maybe that burst will be enough to escape. Who knows? Sometimes, Mars, you have to take a chance. To the stars!"

With that, Oliver Pruitt jumped in and disappeared behind the closed door of his capsule.

"WARNING—NAVIGATION SYTEM FAILURE. THIRD AND FINAL WARNING."

From behind, Cupcake reared up to Mars.

"Cupcake, looks like we gotta launch ourselves," he whispered. "I don't even know if my friends are OK. Or if Oliver Pruitt . . . ?"

Cupcake nudged Mars into the last pod. The unit had seemed small, but there was surprisingly room enough to squeeze in a baby tardigrade. Quickly, he buckled up. "OK, girl. We're going to do this." Mars eyed the dashboard, breathing fast. "Where is the blue button?" He saw it and pressed it. "I wonder what it does. Who cares at this point, right? OK, Cupcake, here we go." Then Mars pushed the green button and felt a supersonic blast . . .

2
ALT

Mars opened his eyes to the sound of a bell ringing. He felt his legs wobble, and he realized he was standing. Not in the compartment of the launch pod, but on solid ground. In fact, he was standing in the hallway of . . . H. G. Wells Middle School? The bell continued, then stopped. It was the first-period bell—a sound Mars had heard every day in sixth grade until he'd stopped going to school. In fact, he'd stopped being on Earth. But now, for some unexplainable reason, he was back in school.

"Yo, Earth to Mars," said a voice. It was Jonas, standing next to him. They were in front of their lockers. "Five days, I know, I know. You don't have to keep telling me."

"Five days?" Mars repeated. Dazed, he sucked in his breath, wondering what had happened. Wasn't he inside the cramped pod with Cupcake? The blast of the pod launching had shaken him to the core. But surely it couldn't have brought him here. Could it?

"That's what you just said," Jonas said. "Until you went into that trance just now. But we all know. We get it. Five days."

"Five days . . . ?" Mars repeated for the second time.

"Five days since Caddie went missing," another voice said.

Mars whirled around to find Aurora. She had come up from behind while he and Jonas were talking. Her hair was a plain dark brown, neatly parted to one side. Gone were the plastic ties and jagged bangs. He looked closely. Was that a barrette in her hair?

"We know, Mars," she said. "Five days since she's been gone, and now you're like, we gotta find Caddie. Even though everyone knows Ms. Safety First is probably fine."

Jonas snickered. "Yeah, Caddie's gotta be careful like Mars gotta have his headphones."

Mars reached up and was shocked to feel his familiar wireless headphones hanging around his neck. Not only that, he was wearing the same hoodie his mom yelled at him all the time to wash. Same hoodie. Same headphones. Same school. But something was very, very different.

"Wait, *Caddie* is gone?" he asked. "But this has happened before. Except it wasn't Caddie."

"What happened before?" Jonas asked. "Us being late to class? 'Cause that's what's gonna happen now."

"No! Not late. It was Aurora who was supposed to be missing. Not Caddie."

"Gee, thanks, Mars," Aurora said. "Way to make me feel needed."

Mars shook his head. "Sorry. That came out wrong." He tried to clear his head. What was going on? It was like he was in some bizarre dream, only it felt like a nightmare, too.

Meanwhile, Aurora and Jonas started walking. "Come on, Mars," Aurora said. "Jonas is right. We'll be late, and you know what that means."

Mars hurried next to them, still dazed and disoriented. "Detention, yeah," he mumbled.

"Detention?" Aurora repeated. "Wait, what planet have you been on?"

Did she really just say that? This was getting weirder and weirder.

"Guys, you have to believe me." He swallowed. "Something unexplainable is going on."

"What's unexplainable," Jonas said, "is how come Mars isn't wet when he just came to school? Are you some miracle maker that rain doesn't stick to you?"

"Huh?" Mars said.

"It's pouring outside!" Aurora said. "Good thing I had an umbrella. You know Mars never has one, right, Jonas?"

"Well, he doesn't have to if he's a miracle maker!"

Mars felt a sudden jolt to his shoulder.

"Out of my way, Martian Patel," said Clyde Boofsky, barreling through the hall.

It was him again, the Boof. Only . . . ?

"Watch where you're going, Boof," Jonas called out. "Though you probably need GPS to find your turd-size brain."

Clyde flipped his finger and kept walking.

"I was supposed to say that." Then Mars noticed something else. "Jonas, you're *short!*"

"Ha, ha, we can't all hit our growth spurt like you, dude," Jonas said good-naturedly.

Growth spurt? Mars started to panic. There were so many things he could explain away in his head, but not the fact that now he could see the top of Jonas's Mariners baseball cap.

"No, I'm sorry, Jonas. That's not what I mean. You don't get it. You used to be tall, like, way taller than me." Mars could feel himself stumbling over his words. But what was the *right* way to explain the impossible? "All of this has happened before. Only it was Aurora missing. I swear. And Caddie was with us when there was a Code Red."

"Code Red?" Aurora stopped walking. "Like a drill?"

"No, like a *real* Code Red," Mars said desperately.

Suddenly a siren blared through the school, echoing down the halls.

"Attention, attention, students and faculty. This is a Code Red. Please remain calm and proceed with lockdown protocol." The announcement came over the PA.

Aurora and Jonas glanced at Mars.

"How did you know that?" Aurora asked.

"That's what I'm trying to tell you!" Mars looked at them. Did they finally believe him?

The PA repeated. "This a Code Red. Please proceed with lockdown protocol."

Around them students started running, teachers calling out to them in the hall.

"Well, shoot, maybe it is a Code Red," Aurora said.

"Or a drill?" Jonas said.

"No, I told you, it's real," Mars said. Maybe they were finally getting it. "This is when we go to the janitor closet."

"Hey, that's not a bad idea," Jonas said. "Come on."

"Yes, no . . ." Mars said. "Wait, guys!" Jonas and Aurora were already two steps ahead of him.

"We repeat. This is a Code Red. Please proceed with lockdown protocol."

Mars ran behind Aurora and Jonas as they headed to the janitor closet.

"Hurry, Mars. You don't want Fagan seeing you," Aurora said. "She likes us, but you know how she is about the rules."

"Since when does Principal Fagan like us?"

Aurora gave him a strange look. "You're being weird, Mars. She's liked us since always. We're the good kids, remember? Quick." She pulled him inside the closet and closed the door.

"When were we the good kids?" Mars burst out.

"No offense, but you're starting to get on my nerves, Mars," Aurora said. "Ow, Jonas! You just elbowed me!"

"Well, watch where you're sitting, Aurora."

Aurora rubbed her arm. "Dang, now we're missing class because of this annoying drill."

Mars leaned forward and clutched his head in disbelief. Everything was repeating itself, from the janitor closet to Jonas elbowing Aurora. Only it was Caddie who was supposed to be here. But he'd told everyone that already. He felt his head throb. Now *he* was the one getting the headache, too. Outside he could hear the siren going as he tried to make sense of this strange reality.

"Let me see if I can get this straight," he whispered. "If Caddie's gone and Aurora's here, then what about Toothpick and JP? Are they around?"

"Of course," Aurora said. "Where else would they be?"

"But Aurora," Mars said. "Don't you remember the launch pod? The Martian Colony?"

"Launch pod? What are you talking about, Mars? A Martian Colony?"

Jonas snickered. "Sounds like my video game. You sure know how to spin one, Mars."

"But I'm not spinning anything," Mars said, frustrated. What would it take for his friends to believe that what he was saying was true? "I've done all of this before. The Code Red, the closet, us here. I just need to know what's happened to Caddie."

"There he goes again about his girlfriend, Caddie," Jonas muttered.

"She isn't my girlfriend!"

"Right, you just talk about her all the time!"

"What!"

"Sometimes people go on vacation," Jonas said. He suddenly bent over. "I gotta go."

"You got to go where?" Aurora asked.

"You know, like, I gotta go!" Jonas stood up, almost knocking over a mop.

"No, you can't go!" Mars exclaimed. "This has happened before, too. Don't do it. It's bad."

"Yeah, but I gotta use the bathroom or it's going to be—"

"A Code Brown in my pants," Mars finished. "That's what you said last time. It's because you forgot to take your pills."

"Whoa, how'd you know?" Jonas moaned. "Sorry, I'm outta here." He reached for the doorknob. "Don't worry, Mars, I can handle it." Jonas opened the closet door and stepped out. "See you on the other side," he said, and shut the door behind him.

"I don't believe it," Mars whispered. "He said that last time, too."

"Mars, he'll be OK," Aurora said. "He's right—he can handle himself." She paused. "Mars, sorry about what I said a minute ago. You're not getting on my nerves. I mean, you are a teeny bit, but I know you didn't mean you wish Caddie was here *instead* of me, right? Because now that we're alone, I wanted to ask you something. I know you might like Caddie, but since she isn't here and the school dance is coming up, I was thinking . . ."

"I can't talk about the school dance right now!" Mars cried. He stood up. "This is bad. I've got to go out there. Jonas needs me."

"But Mars—" Aurora called out.

Mars burst out of the janitor closet. Just a few minutes ago he had been in the launch pod with Cupcake. What had happened to her? And his friends? And Oliver Pruitt? Either he was in a dream or . . . Toothpick's words came suddenly back to him. *It's probably a wormhole. That's the only force capable of pulling us this way.* He ran to the bathroom. The last time he'd been through this scenario, Jonas had disappeared.

"Jonas, Jonas are you there?" he shouted.

He stopped at the door.

"Hey Mars," Jonas said from the sink. "Yeah, I'm here. Where else would I be?"

Mars was stunned. Everything that had happened before was happening now. Except Caddie was gone. And Jonas was here. In the bathroom where he said he would be. "I—I don't get it," Mars stammered. "If you're here, then . . . where am I?"

FROM THE PODCAST

Hello, podcast listeners!

Today the questions go deeper.

It's about asking ourselves, what's real?

Is there a higher consciousness?

Can we choose who we want to be?

Because maybe I want that pair of alligator-leather shoes.

Maybe there's someone I should spend more time with.

What do you want?

Or more importantly, what will you give up,

to get what you want?

Because remember,

THERE'S ALWAYS A PRICE! Ha!

To the stars!

23 Comments ⊗

staryoda   45 min ago
ur annoying

allie_j 33 min ago
u have a point

allie_j 33 min ago
do u mean how much is it to go to Pruitt Prep
also is there a discount since ur missing

galaxygenius 20 min ago
I wanna eat galaxy clusters kinda always

oreocookies 16 min ago
real is what you make it

thisismars 14 min ago
is this real????

3
ENRICHED

OK, Mars had gone through a wormhole. Maybe that's what it was. A weird wormhole where he'd jumped back in time to his old life, except with some crucial differences. Aurora was here. Jonas, too. But Caddie was gone. Who else was missing from this life? What about his mom? He really needed to see her. *Now*. He missed her, and he had so many questions about *everything*.

He made it as far as the front doors of the school, and then he saw it was pouring outside, the sound of the rain coming down like drumbeats on the corrugated awning outside the doors. The rain seemed unusually hard and unpleasant. By the time he got home, he would be a soggy noodle. Maybe it was better to hang out a little longer here. His mom was probably still at work, and the Code Red seemed to be over as everyone started returning to class. And if he did stay, he could try to find out what was going on. Like where was Caddie?

Even after all this time, Mars still remembered that she had social studies with Mr. Sequim first period. So he went there next, now that everyone was back in their seats after the Code Red. Maybe Aurora and Jonas were wrong and Caddie had been coming late to school, slipping in unnoticed. He tried to think of another explanation as he got to Mr. Sequim's door. But when he peeked in, Caddie's chair was empty. He knew because in every class she had, Caddie always took the seat closest to the door. That was Caddie. Around the corner was the sixth-grade hall, so he went there next to try her locker. When it wouldn't open, he used a paper clip he saw lying on the ground to pry the door open (a trick he'd learned from Aurora—the old Aurora, at least).

Caddie's locker was empty, too. No backpack, no books, no flannel jacket.

Down the hall, he saw Principal Fagan talking to a student. He tried to scramble away, but it was too late. She had seen him. "Mars," she called to him. "Please come see me."

He walked to her reluctantly. "I was just on my way," he started. "Since the Code Red is over."

"Great to see you, Manu," Fagan said. "I appreciate all the hard work you and your friends are doing on the rain project."

"Rain project?" Mars stammered. "Are you sure?"

"You saw how much rain we were getting and decided to do something about it," Fagan said, smiling wide. "Now the H. G. Wells outdoor swimming pool is the talk of Puget Sound!"

"Right!" Mars said.

"That Aurora was so resourceful, getting a contractor to build the pool using funds from a school grant," Fagan said. "And the way that Toothpick and JP designed a water filtration system all by themselves? Just incredible."

Actually that *did* sound epic. He crossed his arms. "So what did I do?"

Fagan just smiled as she walked away. "Mars, Mars. Always so modest. I hope you're not late to class now."

For a moment, Mars stood in the hall, blinking in bewilderment. Fagan thanking him? This was a totally different world. An alternate Earth. But instead of reveling in it, Mars decided he'd had enough. He headed straight into the gym and hid behind the bleachers. Safe at last. From everyone.

From here, he could see the rain as he looked out the giant windows flanking the gym. Man, it *was* raining hard. Aurora had been right. He didn't think he'd ever seen so much rain in Port Elizabeth. In fact, now that he thought about it, there had been so many comments on Oliver Pruitt's podcast about the weather—not just about rain, but flooding, too. And throughout the world. Kids had been posting those comments when he was still on Mars. But he hadn't had time to think about it then. Not with all the stuff that had been going on at the Colony. Now that he was here in this alternative world that seemed to predate everything, even his trip to Mars, the rain was even worse.

Was this climate change? Or something bad about Alt Earth?

He sighed, feeling his spirits sink further. Nothing was making sense. Not the weather, not Fagan, not school, not anything. Why was Caddie gone? And if he'd really traveled through a wormhole, why hadn't his friends and Cupcake traveled with him, too? He wondered then if there was some other version of himself running around on Alt Earth, too. *That* would be freaky. He wasn't sure he'd want to meet that alternate Mars. Maybe that Mars had done something for the pool, too. Like peed in it.

Mars reached for his backpack and opened it. He wasn't sure how he even had it or where it had come from, except that he'd found himself wearing it along with his headphones and clothes when he was at the lockers with Jonas and Aurora. He felt his stomach growl as he rummaged through the backpack, and oddly, he found a bagged lunch inside. A peanut butter and jelly sandwich with potato chips and a box of raisins. OK. He pulled them out and started eating.

It was good to eat. He hadn't realized he was so hungry. He rummaged some more and pulled out his phone. Had that been there all this time, too?

He opened his messages, which were filled with texts from Aurora: *Where are you? Where are you? Where are you????* There were no other texts. It was like his whole life from before had been erased. He thought for a moment and started a new text. He wasn't even sure she'd receive it, but he had to try anyway.

Mars · Caddie

Mon, Oct 19, 12:20 pm

Mars

I'm back on earth only it's alt earth

and ur gone, not aurora

Am I dreaming?

I know I say I hate it but I rly wish u could

read my thoughts and tell me wut to do

∩

For the rest of the day, Mars decided to go to his classes: social studies, technology, math. He still remembered his sixth-grade schedule, too. None of his friends were in these classes, except for math, where he usually sat behind Caddie, but today, there was an empty desk in front of him. When the last bell rang, Mars stepped out of class and Aurora accosted him.

"There you are," she said. "You've sure been hiding yourself."

"Um," Mars said. Aurora, with her neat brown hair, frankly made him nervous. Since when did Aurora look so . . . groomed?

"I know you're not yourself today, Mars," Aurora said. "Like maybe that Code Red rattled you. But you've got come back to reality. Just follow me, OK?"

Mars relented. He didn't want to, but Aurora always had

this way of making him do what she wanted. "I guess we're going to detention," he said wearily. So far he hadn't seen Toothpick or JP. Maybe they would be the same. Maybe that was what he needed. A little bit of normalcy.

"Why do you keep bringing up detention?" Aurora gave him the same baffled look he was used to getting from her now. She opened a door to their left and Mars found himself in a bright, sunny classroom he had never seen before.

"What is this place?" Mars asked. Did detention look better on Alt Earth, too?

"Enrichment, of course!" Aurora gave him a light punch in the shoulder. "Look, Epica's here already." Aurora waved to Epica Hernandez, who was seated at one of the desks. Epica waved back breezily to them.

"Mars!" she squealed. "We're getting new planners today, and I've color-coded mine already!" In the old world, Epica was a 4.0 student, Toothpick's girlfriend, and a pain in the butt. She looked pretty much the same here, too.

Aurora pointed to Mars's headphones. "You better put those away. Mr. Q doesn't like it."

Before Mars could respond, he looked toward the front of the room and found his detention teacher sitting behind the large desk. Only Mr. Q wasn't wearing his customary black-rimmed glasses and checkered shirt. Instead, he wore gold-rimmed spectacles and a merino wool sweater with beige slacks. He also sported a crew cut, and a leather briefcase rested on his desk, even though the old Mr. Q was vegan and supported animal rights, and would never use products made from "dead animals." Their old detention teacher had been socially conscious but, as Mars would later find out, totally evil.

"Mars, come in, we're getting delayed," Mr. Q called out in a singsong voice. "We have so much to talk about!"

Mars backed away and collided into someone else.

"Oof." Powerful arms wrapped around him. "I like hugs, but watch where you land, bro."

JP grinned, and for a moment Mars's spirits lifted, hearing the familiar lilt of his friend's voice. Then he saw something that made Mars stop cold. *JP was wearing a skirt.*

"But you hate skirts," Mars croaked. "You say they make you itch."

JP put their hand on their hips. "I think they show off my legs. Epica said so, right Epi?"

"Bestie!" Epica crowed and made the peace sign with two fingers.

Epica, JP's arch nemesis, was now a *friend*?

"Mars isn't himself," said Toothpick, who was now standing behind JP. "That's what Aurora said. Maybe he's confused."

"I'm *not* confused," Mars said. "And . . . where's your glasses, Toothpick?"

"I don't wear glasses," Toothpick said. He smiled calmly, but his eyes were dull. "You know that. Unless you bumped your head."

"Mars bumped his head," Aurora agreed. "It all makes sense."

"No worries," JP said. "We'll just get Mars to sit down, and he'll feel better."

The three of them circled around Mars, blocking the doorway. They all wore the same expression: gentle smiles, but with something strange and sinister lurking in their eyes. He heard Mr. Q getting up from his desk.

"Yes, we need to make Mars feel better," Mr. Q said. "Come, Epica. Let's help Mars."

Epica jumped up. "Gladly!"

"No," Mars said, panicking. He saw an opening between JP and Toothpick. He pushed through with his shoulder and ran down the hall. There was something off about his friends, but there was no way Mars was hanging around to find out what it was.

"Mars!" Their voices called out to him from the classroom. "Mars!"

Once Mars was in motion, he picked up speed. He ran faster and faster past the sixth-grade wing. He had to get out of here. It was all strange and wrong and . . . dangerous.

In his pocket, he felt the outline of something sharp. The keys to his apartment.

"Ma," he whispered. It no longer mattered that it was pouring outside. Mars would take the rain and anything else, just to get home.

When Will the Rain Stop?

Port Elizabeth, WA—Rains continue across the Pacific Northwest, upending everyone's plans.

"We were really looking forward to the annual sailboat race," said Sid Bailey, owner of Port Elizabeth's sailing club. "You can't sail in this kind of rain."

It turns out you can't do other things in this kind of rain either. The farmers' market, which kicks off in May, has been shuttered, along with the H. G. Wells School Fair, baseball tryouts, and the Freemason's dog run in Shoshone Park. Farther north, apples are rotting in the orchards in Port Richard, soil is getting soggy, and so are we. Local meteorologist Cynthia Han says that the rest of the nation is suffering from other unprecedented weather: hurricanes, tornadoes, sleet, hail, and in some areas, extreme drought followed by brushfires nearly impossible to contain.

"Something is going on," Han says. "It's not just rain in Port Elizabeth. Our nation is facing dire circumstances—a rapid escalation of events that has the whole meteorological community reeling."

Meanwhile, picketers in the state capital, Olympia, are carrying signs saying "Climate Change Is Real!"

Is this just a case of some rain? Or are the picketers onto something? ▪

4
THE MOLE

■■■ s Mars ran home, he tried to squash the fear that
■■■■ bloomed through him. Those people he'd left behind
■   ■ were *not* his friends. They looked like them and spoke
like them, but their soulless eyes and the way they drew
around him scared Mars to death. He had to get home. Maybe
his mom would help. Maybe she would be the same and take
care of him. She had to. Otherwise, Mars didn't know what he
would do next.

By the time he reached his block, the rain had drenched
him to the bone and the smell of sea water and pine hung
in the air around him. Well, at least it *smelled* like Port Elizabeth. And the road with its familiar pothole near Kamiakan
and Elm was still there, now overflowing with rainwater. He
remembered playing a game with Caddie, throwing pebbles
inside that pothole from the curb. That seemed so long ago, in
a world where Caddie still existed. Where was she now?

Mars turned onto Chinook. His street. With the same telephone pole, tailor shop, and Douglas fir that dropped needles everywhere opposite his apartment building. It was all the same, only with the parked cars and awnings and sidewalk getting pelted by rain. Was that his bike in the bike rack? Through the curtain of water cascading over him, he stopped to feel the wet seat. The tear in the middle where he'd snagged it with his lock was mysteriously gone. The seat looked brand-new. The handlebars were straight. Gone were the scratches along the metal frame. But it was definitely his bike. Then the rain was too much, and he ran to the front door, jamming the key in quickly.

Inside, the air was dry and warm. He took the stairs two at a time, leaving pools of water behind him where his feet struck, until he reached his apartment and unlocked the door, grateful to be home. Inside the door, Mars stopped in surprise.

The apartment was unrecognizable.

Gone were the folding chairs and futon in the living room. Gone were the boxes that had never been unpacked and had become de facto side tables. Gone was the dining table that leaned to one side. There was now a pair of twin leather sofas and wingback chairs. A brand-new dining table for six gleamed nearby, and in the corner, a baby grand piano. There was an aroma in the air, too. The smell of . . . cooking. The door to the kitchen swung open.

"Mars!" Saira Patel wore a camel-colored pantsuit and pearl

necklace. Her hair was coiffed in a bun and she held a ladle. "Mars, you're soaked! Come, come in quickly. What are you doing home from school already? What about enrichment?"

"I—I—" Mars felt his mouth go dry. In this world, was his mother evil and strange and going to do weird things? He wasn't sure, but it was still his mom. And it had been so long since he'd seen her. Without another word, he rushed into her arms.

She embraced him. "Beta," her familiar voice murmured. "Let's get you some dry clothes."

"I missed you," he said, his voice muffled. His eyes grew wet to match his clothes. He hugged her harder, breathing in the scent of her, of sandalwood powder and soap, which he recognized, and something else, a sweet, fruity perfume that was new.

"Mars, what's come over you, darling?" She stroked his wet head. "No worries. Maybe you had a bad day? There are fresh clothes right here in the basket. I was doing the laundry."

She handed him a clean sweatshirt and jeans. He took them from her and changed into the gray sweatshirt that said SCIENCE OLYMPIAD. It smelled fresh, like detergent. "I've made some chole and rotis for dinner. You can eat now. Then I have to get ready for class."

"Class?" Mars asked as he wriggled into his dry jeans. "What class?"

"Physics," Saira Patel said. "I've got thirty minutes to get to campus, and you know how the traffic gets at this time, especially with all the rain. But Papa will be home in the evening."

"Papa?"

His mother disappeared into the kitchen while Mars took a moment to digest the word. She couldn't mean . . . that would be impossible because . . . his eyes drew to the picture frames that he now saw on the mantel. Pictures of him and their family. Him, Ma, and Oliver Pruitt.

He crossed the room to get near the photos. Oliver Pruitt and his mom were together? Under the same roof? In the photos, they were standing in front of the Taj Mahal, the Eiffel Tower, and the Golden Gate Bridge, and in each one, they were arm in arm, smiling. There were wedding pictures: his mother dressed in a red sari, with garlands around her and Oliver's necks. There were baby pictures, too. So many baby pictures. His mom and Mars in his winter jacket—the orange one that looked like a pumpkin. The first day of preschool. The first day of first grade. The Halloween parade. In all of these, Oliver Pruitt was holding Mars's hand, carrying him in his arms, or bending down and smiling radiantly. There he was, putting to rest any doubts Mars might have had on board the spaceship, ever since the day Oliver Pruitt had dropped that bombshell on him in the Old Colony on Mars. Oliver Pruitt had been telling the truth.

"I'm going to be sick," Mars said. He said that, but the feelings inside were something else. An intense longing and hunger for all of it to be true instead.

"What's that?" Ma asked from the kitchen.

Mars quickly sat down at the dining table when his mother came out. In her hand she had a full plate—steaming chole, rotis, and some apple slices.

"Don't talk, eat," she said. "You look funny, Mars. You will feel better soon if you eat."

He obeyed, tearing a piece of roti as his mother spoke. She told him about her class, about the test no one seemed prepared for, and how she had to go over everything again. She chatted about tickets to a play in Seattle that Papa had gotten for them, about a note from the school about the science fair, and whether Mars was ready to show off his experiment (a wireless helper drone—what a clever idea, Mars!).

The more she talked, the more Mars sank into doubt. School had been weird; his friends had been scary. But his mother here talking to him was undeniably nice. She had made hot food for him, she had clean clothes waiting for him, and she looked so professional and happy, bursting with news of the day. And Mars now had a dad. A dad who wasn't just an idea, but a person who bought tickets, attended his science fair, and left messages on the phone. Mars even saw a pair of alligator-leather shoes (alligator!) lined up near the front closet, evidence that Oliver Pruitt not only lived here but was an integral part of their lives. Most of all, Ma looked so happy!

Saira Patel got up from the dining table. "You take your time and eat. I'll call the middle school and let enrichment know you're home. Papa, too. Maybe he can come home early while I'm at school. It will all be OK."

"Sure, Ma," Mars said. "You'll see me in the stars, right?"

He saw her hesitate as if she didn't understand.

"You know, that saying of yours, right?"

"Of course!" She smiled instantly. "Of course I know about that expression, beta!"

Mars watched her lean forward to lift one of the empty plates from the table. As she did, his eyes went to her left wrist. The one with the small black mole on the inside that was always there. Only it wasn't. He stared, his eyes darting to her left then her right hand. No mole at all.

He swallowed. The same dread came rushing back. He was noticing something else now. He could hear the rain hitting the windowpanes on one side of the apartment near the living room, but not on the other side near the dining area. There, the window was dry. Wet on one side. Dry on the other. Somehow not matching up.

"You OK, Mars?" Saira asked, appraising him. She seemed to notice a change.

"Yeah," Mars said. He put his spoon down. "Actually, I'm kind of tired."

"You don't have a fever, do you?" She reached with her hand, the one with the missing mole.

Mars got up before her hand touched his forehead. "No, just tired. I'm going to sleep. In my room." With effort, he walked slowly, taking care not to speed up or draw attention to himself.

"OK, beta, maybe I'll call Papa now," he could hear his mom's voice behind him. "We don't want you feeling bad now, do we?"

Inside his room, Mars closed the door. Then he locked it.

He wasn't sure what was worse. Seeing his friends act weird and threatening, or his mom act weird and nice. But the mole being gone, the rain not matching up, his mother not remembering saying she'd see him in the stars . . . were these signs that something shady was going on? Or was he losing control over his mind?

He sat down on his bed, seeing the same bedspread that had always been there. This was undeniably his room. The bed was the same, the toy rocket near his pillow, still there. What if this really *was* his life? Enrichment? His friends being good students; his mom a happy college professor; Oliver Pruitt, his dad, now a part of their lives? A small voice inside his head spoke to him. One he could hardly ignore: Was it all so bad? What if his mom didn't have a mole on her wrist? Maybe she got it removed, or Mars had simply imagined it. And so what if the rain was bad, and the flooding was bad, and it rained just near the dining room . . . so what? *Isn't your life better than the one you left behind?*

A great ball of fear invaded his stomach. Everything was better, and yet . . .

Outside his window, Mars heard a new sound. Not the rain. But something else—a familiar buzzing. He ran to the window, pushing the curtain back. There against the glass hovered a familiar object. Mars could hardly believe his eyes. Quickly he pushed open the window to let the drone into his room before slamming the window shut to keep out the rain.

"Droney!" Mars whispered.

"Affirmative," chirped the drone. He circled the room, sprinkling rainwater everywhere. This was not just any drone. This was Droney, Toothpick's repurposed Pruitt drone, the original seal scratched off so that everyone could easily recognize him. It was the old Toothpick with glasses who had captured and reprogrammed Droney. Not the new Toothpick at school who suggested that Mars had bumped his head.

"What are you doing here?" Mars asked, holding his breath.

Droney continued hovering. "Mars Patel, I have intercepted an important message for you."

5
BREAK AWAY

An important message for me?" Mars asked, flabbergasted. Before he could say anything, there was a pounding on the glass. Mars jumped a mile, not expecting a second appearance at his window.

This time it was a person. JP was standing on the fire escape, and they wanted to be let in.

"Mars, it's me," JP said. They continued tapping, this time a little less forcefully, but JP was urgent. "Mars, you gotta let me in, it's pouring out here, bro. I'm turning into soup."

Hearing JP's voice at that moment felt like a trip back in time, where everything dependable and good about JP could be heard in their voice. And now here was JP again, rapping on the window.

"I need to know how you are, Mars," JP said. "You bolted out of enrichment. We need to know you're OK." The rain was falling steadily, making JP look like a drenched cat.

Mars hesitated. It was JP. But something was holding him back. He could still remember JP, Toothpick, and Aurora surrounding him at school. And not in a good way.

"You're killing me, Mars," JP said. "I'm soaked, and you KNOW I hate being wet. And look at me—I even went home and changed out of my skirt because of you."

JP did look wet and miserable, and Mars knew just how much they hated being wet. His hand reached for the latch on the window. Would it be so bad to let JP inside?

Just then, there was a knock on his bedroom door.

"Mars?" The door jiggled. "Is someone else there? What's going on? I need to get to work."

"Coming, Mamaji," Mars said. He glanced at JP, who had started jumping up and down now.

"Lemme in first," JP said. "You got to let me in."

JP kept jumping up and down while the banging on the door continued.

"Mars, let me in, beta," his mom said. "Something's going on."

Mars looked from the window to the door. How could they both be clamoring to get in?

"You are getting hit from both directions," Droney chirped.

In the midst of everything, Mars had forgotten about Droney.

"Droney!" he exclaimed! "Who do I let in? My mom or JP?"

"Arriving at a smart decision should be made after considering all information," Droney said.

"What information is that?" Mars looked hastily from the jiggling door to the fire escape outside his window and suddenly noticed what JP was wearing. As they jumped up and down on the fire escape, Mars saw that JP had changed into sweatpants and their soccer cleats. Cleats! Mars remembered all the times he'd heard JP say how it was super bad to wear soccer cleats off the field. It was the number-one way to bust the bottoms. They always made a point of carrying around flip-flops so they could change as soon as they finished a game. Yet here was JP, wearing cleats on the metal bars of the fire escape.

Meanwhile, the bedroom door jiggled wildly. "Mars, I'm coming in using a pin," Mars's mom said.

Mars was shocked. *That* was so unlike his mom, too, who *always* respected his privacy. Would she really pry open his door?

"You must listen to the important message," Droney said.

"Quick, Droney," Mars said. "Tell me!"

"I think I have to break this window down," JP said. "Like, for your own good."

"Playing back message," Droney announced. There was a whirring sound.

"Mars, you need to break away."

"Caddie!" Mars immediately recognized her voice. His heart sailed. "That's Caddie's voice!"

"A recording," Droney informed him. "Not Caddie."

"What does she mean?"

"Mars, you need to break away." The recording went into a loop. *"Mars, you need to break away."*

Break away? From what? It was so weird hearing Caddie's voice coming from Droney. Almost like she was here in the room with him. If only she were!

There was the sound of something being inserted into the lock. More jiggling.

Next to him, JP was beating a heavy branch against the glass.

"Droney, I'm running out of time!" Mars cried out.

"Mars, you need to break away."

There it was, Caddie's voice again. Mars had a sudden thought. What if Caddie *was* trying to help him? What if she had sent Droney to tell Mars what to do?

"She's telling me to break away, Droney," Mars said. "How do I do that?"

Break away. Break away. Break.

Mars closed his eyes like he used to see his mother do before she said her prayers. Concentrating, focusing, going inward. None of this was real. JP on the fire escape, his mom jiggling the lock, the rain on one side of the apartment and not on the other. And maybe he couldn't break out, but he could break in. Find himself. Where it began. Him, the launch pod, Cupcake, and somewhere out there, Caddie.

"Must break away . . ." he whispered.

Then the walls around him disappeared.

6

CRASH LANDING

Mars's back ached. He was in a ball, his knees up as if he were bracing for impact. Around him the walls shook. Tight walls surrounding him like a pod. The launch pod. Something roared next to him. Not an adult roar. A kid roar. But nevertheless by a creature of fair size.

"Cupcake!" His tardigrade, who was strapped in next to him, grunted. "Where am I? Did I come back?" Mars pressed a button in front of him on the control pad. "Computer, where am I?"

The guidance navigation control system kicked in.

"You can call me Chiron," responded the computer interface. "We are approaching Earth's atmosphere at an altitude of twenty thousand feet. The heat shield has been activated for entry."

"Earth!" Through the tiny square of reinforced glass overhead, Mars could see flames surrounding the pod like a halo of light. "But I was just there!"

"That would be negative," Chiron said. "You are due for landing in approximately fifteen minutes if you survive initial entry, descent, and landing."

"If?" Mars squeaked. His mind was trying to catch up on all the things Toothpick had told him about EDL. He remembered that entry was the most deadly part of returning to the surface. The friction from the air would heat up the surface of the launch pod, and the heat shield was there to protect them from exploding.

"Cupcake, you have to believe me," Mars said. "I was on Earth. But it was Alt Earth. Aurora, Toothpick, JP, and my mom were there, but something was really off. Something diabolical. Now I'm in the launch pod, heading back to Earth. Does that make sense to you?"

Cupcake just grunted again.

The launch pod rattled even more intensely as Mars peered through the glass to see sparks bursting around the pod. He just hoped the heat shield would hold.

"The heat shield gives us some serious superpowers, bro," JP had told him while they were still on board the *Manu 1*. That was when flight manuals were floating around the cabin as Toothpick pored through them, committing entire sections to memory. But JP had read through them, too, and unlike Toothpick, JP's approach was pragmatic and quick. "Just tell me what I need to know to survive" was their motto.

If JP said the heat shield would protect Mars, then JP was

probably right. But that was then. Would JP say the same thing now? What if Mars was in another wormhole flying down to some other version of Earth, where the laws of heat resistance were different?

"Maybe this isn't real either," Mars murmured to himself. Then he had to stop talking because the rattling was so intense it felt like his face would fall off.

"Atmospheric altitude reached," Chiron informed Mars.

As they continued their descent, Mars thought of the space movies he'd seen where the hero reached Earth despite improbable odds. He thought of the astronauts making touchdown in the water, then bobbing up to the surface. His mind drifted to Oliver Pruitt, his . . . dad. Pictures of him and his mom on the mantel. In spite of everything creepy and glitchy about Alt Earth, seeing those photos filled a hole in Mars that he hadn't known was there. They were photos he'd never seen anywhere else. Oliver Pruitt standing with his arm around Mars's mom, who was carrying Mars, and smiling at the camera. They looked like they were really together, in love. And in that alternate world, the three of them were . . . a family. Mars blinked hard. *Time to get real*, he told himself. He had to be ready for whatever was down there, for better or worse. At least he had Cupcake with him this time.

As they descended, the view outside his window began to change. The dark of space was being rapidly replaced with something else. Sky. Clouds. And below him, the great, vast stretch of solid Earth and sparkling ocean. Mars gasped. God! It was so beautiful. So much more so than the terrifying sprawl of Mars. This was where he was from, and home would always be beautiful.

"Cupcake, it's like we're in a movie!" he said with effort as their bodies continued shaking inside the pod. He was scared and hopeful and exhilarated all at the same time.

"Altitude of nine thousand feet and descending," Chiron said. "Parachute deployment commences."

A pair of bright orange parachutes released from the launch pod and billowed above them, slowing down the careening pod as it sailed closer and closer to the straddling acres of lush green forest and brilliant blue ocean. One by the one, the rest of the parachutes opened—a total of ten—until it seemed the pod was floating like a feather to Earth. Finally, they reached a line of pine trees, cutting through mist, and Mars's pod made contact with the ground with one soft thump.

"Launch pod has successfully landed at T minus thirty minutes," Chiron informed them. Overhead lights flickered on.

"Thank the stars!" Mars pulled off his straps and gave Cupcake a tremendous hug. Cupcake responded by bumping up against him with her snout. "Chiron, where did we land? What do we do next?"

"You have landed in the Cascadia subduction zone," said Chiron.

"The what?"

"The main tectonic plate system of the upper Pacific North-west. To your right is the border of the Quinault Rain Forest. To the left is—"

The rest of the computer's coordinates were drowned out by a furious rapping on the door.

Rap, rap, rap!

Then the hatch was unceremoniously pried open.

Two familiar faces peered in with a slice of sky framing them from behind.

"It's them! And they're alive! Mars, tell me you're alive, buddy!" JP's voice filled the cavity of the launch pod.

"JP! Toothpick!" Mars cried. "I'm so glad to see you. Tooth-pick, you have your glasses on!"

"Well, affirmative," Toothpick said. "Otherwise I would lit-erally not be able to see."

"And JP—you're NOT wearing a skirt. And . . . you cut your hair."

JP laughed. "Um, thanks?"

"Sorry. Everything's all happening so fast," Mars said, scrambling to his feet. "But tell me you're JP, right? The real one and not some weirdo trying to break into my room."

JP and Toothpick looked at each other. They reached in to help Mars out of the pod.

"You don't know, like, how happy and relieved I am that you're alive!" JP said, hugging Mars tightly. "But just to clarify. Yeah, it's me, all right. But *I'm* not the problem."

Mars and Cupcake had landed in a grassy clearing west of Olympic National Park. A gentle mist hung in the air, and Mars could hear warblers and winter wrens. The sound immediately relieved Mars. There was no birdsong on Alt Earth. There had been too much rain. Here the air smelled sweet, everything was crisp and bright, and the ground was pleasurably soft under Mars's feet as the group made their way from the landing site to the parking lot. Mars could feel the tension drain from his neck and shoulders. It was good to be back. Like, really back.

"Who drove you?" he asked. "Is one of your parents waiting in the car? Because how are we going to explain the launch pod? Or Cupcake!"

"Relax," JP said. "We got it all under control. But tell us, what happened to you, bro?"

So as they walked, Mars filled them in on Alt Earth. "It felt like an alternate reality. But then I figured out, Toothpick, it was a wormhole. Like what you were saying. It was pretty wild."

"Sounds wild, all right," JP said.

"How did you know where to find me?" Mars asked.

"Toothpick picked up your signal, right, Pick?" JP asked.

"Yes. We all landed safely—JP, Aurora, myself. The two pods that were missing had Oliver Pruitt, who remains at large. And you, Mars. But your pod had a tracking device. That's why we were able to detect your signal. We knew where you were positioned and where you were landing."

"What happened to Oliver Pruitt?" Mars asked. "Did he . . . um . . . ?" He was unable to finish the sentence. He hadn't told them about the photos on the mantel in his apartment. The ones in which they were a family. There was still no way to describe that.

"Nah," JP said immediately. "Pruitt's been straight up doing his podcast. We just don't know from where. So he's OK, and he's probably MIA on purpose because he's Pruitt." They ran their hand lightly over their hair. "What do you think of the buzz cut, Mars?"

"I like it," Mars said. "It's you."

"I know," JP said. "There's like a lot of wind on my neck now, and when I turn my head, nothing moves! And no more combing in the mornings. Free at last!"

Cupcake had been following along next to them, but she suddenly stopped, pricking her nose up in the air.

"What's wrong, Cupcake?" Mars said. "We're almost there. Aren't we?"

Toothpick nodded. "The parking lot's over there. Although . . ." His voice trailed off curiously. "Not sure yet on the logistics of fitting a baby tardigrade in the back. Oh, well."

As if on cue, Cupcake bolted.

"Cupcake!" Mars called out.

Cupcake continued running, undeterred, heading for the trees.

"Hmm, was it something I said?" Toothpick wondered. "We do have the moonroof."

"Hang on! Wait!" Mars started to run. But he was no match for Cupcake's speed. After a few yards, he stumbled, falling hands first onto the soft grassy ground. "Cuppyyyyy!" he yelled.

JP helped Mars up as they watched Cupcake disappear into the woods.

"She's so young," Mars said, agitated. "And she's never been on Earth. What's she going to do out there? What if someone else finds her first? And does something to her?" He tried to run again, but JP held fast onto Mars's sleeve.

"Mars, Mars," JP said.

"Let go of me! I have to go after her. She won't be able to—"

"You gotta let her go," JP said. "We've got an SUV, and Cupcake is, like . . . the size of one. And maybe she needed to go. You know how the tardigrades are. They've got minds of their own."

"But we have to keep Cupcake safe," Mars said. "She needs to come home with us."

"Yeah, maybe she will," JP said. "Give her some space."

They fell silent as the birds resumed their singing.

"You really think she'll find her way back?" Mars asked finally.

"The odds say yes," Toothpick said.

JP nodded. "Remember how they knew how to get us to the

Old Colony back on Mars? I swear. They're either mind readers or fiendishly smart."

Mars gave a tiny smile. "Fiendishly smart. I like that." He wiped the dirt off his knees where he'd fallen. "All right. I'm going to trust you, JP."

"Now we're talking," JP said.

The three of them walked toward the parking lot that was only a few yards away.

"Well, one thing's for sure," Mars said. "I can't wait to get home and see my mom."

Toothpick and JP glanced at each other.

"Mars, your—" Toothpick started, but JP clamped their hand over his mouth. "Ummfph," he said instead.

Mars stared at them. With a start, he realized that while he had been telling them about Alt Earth, JP and Toothpick had been strangely silent about whatever had happened on their end. By now they'd reached the parking lot, which was empty except for a large Chevy Tahoe parked in the dead center. There was no one waiting in the driver's seat.

"Why is no one in the car to pick us up?" Mars asked. "What are you not telling me?"

WHERE DID THEY GO?

JP sighed. "There's a lot to tell, Mars, and we still don't have all the answers." They nodded toward the car. "Why don't you hop in? Pick, unlock the doors, will you?"

Toothpick fished out a key from his pocket and clicked it. The Chevy immediately beeped.

"*You're* driving?" Mars was surprised to see Toothpick get into the driver's seat.

"Shotgun!" JP called out. "Get in the back, Mars."

"But . . . but . . ." Mars sputtered. "Isn't this illegal? Where's your mom or dad, Pick?" When no one responded, Mars figured he had no choice but to climb in the back.

Maybe he was wrong. Maybe this *was* another Alt Earth. With birds and grass and Cupcake leaving him behind in the dust, and now Toothpick about to drive them to their demise. The back seat was filled with stacks of papers, a box full of rain gear and tactical equipment, a tent, and a small Bunsen burner as well as blankets, a few pillows, and several plastic jugs of water. "What is all this stuff?" he asked nervously.

"I like to be prepared," Toothpick said, slipping on a pair of aviator shades. "Buckle up, everyone. We're going for a ride." He reversed the SUV with a screech, and they roared out of the parking lot.

"Slow down!" Mars yelled in panic from the back seat. He closed his eyes. Maybe if he thought really hard, he'd be back in the launch pod again, flying down to the real Earth, and this was all just a passing dream. But even with his eyes closed, he could feel the car surging across the road. After a moment he opened his eyes. Nope. Toothpick was still in front, driving a monstrous SUV.

"I know you're grappling with this new normal, Mars," Toothpick said to him in the rearview mirror. "But let me assure you, I've clocked over three hundred hours of driving time since we've been here. Not only that, Droney helps me better than GPS." As if on cue, Droney, who had been in sleep mode, whirred to life on the dashboard.

"Greetings, Mars Patel," Droney said. "Where do you wish to go, Randall Lee?"

"Going home, Droney. Check for traffic," said Toothpick. "And remember, don't call me Randall. Just say Toothpick."

"Roads are clear, Toothpick," Droney said, correcting himself. "Mild congestion at exit 14 but it is nothing you can't handle."

"Excellent!" Toothpick reached up to adjust the rearview mirror as they entered the freeway.

"Oh my god," Mars muttered, his eyes glued to the road. "Tell me we're not going to end up in the Pacific Ocean."

"Negative, Mars," Toothpick said cheerfully. "Droney literally knows everything about the road. I've even programmed him to be more conversational. So don't worry. I've never been in an accident, though—full disclosure—I *am* a speed demon."

"Accelerating to eighty-five," Droney said. "Cool!"

"Toothpick can do zero to eighty in twelve seconds," JP said. "Let this baby rip, Pick!"

With that, the SUV veered into the left lane and shot down the highway. At first the sheer speed was terrifying. But after a few minutes, Mars had to admit that Toothpick seemed to know what he was doing, and his driving was smooth, steady, and comfortable. Gradually, Mars let go of the seat he'd been gripping.

"All right, so how come Pick is driving?" Mars asked. "Won't his parents be mad about Pick's three hundred hours involving their SUV?"

"Well, that's the thing," JP said. "They aren't mad because, uh, they're kinda not here."

"Where did they go?" Mars asked cautiously, wondering if something awful had happened to Toothpick's parents. What else could explain him taking over the family car?

"We don't know where Pick's parents went," JP said. "Or if

his parents went where my parents went, and Caddie's parents, and the teachers at school, and your mom, too."

Mars blinked. "My mom? And all our parents?"

"Not just our parents, Mars," JP said. "*All* adults. And we don't know where they are. But they're all GONE. POOF."

"Poof?" Mars repeated.

"Vanished without a trace," Droney interjected.

"You're joking, right?" Mars said, still not comprehending.

"You better believe it, baby," Droney warbled. "Kaput!"

"Droney, can it," JP hissed. "Pick, make him stop."

"Sorry, sometimes he takes convo mode too far," Toothpick apologized. "Droney, hibernate for five."

Droney whirred to a stop.

JP turned around anxiously. "How are you taking all of this, Mars? You doing OK?"

Mars was looking out his window at the other vehicles on the road. For the first time he was noticing how in every car, a kid was in the front seat, driving. Some were teenagers, but there were also kids who looked like they were ten or even younger. There were no adults anywhere as far as Mars could see. The enormity of the situation began to sink in.

"It doesn't make any sense," Mars said, stunned. "Where did they all go?"

"That's what I'm trying to tell you," JP said patiently. "Nobody knows. When Toothpick and I got here, we asked the same question."

"That's right," Toothpick said. "At first we didn't believe what the kids told us."

"Yeah," JP said. "According to them, one day about a year ago, they all woke up and found everyone over the age of eighteen gone. We're not sure, but Toothpick and I think that's the same time we lost the signal from Earth on the *Manu 1*. Day Zero. When it all began. No adults. No grown-ups operating the gas pumps, picking up the garbage, delivering the mail, no teachers at school, and worst of all, no parents. All of them just plain gone. At first the kids were like, where did they go? It was like that episode of *Gone, Zombie*, only it was the adults gone, not the zombies."

"Great episode," Toothpick said, making a sudden lane change that sent Mars lurching to the right. He pushed himself back up, barely noticing as his thoughts raced. His mom was gone? Like, she wasn't there in the apartment?

"Then they got used to it," JP was saying. "So did we, I guess, now that we've been here six months. I still really wish Mom and Dad were here. It's tough. But it's like back when there were all those missing kids, and Pruitt was responsible. There was a reason. There has to be a reason for the missing adults, too. We just don't know what it is yet. But in the meantime, Toothpick learned to drive. And I'm cooking up a storm. Last night Pick and I had stroganoff!"

"Tasty," Pick said.

"Wait, wait," Mars said. "Back up. Did you say six months? You've been here *six months*? But I just got here, and I was on

Alt Earth for, like, a day!"

"Maybe in your mind you were," JP said. "Or maybe the wormhole scrambled up the time. All we know is that you've been orbiting Earth for the past six months. We tracked you. We tried communicating with you, but it was radio silence. Then today Toothpick's software detected movement. I think your navigation system alerted us. So Toothpick plotted the coordinates, and that's how we got here."

Mars sat back. It was all a bit too real. Or not. "How do I know I'm not just in some other wormhole?" he demanded. "How do I know *this* is real? Or you're both real?"

Toothpick exited the highway. "Mars, you're asking the age-old existential questions: What is real? Am I real? For that I don't have the answer. Neither does Droney."

"I think, therefore I am," Droney chirped, whirring back to life at the mention of his name.

"Great," Mars muttered.

"But Mars, I'm just as real as you are," Pick said. "I think you have to just go with that. If we're in a wormhole, then we're in the same wormhole. But we *are* back on Earth. It's just that Earth . . . is different."

"And worse!" Mars said. "No parents, no Caddie, and . . . hey, just a sec."

"Wait for it—Mars is about to have a revelation," JP said.

"It took him long enough," mused Toothpick. "Twenty-three minutes since he landed."

"Maybe he was disoriented by your driving, Pick."

"Where's Aurora?" Mars asked flatly.

"No worries," JP said. "She made it back. Listen, Mars. You must be starved. I know I am."

"Actually, I feel like I'm going to barf," Mars said plaintively.

"That's just the landing still affecting you," JP said.

"But what about Aurora? Is she OK?"

"She's fine, Mars. Trust me," JP said. "But right now, it's time for sustenance. Pick, let's stop for food. In all this excitement, I didn't have time to cook."

A few minutes later, Toothpick turned into the drive-through for Burger Heaven. "JP thinks the burgers here are 'out of this world.' But since we now have a point of reference, I can assure you they're not."

"Thanks for the PSA, Pick," JP said.

They pulled up to the drive-through window with a girl who looked like she was about nine taking orders. "Good evening, gentle people. What can I get you?" she asked, revealing a mouth full of braces.

"Hi, Evie," Toothpick said, resting his aviators on his head.

"Oh, it's you, Toothpick!" Evie squealed. "I didn't recognize you in your shades. Oooh, it's JP, too!"

"Hey, friend!" JP said easily, waving.

"What will it be?" Evie asked. "The usual?"

"That's right," Toothpick said. "Which would be one Olympia burger with all the trimmings, one veggie burger with onions, and you?" Toothpick turned around. "What would you like?"

Mars frowned. "I'm too discombobulated."

"You still need to eat," Toothpick said. He turned back to Evie. "How about a large order of fries and an apple pie? And three Cokes."

"Anything for you guys! Be right back!"

Mars sighed. "She looks like she barely reaches the counter."

"That's why she's standing on a stool," Toothpick said. "She turned eight last week."

"Also . . . is it my imagination, or did she treat you both like rock stars?"

"Eh," JP said. "It's a new world, bro."

Evie came back a few minutes later with their order. "Will that be all?"

"Yes, please." Toothpick held up his phone to be scanned.

"You're paying with your phone?" Mars observed after Toothpick rolled up his window.

"We don't use paper money or cards anymore," Toothpick said. "Bad for the environment. There was a Sustainable Commerce Committee vote."

"Eat up," JP said, watching Mars. "You can have half my burger if you change your mind."

"Or mine," Toothpick said. "Though I'm mostly vegan now. Smaller carbon footprint."

Mars chewed his fries silently as they drove down the familiar streets of Port Elizabeth. This version looked just as convincing and familiar as the last one he had been in, but the evidence was everywhere. No adults—in the restaurant windows, on the sidewalks, in the cars.

They pulled up to Mars's apartment building, and Toothpick turned off the engine.

For a few minutes no one spoke as they ate. Now that Toothpick and JP had caught Mars up on this new version of Earth, it dawned on Mars that he would have to go home to an empty apartment. No one would be there. Definitely not his dad. And not his mom, either.

JP turned around, holding Mars's backpack. "I thought you might want this. It's got everything. Your headphones, your phone, some of your stuff from school. Remember that day you disappeared from the parking lot and got taken to Pruitt Prep? Well, we've had your backpack ever since. It's been in my room. I found it when I got here six months ago." They handed the backpack to Mars, who still hadn't said anything. "I'm sorry, Mars. If it helps, I can come up with you. Or you can stay over at my place. The first night is brutal. Like, all kinds of thoughts going through your head. But it will get better. You'll see."

Mars crumpled up his empty bag of fries. "No, I'm OK, JP. I think I need to be by myself tonight. Sort it all out. But it's like you said. When the kids went missing, there was a reason. Now the adults are gone. And there has to be a reason for that, too. Didn't you say Oliver Pruitt is still running his podcasts?"

"You think Pruitt is the reason the adults are missing?" Toothpick asked.

"Isn't he always the reason we're miserable?" JP said.

Mars winced. Normally he would have agreed. But now that same guy was his dad. Which made Mars feel responsible, even though he wasn't.

"Maybe. But it's worth trying to find out what he's doing with all those podcasts," Mars said. He yawned. "Wow, I guess I'm tired." Actually, he was totally exhausted.

"Just chill tonight," JP said as Mars got out of the car. "You've been through a lot. Rest up and we'll see you tomorrow, bright and early. Pick, let's go. I got tomorrow's menu to plan."

Mars · Ma

Wed, May 20, 8:20 pm

Mars

I'm standing outside our door

I wanna go in but not yet cuz you won't be there

Weird seeing u on alt earth

so happy u were a prof!

And . . . nvm about the photos bc that made me sad

I want us to be a family again

But don't worry i'll be brave

i'll find u

See u in the stars mamaji

8

A FRESH CLUE

It was dark inside his apartment when Mars let himself in and turned on the lights. The last time he had been here was on Alt Earth. Gone were the fancy dining set, the leather couch, those unreal photos from the mantel, and with them, all traces that Oliver Pruitt and his mom had ever been together. This was the old apartment, the one Mars remembered, but even this one had changed. The fridge was empty. There was no box of the Galaxy Clusters cereal his mother would stock in the cabinet. There was no laundry waiting to be washed or garbage to be taken out.

Mars went into his mom's bedroom. The bed was there, as was the cotton bedspread from India with the elephants on it. In the closet were some generic items of clothing—a few pairs of pants, a sweater, one or two shirts. His mom's standard black turtlenecks and leggings that she wore all the time were missing. The drawer next to her desk was emptied of everything except a few paper clips, one pen, and a post-card of the Seattle Space Needle. When had she even bought this? He had gone there on a school field trip once, but never with her. He turned it over and read the short description on the back. *In the heart of Seattle, the Space Needle was built for the World's Fair in 1962. Take the 43-second elevator ride to the top to see stunning views of Seattle, Puget Sound, and the Olympic Mountain Range. Don't forget to stop for snacks and your favorite beverage!*

The postcard was otherwise blank. He left it in the drawer. Where was his mother? Where were her things? Why did the place feel empty, but as if his mom had still left a few things behind? Like this bedspread. He sat down, his legs dangling off the bed. An incredible sadness weighed on him. He'd never felt this way, not even when he was in the Martian Colony and didn't know where Aurora had gone or whether he'd ever find her. Back then, he'd assumed his mother was still *here*.

"Mamaji," he whispered. "It's all my fault." She had been here before he'd made the terrible decision to leave. And now that he'd finally returned, she was gone.

As he walked down the hall, he passed the door to the puja room, where his mother would light the diya every morning. It was a small room, intended as a pantry, but she had kept it clear of everything except a few shelves where she had set up a small puja area. There she would light the diya, a small brass stand with a tea candle inside it, and sometimes she would lay fresh flowers, too. In front of the shelf, she kept a bamboo mat for sitting on. His mom wasn't that religious. But she lit the diya each morning without fail, and she would sit in front on the mat for several minutes with her eyes closed, lost in meditation. Once she said to him, "Mars, lighting the diya is a way of remembering home."

He sat down lotus-style on the bamboo mat without turning on the light. It was kind of nice. Quiet, peaceful. There was even the faint smell of incense, which he liked. He closed his eyes, trying to meditate like his mom did. But instead his mind wandered, and he thought about Alt Earth. It had been strange to see Aurora all clean-cut and dragging him to enrichment. And his mom had seemed happier than he'd ever seen her. Still, Alt Earth wasn't that great. His friends had been overwhelmingly creepy. And the last thing he remembered his mom doing was trying to pry open his door. The only thing that had felt real was hearing Caddie's voice through Droney. She was the one who had saved him.

What would she tell him to do now? With Caddie, it was always about being honest and speaking your truth. He opened his eyes. "Ma," he said out loud. "Where did you go?"

For a moment, he waited.

No response.

Mars waited some more in the silent apartment.

Still . . . nothing.

He sighed. He would have to figure it out on his own. Just like he'd told JP in the car.

Mars was about to leave the puja room when he thought he should light the diya. Maybe his mom would like it, knowing he was remembering home. He turned on the light to look for matches. As he hunted around the shelf, he noticed flower petals arranged in a half circle around the diya. Mars held one up. It was a fresh rose petal, still moist. How had they gotten here? No one else could have prayed here, and certainly no one else had placed petals around the diya.

A new life breathed into Mars.

His mom had been here!

As if . . . to leave him a clue.

"Mamaji, I'm going to find you," he whispered.

What had he done when Aurora went missing? What did he and his friends do when something didn't add up? They looked for clues. They paid attention. They worked together.

Mars found the matchbox at last and struck a match. As he watched the flame flicker on the candle, he felt a new hope flicker inside him, too. The petals were the first clue. Now he knew there would be more.

FROM THE PODCAST

Hello, podcast listeners!

It looks like everything is going swimmingly!

Nasty rainstorms? Forest fires? Greenhouse gases?

Gone!

It's funny how all those things seem to

vanish now that the grown-ups have said adieu.

I think you're finally discovering your potential.

I think you're finally realizing just what

you can do with kid power.

BUT BE CAREFUL!

Remember: power corrupts. Ha, ha!

To the stars!

---

17 Comments ⌃

staryoda   *45 min ago*
Hey OP glad UR gone!!!

allie_j *33 min ago*
he's still there or how r we getting the podcast

andromeda *17 min ago*
no adults is lowkey cool

staryoda   17 min ago
no to power grabs

galaxygenius   16 min ago
it stopped raining all the time #howitbegins

oreocookies   10 min ago
no more pollution I can breathe #howitbegins

galaxygenius   9 min ago
I miss my dad :(

allie_j   8 min ago
I miss my mom :(

neptunebaby   2 min ago
I wanna know where is #marspatel

9

SCHOOL AGAIN?

Mars was still in bed when he heard a car honk outside. He rolled over and tried to go back to sleep, but the car honked again. And again. Then his phone rang.

Mars sat up instantly. "JP?" he said groggily, seeing their name on his phone.

"Mars, tell me you're ready. Pick and I are waiting downstairs."

"Ready for what?" Mars looked at the clock on his dresser. 7:20.

"School, what else?"

Mars struck his forehead. "You still go to school? I thought there weren't any adults."

"That doesn't mean we can't still be learning. And we'll be late if you don't get your butt down here in five."

"All right, I'm coming," said Mars. A few minutes later he

was downstairs in front of his building, running his fingers through his hair.

"You look beautiful. Climb in," JP said. This morning, they were wearing a beige tunic and denim shorts, along with their favorite orange scarf.

"Did I tell you that on Alt Earth, you were wearing cleats when you were trying to break into my room?" Mars said.

JP shuddered. "No wonder you knew I was a fake. What's the first rule of soccer?"

"Never wear your cleats off the field," Toothpick said automatically. He was wearing a light green polo shirt and khakis and his hair was swept back with product.

"Pick, you're looking snazzy," Mars commented. "What's the occasion?"

"This is how I dress for school now," Toothpick said. "I think it looks more professional."

"Yeah, Pick got rid of his man bun as soon as we landed," JP said. "Too bad. I liked it."

"It was itchy," Toothpick said.

Mars unconsciously felt his own hair. The last time he'd cut it, he was on the *Manu 1*, and since then it had grown in thick curls over his ears and neck.

"Mars, before I forget." Toothpick handed Mars a stack of books. "That's all your books for seventh grade—science, history, Spanish, and Algebra 2. I know you didn't technically pass Algebra 1, but since you've been on a spaceship and piloted a launch pod, that should count for something."

"Remind me again, why are we still going to school?" Mars asked as he put the books in his backpack.

"At first when the adults disappeared, the kids just did whatever they wanted," JP said. "But after a while they got bored and lonely. So they started going to school. The older ones study YouTube videos and teach the younger ones. The younger ones ask a lot of questions. We try to solve real-life problems, like where does all the garbage go when you pick it up from the curb? How about something better than just dumping it in a landfill? That kind of thing."

"We calculated rates of decay of banana peels," Toothpick said. "That was satisfying."

"It's been a blast. Then after school, we go to work," JP said.

"Like a job?" Mars asked. He thought about Evie at Burger Heaven yesterday. It hadn't really registered until now that she was *working*.

"Sure," JP said. "I work at the sports clinic. I set broken bones, give shots. Heck, I've even done stitches. The only thing I don't do is surgery. I hate the sight of blood."

"I guess I know where to go if I break a leg," Mars said. "What about you, Toothpick?"

"I run the Northwest power grid," Toothpick said matter-of-factly as he pulled out of the circular driveway.

"For the *United States*?"

"Sure. Helps me keep track of our energy usage. We don't want to fall into the same bad patterns as our parents." Toothpick pointed toward a hill in the distance. "You can't see it, but we're building windmills over there. We're also updating our transmission lines and distribution centers, and burying electrical lines. We're totally going green."

"We're using eco-friendly stuff at the sports clinic, too," JP said. "Like biodegradable casts and finger splints."

"That's awesome," Mars said. "Just kind of . . . sudden. Like, we were doing bar graphs in sixth-grade math last time I was here."

"Here, I bet you haven't had breakfast." JP handed Mars a stainless steel container.

Just then Toothpick went over a pothole.

"Pick!" JP wailed. "You almost made me drop Mars's breakfast!"

"Apologies," Toothpick said.

"So folks, you won't believe what I found in the apartment last night," Mars said as he placed the container on his lap. "Fresh flower petals where my mom prays. Which means she's been to the apartment."

"But Mars, that's impossible," Toothpick said.

"I'm telling you what I saw," Mars said. "I think it's a clue."

"Our data shows that there have been no adult sightings across Washington State for the past year," Toothpick said, "or the continental United States. We've been keeping tallies."

"What about the rest of the world?" Mars asked.

"That, too, though we're still syncing world data," Toothpick said.

Mars opened the container and found a stack of blueberry pancakes, a metal fork, and a small vial of maple syrup. "JP! Holy cow, thanks." He scarfed down his pancakes with syrup and got some on himself when Toothpick hit another pothole.

"Transportation really needs to fix those," Toothpick said.

Mars swallowed his last mouthful of pancake. "I thought all the adults are gone."

JP turned around with their thermos. "Want some lemon-ginger tea? It's surprisingly refreshing." Mars shook his head. "Also, just 'cause the adults are gone doesn't mean we're at a standstill. Port Elizabeth has an eleven-year-old mayor. And kids are running all the major services like sanitation, utilities, transportation, and public health."

"When kids stopped going to school and staying home, everything was fine at first," Toothpick said. "Then food ran out at the grocery store. The power grid got overloaded. Kids didn't have enough money. They realized that if they didn't solve these problems, there would be an economic and social collapse of epic proportions."

"That's Toothpick's fancy way of saying some serious doggie doo would be hitting the fan," JP said.

"So they held emergency meetings in communities,

metropolitan and rural areas across the world," Toothpick said. "They used their phones to vote."

"To vote?" Mars asked.

"On everything. Who would be in charge of what and when? Each phone gets a single vote."

"One vote, one kid," JP said.

Mars scratched his head. "That seems like it could get complicated really quick."

"But it worked *enough*," JP said. "Enough for whoever had phones to get organized. Now today, we're *humming*. Which shows you, kids can get it done. Watch out, Pick! It's red!"

Toothpick slammed on the brakes at the traffic light. "Not only that, climate change has reversed," he said. "With the adults gone, travel has dropped, and carbon emissions. We've switched to natural gas, wind, and solar power. Did you notice how clear the sky was last night?"

"Um, actually, I conked out," Mars said. He had lay in his bed, the familiar weight of his blanket on top of him, thinking he would never fall asleep. He desperately hoped that he would hear the turn of the front doorknob and it would be his mom walking in. He stayed up as long as he could, his ears pricked, but in a few minutes, he was out. He was just too tired.

"The floods and wildfires have been contained," Toothpick said. "The weather is normal."

Normal. Mars said the word in his head. He'd almost

forgotten what it meant anymore. "Sounds great, Pick. Still, don't you think there must be an explanation for the missing adults?"

"Maybe, but we keep running into dead ends," JP said. "But if you think your mom was in the apartment, we'll investigate." They turned up the volume on the radio, which had been playing on low the whole time. "Hey, check out this song. I love it."

"When you're nobody you got nothin', but when you're with me, we can be somebody, and that's somethin'."

JP hummed along. "Sing it, friend!" they said to the radio.

As Toothpick turned into the school parking lot, the song ended, and a commercial came on.

"Have you found it easier to breathe the air outside?" a familiar voice began. *"Is there less traffic on the road?"*

"Hey," Mars sat up. "That sounds like—"

"Oh, lookie, we're at school," JP said quickly. "Time to—"

"Stop, don't turn it off!" Mars leaned forward to pull back JP's arm.

They gave a sigh and dropped their hand to their lap.

". . . clean air, quiet streets, and time to do what you want," the voice continued. *"And if you vote for me, I promise we'll keep finding more ways to make our world better."*

"That isn't . . ." Mars's voice trailed off, surprised.

"Vote for me and, unlike my competition, I promise I will never look for the adults."

JP said, "Pick, kill the engine or I'll be sick."

Toothpick turned off the ignition.

"Let's go, Mars," JP said. "Busy day." They jumped out of the passenger side.

As they walked to the school building, Mars turned to JP. "That was Aurora, wasn't it? Why didn't you want me to hear? Is she OK? Why does she want people to vote for her?"

Before JP could say anything, a boy in a green T-shirt approached them.

"Hey, are you Mars Patel?" he asked.

A few kids gathered around them. A murmur ran through the crowd.

"Is that Mars Patel?"

"Back at H. G. Wells?"

"Dude, it *is* Mars!"

Mars looked from face to face, bewildered. He recognized many of them. But he'd never expected that they would know him back. "Hey, everyone," he said uncertainly.

The crowd grew as they gathered around, pushing one another to get to the front.

"It's Mars, all right!" JP announced to everyone. "But give him some space, kay kay?"

"Yeah, sure, of course . . ." The kids backed away respectfully as Toothpick, JP, and Mars entered the school building. But the voices continued to buzz around him inside.

"I don't get it," Mars whispered to JP and Toothpick. "Why do they care that I'm here? Like, I'm used to being invisible."

"The same thing happened to us when we got here," Toothpick said. "Remember Evie at Burger Heaven? She's still starstruck. But you've been gone longer."

"So?" Mars said. "I'm the guy who's always in detention."

"I don't think you get it," JP said. "Everyone has been talking about you on social media. They know you were on Mars. They know about all of us. But they think you're the first one to take on Oliver Pruitt. That makes you a legend. Word has it that they think you brought down the Colony."

"But that's not true!" Mars said. "It was the volcano."

JP shrugged. "Sometimes when they hate someone as much as they hate Pruitt, they have to put their love somewhere else."

"Hey Mars! Can I get your autograph?"

"Mars, you're back! Can I get a selfie with you?"

Kids jostled one another to get a photo of Mars.

"Mars, no hard feelings, right?" To Mars's shock, the Boof was standing in front of him. This was the same Clyde Boofsky who, along with his awful friend, Scott Bane, had made Mars's life miserable for as long as he could remember. Now the Boof was apologizing?

"Sure, Bo—Clyde," Mars said.

The Boof lifted a fist up, which Mars bumped with his own.

"Hey everyone, leave Mars Patel alone or I'll smash your face in," the Boof said gleefully, turning around and punching the same fist into his palm.

Immediately the crowd dispersed.

"What just happened?" Mars asked.

"Beats me," JP said. "The Boof was always a strange one."

As the crowd thinned, the seventh-grade wall soon became visible.

"Like, even weirder than . . ." Mars stopped as he stared ahead, his mouth agape.

"Methinks he found out," JP said.

"A fair deduction," Toothpick said.

On the wall facing them, Mars saw a poster with a giant, life-size image of Aurora. Her hair wasn't purple-tipped like it had been in sixth grade, or clipped back with a barrette like it had been on Alt Earth. The Aurora in the poster was sporting a blazer with her hair cut to her chin, and she was wearing black-rimmed glasses. Under her image were the following words:

YOUNG PEOPLE RULE THE WORLD.
LET'S KEEP IT THAT WAY.
VOTE AURORA GERSHOWITZ
UNITED STATES PRESIDENT

Mars looked from JP to Toothpick as kids slid past them in the hall.

"She's running," he said, "for president?"

10

CAMPAIGN

Aurora adjusted her black-rimmed glasses as she stood in front of a mic inside the Pruitt Prep auditorium. Her eyesight was actually fine, but wearing the nonprescription glasses gave her what she thought was that "Caddie" quality. Everyone always seemed to like Caddie for some reason, and if there was a way to copy likability, then why not?

Aurora glanced around the now empty auditorium of the school. It had been six months since she had returned from Mars to discover an Earth without adults. She did not miss her own parents. Her father had abandoned them years ago, and her mom had been mostly MIA, except for the brief encounters in their apartment when she would say stuff to Aurora like, "Throw out the trash, will ya? I'm gonna be out," and then be gone for days, even weeks. For years, Aurora had had to fend for herself, living under the shadow of her mostly absent mother, while a slow rage brewed inside. Now that Aurora was back on Earth, she had no need to find her father or her mother or any of the other mindless adults who had screwed over her generation.

Instead, Aurora saw an opportunity. In the void left by the adults, Aurora had quickly assumed authority. It didn't hurt that she'd become an instant star, along with Toothpick and JP, when they were discovered emerging from their launch pods. But she'd also had practice being Fang, the leader of the Martians, the rebel group of kids who'd splintered away from the Colony in protest against Oliver Pruitt. The key was to tap into feelings that were already there and amplify them. With the Martians, it was telling them that Oliver Pruitt had taken advantage of them.

It turned out she could say the same thing at Pruitt Prep. All along, Oliver Pruitt had promised students the world if they came to his school. And where was he, once he had failed to run a colony on Mars? Missing. Disgraced. Were any of them better off? Had it stopped raining? Had it stopped flooding? Was anyone taking care of global warming, pollution, or raising the minimum wage?

Of course not. Not until the adults were gone and the kids took charge. First thing they had done was abolish the head government in every country around the world. In its place, it was one kid, one vote. Everyone voted on everything everywhere. New rules. New electronic money and no one was allowed to go hungry or not have a place to live. It was amazing how much you could do if you had a roof over your head and enough to eat. Then it was decided that in one year, each country would hold elections for president. After that, the job of all the presidents was to get together and talk about what *the kids* in their countries wanted, without bossing over anyone else. Like real leaders should. Fine. Aurora could do that. Be a leader, that is. Of the United States. But first she needed to convince everyone that she was the best person for the job.

She started with Pruitt Prep. She held assemblies, gave speeches, and chose the right people to help her. Like Jonas. Loyal, laid-back Jonas, whom everyone liked. In no time, she became the new head of Pruitt Prep, and Jonas became her trusted assistant. So far, the school's output had been magnificent: a line of self-driven cars that used a combination of solar power and garbage to run instead of gas, artificially intelligent teachers, medical personnel, lab-produced meats and vegetables, "exploding" candy (which admittedly was kinda weird), infinity lighting for classrooms and parking garages, and over a hundred new household gizmos and gadgets waiting to be sold online. And that was just in the last six months!

Now that Aurora had proven herself at Pruitt Prep, it was time to achieve her higher goal. For Aurora, the White House was the real pinnacle of success. She had only one competitor, thirteen-year-old Xavier Psai from Arizona. He was running on a campaign to find the adults, but so far, that was gaining little traction. The polls showed she was crushing him.

There was just one problem. Mars was missing. He had not turned up in an emergency launch pod like Toothpick, JP, and she did. And sure, Mars not being there didn't change Aurora's plans for running for president. But his absence pricked at her conscience. Sometimes she woke up at night in a cold sweat. A strange guilt pervaded her, a feeling she wasn't used to having. Of course, it wasn't her fault she was back on Earth and he wasn't. If anyone, Pruitt was to blame, along with his malfunctioning launch pods. (There was also a rumor that persisted about Pruitt being Mars's dad.)

Still, Aurora felt uneasy, even sad, that Mars had been gone for so long with so little explanation. What if something had happened? What if Pruitt had banished Mars somewhere into deep space? Should she try to rescue him like Mars had rescued her? Aurora had no idea where to even look.

Lately, there had been rumbles among the students at school. They all knew Mars was gone. To them he was an enigma and a hero, the original Martian, even though—hello?—Aurora had gone to the Red Planet before him. Something about Mars fed a hunger in them. He was the one who'd first stood up to Pruitt, the adult who had morphed into enemy number one (no small thanks to her!). Mars was also Pruitt's supposed son, which gave him nearly cult status. It was hard to compete with that. Next to Mars, Aurora knew she was a second-choice leader, and that her chance to win would (unfairly) change if he should ever come back. If he did, who knew? He might even get elected president. So for right now, Aurora tried to pretend Mars away from her daily life. It was the only way for her to deal.

As she stood in front of the auditorium now, she glanced over her notes one last time. In a few minutes, the students would come pouring in for their weekly assembly. As principal of Pruitt Prep, she used assemblies to share with students a list of accomplishments (mostly hers) and directives, and she now used the meetings as a place to continue forwarding her candidacy. As she reviewed her notes, she felt a tap on her shoulder.

"Aurora, how's it going?" It was Jonas, who had grown even taller during the year since she'd been gone. He towered over her, reaching a height of nearly six feet. He tried to stand respectfully, but he was Jonas, and an easy casualness followed him everywhere. He was slouching now and grinning. What could he be grinning about?

"Jonas, did you bring the thumb drive like I asked?" she said.

He nodded and handed it to her. She inserted it into her computer. "OK, be on standby. I'll need you to hand out the flyers when I tell you."

"Hey Aurora, I've got some epic news that I discovered from last night's satellite feed."

"Oh, really?"

Jonas grinned wider. "Last evening at 1900 hours, guess who was spotted entering a Chevy Tahoe in the Lake Quinault parking lot of Olympic National Park? I'll give you a hint. His name rhymes with stars!"

Aurora felt the blood drain from her face. "You mean . . . Mars? Quick, get me a list of all registered vehicles in the—"

"Done!" Jonas was triumphant. "The car is registered to a Mr. Randall Lee with the license plate TOOTHPK. Plus, he and JP McGowan were seen entering said Chevy Tahoe with said person, Mars Patel!"

"Fabulous," Aurora said faintly.

"Wait till everyone hears! They're gonna be so happy! Mars is a legend, right?"

"Wait." The wheels in Aurora's mind were spinning. "This could be good for everyone. But we have to own it, or the news could go in the wrong direction."

"I'm not following, AG," Jonas said slowly.

"Don't tell anyone yet."

"But they're going find out. Maybe they already have."

"Invite Mars to Pruitt Prep ASAP," Aurora said. "Send it from ⸻ ‑‑‑t. Make it official. I'll text you the wording."

⸻ phone. "Mars is going to be big, but let him

be big *here.*" She started texting, her thumbs going back and forth rapidly. She had worried about Mars usurping her place one day. But maybe Mars by her side could be a game changer. Like, he could push her campaign so far to the top that Xavier Psai would have no choice but to step down. "You take care of Mars," she said, "and I'll take care of assembly. Jonas, this is only the beginning."

Hello, young citizens of Earth!

Nothing spells progress like

a good leader.

I know because Pruitt Prep didn't

happen by mistake, but through careful

leadership and vision.

Aurora Gershowitz thinks she can rule the world.

She's fierce and determined.

But remember what I said about power—ha, ha!

Meanwhile, wonder how the Mars Colony is faring?

Do any of you, ahem, remember Caddie Patchett?

To the stars!

25 Comments ⊗

staryoda   35 min ago
wut did u do to caddie we're onto you OP #neverpruitt

allie_j   33 min ago
I still think OP might be able to help us am I wrong??

andromeda   17 min ago
OP is the only adult left

neptunebaby   13 min ago
vote aurora #kidpower #neverpruitt

staryoda   9 min ago
or we need #marspatel #neverpruitt

11

MARTIAN MANEUVERS

Caddie sat down at the Command Station next to Daisy and put on her headphones. It was part of her morning routine at the Mars Colony, which started in the dining hall with oatmeal and a glass of fresh-squeezed cucumber juice (greenhouse produced!), then heading to the control room, where Daisy briefed her on the events for the day.

"Good morning, Caddie," said Daisy, whose hair was copper red with gold highlights today. She was wearing a brilliant white Colony suit that had been pressed in the laundry before being dropped at her door in the early morning hours. Daisy being impeccably dressed was a sign that life on the Colony was good. "Are you ready for the day?"

"Absolutely," Caddie said. "Did you get the weather report from Julia yet?"

Daisy messaged the weather tower. "Julia, can you report on today's weather? Over."

Julia's response was swift. "Good morning. We are looking at another gorgeous Martian day. Skies are clear, winds from the south are mild, gearing up for about forty-five miles an hour. Which is good! Over."

"Excellent," Caddie said. She looked over the notes Daisy had prepared. Greenhouse yields were up. Good. The garden team was now making plans to include more complex produce like sweet corn and okra. Lab meats were on target and being reformulated using a soy and nongluten protein formula. There were new hovercrafts in the works at the tech hub, too, along with several rover upgrades for Julia and the other kids who required assisted transports. The latest one had lengthened its battery time and allowed for a full range of motion, from upright to sitting to fully prone. There were also several machines used to convert carbon dioxide from the Martian air into breathable oxygen. Even so, oxygen supply levels had been slipping lately. Charging stations were also underperforming. Hmm. Caddie would need to check with Orion. Maybe they were both tech issues.

Still, everything was going better than Caddie ever could have imagined. And when she saw the dining hall filled every day with kids talking and laughing, their faces bright with excitement, she felt a swell of pride. She had done it, along with Daisy, Julia, Orion, HELGA, and even Axel, who had proven to be surprisingly pleasant once he was away from Aurora and their Martian days. There was no more Martians versus colonists. Everyone worked together in harmony now.

But things had been very dire in the beginning. Caddie remembered that awful, uncertain day at the Old Colony, when she'd made the decision to stay behind on Mars instead of flying back to Earth. At first, no one even knew how to get back—they were miles away from the new colony. The space shuttle Julia had used to fly them over was out of fuel, night was falling, and they would soon be out of oxygen. Then the tardigrades came. Unbelievably, Tartuffe, Emi, and Duke had been waiting outside the Old Colony door. Caddie understood their intention at once and directed everyone to hoist themselves on those massive creatures, who brought them all back home.

No one exactly knew how Tartuffe, Emi, and Duke, as well as the dozens of other tardigrades that roamed outside the Colony, had come to live on the Martian surface. They were said to have originated in a lab at Pruitt Prep on Earth, then they were brought to Mars to multiply. Part spider, part wolf, part something that was entirely their own, they were also said to be crossbred for agility and strength. But unlike Muffin, the one on Earth that had been outfitted with armor, these were bare-skinned, with a fine coat of gray fur covering their immense bodies. They were also very fast, moving with breathless ease across the rocky terrain with their eight powerful legs. For the Colony, they were indispensable for moving boulders and turning windmills. It was thanks to the strength of these tardigrades that the Colony had been able to rebuild.

Even so, it had taken weeks before the kids at the Colony had been able to refuel all the spaceships, repressurize the tunnels in the Colony, and start up food production again in the greenhouse. They subsisted on potatoes, packaged soy, and a case of bottled water stored in the emergency shelter. They made use of a single oxygen machine to supply the dorms and then gradually, other parts of the Colony. Eventually Orion was able to build additional machines, and from there, a few months later, classes resumed, renovations got underway, and the kids started to feel hopeful again. Now, a year later, Caddie and Daisy were in charge of a Colony that wasn't just reassembled and repaired but buzzing with plans for the future.

Still, there was one problem that continued to plague Caddie. In the days following the volcanic explosion and dust storm, they had not only lost all contact with Pruitt Prep, but also with the *Manu 1*. Even now, Caddie had no way of knowing whether Mars and the crew had landed safely on Earth. It was a big black hole of information. And there was also the matter of Oliver Pruitt and his relationship to Mars, a secret that Caddie had intuited and kept to herself all this time. She didn't want to share anything without talking to Mars first. If she only could.

"How is Operation Contact coming along?" Caddie now asked Daisy. "Any progress?"

"None yet," Daisy said. "So far, as already reported, no contact achieved with Pruitt Prep or the *Manu 1*. Also, their fuel sources would be past depleted by now and ..." Daisy stopped here, her lower lip quivering. "I'm sorry, Caddie. I know it sounds bad. But it doesn't mean that they *didn't* make it to Earth. Remember, you were able to reach Mars's thoughts, weren't you?"

Several months ago out of desperation, Caddie had tried reaching out telepathically to Mars. It had taken all her energy to send her thoughts across millions of miles without even knowing where he was. *You need to break away,* she had tried telling him. She'd had the haunting sense he was in trouble. And it seemed to have worked; that is, it felt like her thoughts had been picked up by someone. But if it was Mars, why didn't he respond?

"Sort of," Caddie said, trying to explain now to Daisy. "It's like my message was received by someone or something."

"Something?" Daisy asked. "You mean like a computer?"

Caddie shrugged. "I'm not sure, but there was no response from Mars. No thoughts coming back." In the past when Caddie could feel Mars's thoughts, it was like the doors were open. Now they were shut, and she couldn't get in. And the harder she had tried last time, the more tired she became, until all her energy drained away. Orion and Julia had helped her to her room, where she stayed in bed for days.

"I wish I could try reaching him again," she said wistfully.

"Oh, but Caddie, it took so much out of you," Daisy said.

Caddie looked away. "Yeah. But it's not like I can do anything now."

After she'd recovered, she had discovered something else. Her ability to read minds was gone. Every now and then she would get a glimmer of a thought from someone, but largely, her powers were depleted. Perhaps for good.

"Well, we'll keep trying Pruitt Prep," Daisy said. "Orion thinks it's a power-grid issue. He's been working to increase power from the windmills. But part of that depends on the tardigrades turning those levers, and it's been getting harder to motivate them."

"Yes, I know," Caddie said. "I feel so bad for them. I know they're tired. They've got the polo tournament coming up, too."

Tardigrade polo was an unexpected activity that had cropped up in the last year. A year ago, organized sports on Mars would have been unthinkable. But the Colony had surprised everyone. It had been Axel's idea to ride on tardigrades and thwack balls with long sticks, all made with Colony-grade plastic in the maker lab. Orion became interested, too, and so did some of the other kids. In fact, polo fever took hold of the Colony, as a few fledging practices turned into weekly games, a longer tournament, and now the finals. Surprisingly, the tardigrades went along, allowing themselves to be strapped with harnesses, and even seemed to understand the rules of the game.

"The tournament will be awesome!" Daisy said. "When else do we get to root for the best athletes to win? Even if they're eight-legged modes of transportation the size of a pickup?"

Caddie laughed. "They're more than just transport, you know."

Daisy became ultraserious. "Oh, I know. Every time someone climbs on one, myself excluded because I'm terrified of them, I know it's a huuuuuge risk. I don't forget for a minute that they're fierce and totally unpredictable."

Caddie looked thoughtful. "I don't think it's that they're fierce, Daisy. It's that . . ." She remembered when the tardigrades had rescued them from the Old Colony last year. "They've got minds. And we have to treat them with respect."

"Yes, R-E-S-P-E-C-T," Daisy agreed. "And plenty of distance, right?" She shuddered and looked down at her notes on the table. "Also, one last thing, Caddie. There's the question of the podcasts."

"Didn't we agree not to resume them since they drain resources and we're not sure if they're received?"

"Affirmative. But that's not what I mean. Kids in tech hub have reported receiving frequent signals from somewhere in our astral network. The connection's bad, and we can't access the content. But *someone else* is broadcasting. I checked the logs—uploads go back six months!"

"That's promising! It also means we're able to connect out. Full-steam Operation Contact!"

"Roger!" Daisy typed on her keyboard. "As soon as I email the daily communication, I'll try again to connect to Pruitt Prep. One of these days, something has to work!"

Server: ad_astra
Sender: daisy_does_good_deeds
Recipients: colony_peeps
Timestamp: 0815 hours

Good morning, Colony Peeps!

Three cheers for the talent show last night! Weather for today is gorgeous with mild southern winds. Today's lunch is vegan ham sandwiches with marinated tomatoes and Colony olives. Dessert is chocolate brownie surprise (gluten-free option available).

Update: Tech hub is assembling a trial run of Hovercraft RX, a new addition to our fleet of hovercrafts, Orion leading.

Spotted in Tunnel A: Abandoned space boot with broken strap. Anyone want to claim?

Reminder: Tardigrade polo finals this week! Get your Colony spirit on!

Finally, please report to the dining hall this evening at 1800 hours for a live music performance by the Martian Pops. Program includes "Raindrops Keep Falling on My Helmet,"

"I'm Spacewalking on Sunshine," and the perennial crowd-pleaser, "It Takes Two to Make Martian Stew." It will be awesome!!!

Daisy Zheng (she/her)
Colony Chief of Communication (CCC)

12
MEANWHILE

Why didn't you tell me Aurora is running for president?" Mars asked as he followed Toothpick and JP down the seventh-grade wing.

JP sighed. "How do you tell someone, um, your friend has a plan for world domination?"

"Aurora has found another way to use her celebrity," Toothpick said.

Mars thought back to the radio ad. "She said she wouldn't look for the adults." He gestured around him. "But us going to school and work? It's not a solution. We need to find them."

The first bell rang.

"Not arguing," JP said. "But that's the bell, and we're gonna be late. You know Epica."

"Epi just wants everything to run smoothly," Toothpick said. "She's a rules person."

"Why would Epica care?" Mars asked.

"Take a wild guess who replaced Fagan," JP said. "Come on, Mars. We'll show you the board real quick before Pick's girlfriend spots us."

They went up a flight of stairs to an empty science lab.

"Hey, this is the same place I blew up Mrs. Baker's desk with my experiment," Mars said.

"Ah, the memories," JP said. They went to a dry-erase board and flipped it over to reveal a list written in blue marker. "Here's what Toothpick and I have been working on. We came up with different scenarios for Day Zero."

Mars looked at the list:

1. Deadly virus
2. Hoax
3. Nuclear annihilation
4. Computer simulation
5. Aliens

"We've gone through these scenarios one by one," Toothpick said. "Was it a virus?"

"No," JP said. "A virus can't just affect adults and not kids."

"Right. Then we thought, maybe it's a huge hoax. But that would be hard to pull off without someone leaking it on social media," Toothpick said.

"Then I thought, what if it was something nuclear?" JP said. "But where's the radiation? Nada. Also, I thought, what if there was a giant asteroid? But Toothpick didn't even let me put that on the list."

"Our satellites would have detected it before impact," Toothpick said.

"No on a computer simulation, too," JP said.

Toothpick nodded. "There would be some kind of glitch in the system. A bug. But here, everything is exactly the same as before except for the adults. And so far . . . no alien spotting."

"Which leaves us where we are, Mars," JP said. "No leads."

The door to the science lab opened.

"Hey everyone, it's time for class. And tardy is *never* a good look." Epica Hernandez stepped in wearing a heather-gray power suit and red heels. "Welcome back, Mars," she said, flashing him a bland smile. "Now that I'm principal, I want to hear about all about your trip to the Mars Colony. Way to represent H. G. Wells in the universe! But first period has started. I don't want to shut my celebrity student inside detention hall the first day he gets here."

"Hey, Epica, maybe you can shut your—"

"What JP means," Toothpick said quickly, "is that we're just finishing up debriefing Mars."

Epica smiled at him. "Of course, Randall! Oh, Mars—Aurora wants to see you ASAP."

"Me?" Mars said. "But I don't even know where she is."

"She's at Pruitt Prep," Epica said. "She's principal, like I am at H. G." She struck a pose. "And together, we're a force to reckon with."

JP rolled their eyes. "More like the principals of doom."

"I'm going to pretend I didn't hear that," Epica said. "But if I were you, Mars, I would check your messages immediately. You know Aurora doesn't like to be kept waiting." She stepped out of the lab. "Hey, you. What are you doing in the hall without a pass? That's detention for you!"

Meanwhile, at Pruitt Prep, Aurora and Jonas were finishing up in the recording studio.

"OK, play it back, Jonas," Aurora said.

"Sure thing," Jonas said. " 'Aurora Delivers on Her Promise,' take number thirty-two."

"Hello, young citizens. It's me, Aurora. On Mars, I rebelled against Oliver Pruitt's authoritarian rule. When the volcano erupted, I saved the Colony and led a daring mission back to Earth. As the only candidate with true leadership experience, I promise you I will never look for the adults who abandoned us. Instead, we will build a prosperous new path without them. Why should you trust me? Because I've already delivered on one of my big campaign promises. We have found Mars Patel! And he will be a key part of the future we create together!"

"Nice job, AG!" Jonas said. "Though you didn't mention Xavier and his plan to find the adults. Isn't he the one you're worried about?"

Aurora took off her headphones. "Never mention your competition, Jonas. You want the focus to be on you. Please go ahead and send this recording to every screen and media outlet you can." She saw Jonas's expression. "What?"

"Your ad's really great," he said slowly, "but are you sure about that part with Mars? I mean, you didn't *exactly* promise to find him. And now he's part of your campaign?"

"Mars is our friend, Jonas. Don't you miss seeing him? I miss seeing him. And now he's been found. Who cares if I promised that or not. It's still excellent news. Especially for me."

"Yeah, well, I'm just not sure he's going to help all that much," Jonas said. "Since, um, he kinda doesn't want to see you."

"What?" Aurora's eyes narrowed. "We're best friends. Like, he came all the way to Mars to rescue me. I mean"—she cleared her throat—"obviously, *I* was instrumental on that trip back to Earth. But Mars still came to the Colony because it was important. And now? The presidency is *way* more important."

"You don't need to convince me," Jonas said. "But Mars has other ideas. At least his email said so."

"What did he say? Send me that email he wrote."

Jonas opened his phone and clicked Send.

From: thisismars@zapmail.com
To: Jonas Hopkins <jhopkins@pruittprep.edu>
Date: Thursday, May 21, 9:30 am
Subject: Re: Invitation to Pruitt Prep!

Hey Jonas,

Great to hear from you! Yeah, glad to be back!

Listen, I'd love to come but I'm busy. Maybe some other time.

Say hi to Aurora for me.

Peace out,

Mars

∩

"Peace out, Mars?" Aurora repeated. "That's completely unacceptable. I didn't want to do this, but I have no other choice. Jonas, it's time for Operation Limo."

"But maybe you should—"

"This isn't a discussion," Aurora said. "Now!"

Jonas shrank back. "Sure, whatever you say, AG."

He ambled out of the recording studio.

Aurora followed him, storming to her private office. It was a totally exasperating day. Sure, she was glad Mars was back, but she was hurt, too. Wasn't she supposedly the most important person in his life? Why else *had* he come to Mars to rescue her? And now he'd teamed up with Toothpick and JP, who had completely abandoned her. They'd preferred mediocre H. G. Wells to Pruitt Prep and its state-of-the-art equipment, even when she had sent them both exclusive invitations to attend. They'd chosen the Boof, who couldn't tie his shoelaces, over the smartest kids in the world. Headed by her.

And that was their problem: she was in charge, and they couldn't deal. Meanwhile, someone like Caddie could . . . Aurora swallowed. She couldn't bring herself to complete the thought. It didn't matter. Mars would still come through for her. He just needed to understand what was at stake.

Because if Xavier Psai beat her, he would do what Aurora had resisted all along: a coordinated, full-scale search for the adults. Why? Because Xavier was nice. Because he had a conscience. Because he missed his mommy.

Not Aurora. She had bigger and better plans. She reached for her phone to tell Mars. Then she stopped. Because that wasn't the way it would work. No texting from her. Not when there was Operation Limo.

Next to her there was a beeping on the screen. Aurora's eyes flickered to the monitor.

PRUITT PREP MISSION CONTROL: ATTEMPTING CONTACT
PRUITT PREP MISSION CONTROL: ATTEMPTING CONTACT

Aurora's eyes widened. For months, Jonas had tried establishing contact from this end. First there was no signal. Then it kept getting disrupted. The infrastructure had been wiped out by the volcanic eruption. Different students had attempted to reroute the signal but were stymied at every turn. And now, with no explanation, the Mars Colony had reached them.

She looked around. Usually there was a team of kids

monitoring the outside communications throughout the school day. There were daily emails from neighboring communities, utilities companies, and salespeople. But today, the team had been sent to the central office while she and Jonas recorded her ad. Last time she had recorded, a few of them had burst in with a tech support question for Jonas and interrupted her recording.

Aurora opened the message and scanned its contents.

Server: ad_astra
Sender: daisy_does_good_deeds
Recipient: Pruitt_Prep_Central
Timestamp: 0930 hours

Attention Pruitt Prep Mission Control:
Do you read us? We are attempting contact. Please respond by message or radio transmission. We are attempting contact. Status of Colony: excellent. Caddie Patchett, now commander-in-chief. Several missions successfully deployed, including new weather system, reactivation of greenhouse, production of crops, and transportation milestones. But we continue to be without contact to the *Manu 1* (and its crew) or to Earth.

Please respond. Like . . . NOW!!!!!

Yours Respectfully,

Daisy Zheng (she/her)
Colony Chief of Communication (CCC)

Aurora stared at the message on the screen. She felt her stomach churn. The message had come at the worst time. Talking to them now would remind everyone that there was a Colony in the first place. That they had succeeded, that Caddie was in charge, and most of all, they were *surviving*. Surviving meant success. Caddie's success. And Oliver Pruitt's. Which would spell the end of Aurora's campaign. "You always were a do-gooder, Caddie," Aurora whispered.

Her heart raced. For a few moments, Aurora truly hated herself. She thought of all the things she could do, and what she might have been like in a perfect world—the one she didn't live in.

Then she leaned forward and deleted the message. As for the radio call, there was a way to purge that from the system, too. By the time Aurora left the office, there was no trace that anyone had ever tried contacting them from the Colony.

13
MEMORY LANE

"OK, why are we meeting in the janitor's closet again?" JP asked.

"Mars wants to revisit cherished memories," Toothpick said.

"Ow!"

"Sorry," said Mars, righting a mop that had fallen on JP's head. "Yeah, we had some good times hiding here from those awful assemblies."

"Totally," JP said. "Aurora was always pulling the fire alarm or something."

"Last time I saw Jonas in school was in this closet," Mars said. "Before he disappeared after that Code Red. That seems so long ago. And Caddie . . ." His voice drifted off.

"You miss her, don't you, Mars?" JP said. "We all do."

"A lot can happen in a year," Toothpick said.

Mars leaned back against the wall. "I'm here also because

I need a break. Everyone keeps asking me questions about outer space. I can't go to the bathroom or get a drink of water or get to my locker. There was even a news reporter in science class! It feels like the paparazzi chasing me!"

"Whoa," JP said. "Pick and I didn't get reporters. There's something different about you, Mars. Maybe because of who your dad is and—" JP slammed their hand over their mouth.

"JP!"

"Sorry, Mars," JP said. "I meant, I meant—we don't know who your dad is, right?"

"Except that he's Oliver Pruitt," Toothpick said.

"JP!"

"I didn't tell Pick, I swear!" Their voice rose. "I'm a clam, people!"

"JP didn't tell me," Toothpick said. "Everyone knows already because Oliver Pruitt announced it himself on his podcast."

"But he said he would keep it a secret!" Mars exclaimed.

"That's Pruitt for you," JP said. "Are we surprised?"

Outside, the bell for last period rang.

"I still don't get it, Mars," JP said. "Why don't you want anyone to know Pruitt is your dad?"

"At first I hoped he was lying," Mars said, and sighed. "But he wasn't."

"You received the results of a DNA test?" Toothpick asked.

"What? No!" Mars thought of the photos on the mantel in

his Alt Earth apartment. "I mean, I guess I knew he was telling the truth all along. I just didn't want to accept it."

"Makes sense," JP said. They squeezed Mars's arm in the dark.

"But also I don't want people to treat me differently because I'm related to him. I don't want to have special power because of who I am."

"Mars, you *are* powerful," JP said. "And it's not because you're Pruitt's son."

"Really?" Mars asked.

"It's because you took him on, you rockin' space rebel."

Toothpick leaned forward. "Also Mars, there are two camps. That's what the whole election is about, and Aurora's campaign. Some kids are #NeverPruitt. And some kids still believe in him, because they think he might be able to help find their parents."

"Surprise, surprise—guess which side Aurora is on," JP said.

"The question is," Toothpick said, "which side are *you* on, Mars?"

"We have to find the adults," Mars said. To him, it was clear. He needed to find his mom. The other kids needed to find their parents, too. But even the other adults who were not someone's parents had a right to be found. They had a right to continue their lives. "I found those flower petals in my apartment. That's a clue."

"I left Droney in my locker for system updates," Toothpick

said. "But before I rebooted him, he reported that fresh flower petals can last for a period of three days."

"That means my mom was there in the last three days. Maybe she left some other clues, too. I have to go back home. If I can get past the paparazzi, that is."

"I'll go," JP said. "Pick? You game?"

"Affirmative," Toothpick said. "Which leaves one question. Why are we still in the janitor closet?"

"Yeah, our work is done here," JP said. "Love the memories, but—"

Without warning, the door to the janitor closet was wrested open.

"AAARRGH," JP yelled.

Toothpick and Mars held up their hands to block the light from the hallway.

Epica stood there in her pantsuit. Behind her were two teens wearing shades and army-green sweats. "Sorry, Mars," she said. "Gentlemen, grab him."

"Patel." One of teens pulled Mars out of the closet roughly. "You're coming with us."

"Epi," Toothpick said, dismayed. "We had an agreement about the janitor closet."

Epica cast her eyes down. "Randall, babe," she whispered, "I didn't have a choice."

"Hey, that's my friend!" JP yelled as the two teens grabbed Mars's wrists and dragged him down the hall.

Mars wriggled between the two lanky boys. "Where are you taking me? What's going on?"

"You'll find out," said one of them, a thin guy with a sparkly earring in his left ear.

"Yeah, you'll find out," said the other one. He wore thick boots that made clomping sounds on the floor.

"Stop copying me," said the first guy.

Mars could feel their nails digging into his wrists as he tried to slip his arms out, but the two teens were remarkably strong. "Let go!" he cried.

JP tried to follow them, but Epica blocked their way. "You and Randall stay back."

"Who sent those thugs?" JP demanded.

"Epi must have a good reason," Toothpick said. "I think."

Down the hall, Mars kept trying to dig his heels in. "I don't have to go with you," he said, gritting his teeth. "Hey, Boof, look what these guys are doing! All of you . . ."

The boy with the earring hissed at him, "Cut that out if you don't want anything bad to happen to your mom!"

"My mom?" Mars fell silent. Who *were* these people?

They had reached the front doors of the school. Around him a crowd had started to form.

"Tell them to scram, Patel," continued the guy with the earring.

"Yeah, we don't need trouble," said the thick boots guy. "Remember your mom."

"Mars, are you OK?" asked a sixth grader.

"Hey, Mars is in trouble!" yelled someone else. The crowd that had formed was getting agitated. But surrounding the periphery of the school were other teenagers dressed in army-green sweats like the two guys holding him. They seemed ready to attack. Things were going to get out of hand. Behind the crowd stood JP, Toothpick, and Epica, and they look worried, too.

"I'm OK! I'm OK!" Mars called out to crowd. "These are, um, my friends."

At the curb, a stretch limo was waiting. Someone opened the back door from the inside.

Mars eyed the limo nervously. "Where's my mom?" he asked. It was a way to delay getting inside, but maybe one of the teenagers would slip up and tell him.

"Get in, Patel," said the guy with the boots instead.

Mars tried to think fast. If he resisted, something bad might happen to the kids watching. At the same time, he did *not* want to get into the car. Just then Mars heard a deep, throaty cry. From the parking lot, an enormous creature was heading for them, a creature no one had seen before. Well, most people. "Cupcake!" Mars cried out.

The tardigrade roared, sending everyone into a panic, including the teenagers surrounding the school, who scampered back. Meanwhile, the guys who had been holding Mars jumped into the limo.

"You came back!" Mars said, wrapping his arms around the tardigrade's leg. "Atta girl!"

Cupcake nudged him and leaned down so Mars could climb on her back. From up there he saw the throng of kids standing several feet away on the sidewalk. "Don't worry!" he called out to them. "I have a plan! We're going to stick together and find the adults!"

The kids who had been watching in fear as Cupcake reared up now cheered.

"You go, Mars Patel!" someone yelled.

"Peace out, Mars!"

Mars craned his neck and saw Toothpick and JP hurrying down the sidewalk away from the parking lot and looming teenagers, and then Cupcake carried Mars away.

14
SECTOR 4B

As head of security, part of Julia's job was to monitor the weather for any developments that could threaten the well-being of the Colony. Which is why on most days, she spent her time in the weather tower, looking at precipitation data. During the last weeks, Julia had been noticing some strange patterns from one of the weather tracking programs. There had been storm systems, gale winds, and then nothing for days. Then, curiously, a cloud system that lingered over Sector 4B for no apparent reason.

"Why so many clouds there?" she asked Axel, her partner in the weather tower.

"I dunno," he said. "Maybe it's just a malfunction in the satellite images."

"No, they look real," Julia said.

"I can run a script and compare it against cloud patterns

last year around this time period," Axel offered. "Then you can see if it's an anomaly or seasonal."

"Good idea. Thanks," Julia said, surprised. Axel was turning out to be a better partner than she had expected. When he had first started, he'd been dour and disengaged, and once she had found him scribbling graffiti on the walls of the weather room. Julia immediately put in a request for *anyone else.*

"I can't have a teenage mutant ninja whatever running amok in the weather room," she complained to Caddie. "I caught him writing space graffiti on the wall."

"Give him a chance," Caddie said gently. "Maybe the weather room could use astronauts or spaceships or whatever Axel likes to draw."

"No, he was literally writing 'space graffiti' on the wall. And he spelled *graffiti* wrong, too."

"I think he'll surprise you, Julia," Caddie said. "Remember, he's been through a lot."

The next day, he was drawing goblins. "Stop drawing on the walls!" Julia barked.

Then she remembered what Caddie had told her. About giving him a chance. So Julia stuck Axel with a multitude of tasks to keep him occupied so he wouldn't have time to pick up a marker. And then something strange happened. He did everything she asked. And more. Most surprisingly, he wrote a computer program to check for volcanoes by detecting changes in the level of methane in the atmosphere.

"Axel, this is . . . clever," Julia said, surprised.

Slowly, they formed a partnership. He would run the scripts; she would read and interpret. Sometimes he would correct her. Just like how a good team ought to work.

Together, they made so much progress. These days no one got caught unaware in a windstorm while collecting samples on the surface. Greenhouse production had tripled by timing harvest cycles around sun patterns. And in general, kids started to freak out less about the volcano, now that Axel had assured everyone that they would really know if and when it would ever blow again.

But even Axel didn't have a real explanation for the clouds Julia was seeing now. As he worked on his script, Julia mulled over the formations.

It didn't seem like a big deal, really. So there were some clouds. But Julia couldn't shake the feeling that those clouds weren't . . . normal.

She heard a beeping sound coming from her rover. "Low battery," came an announcement.

"Not again," she groaned. "I just bloody charged my rover yesterday."

"Isn't Orion working on an upgrade?" Axel said. "Maybe it's time for a new rover."

"This one's only a few months old. I'll have to take it to tech and see what Orion says."

"Caddie's on the line from control." Axel pressed the intercom. "Wassup, Caddie? Over."

"Hi, Axel," Caddie said. "Daisy is here with me, too. Over."

"Hi, awesome weather team. Over," Daisy said.

"Orion is reporting a power outage," Caddie said. "Charging units aren't charging either. Over."

"Exactly!" Julia said. "I thought it was just my rover. Over."

"Lemme see what Orion says," Axel said. He conferenced in the tech hub.

"This is HELGA," announced a familiar robotic voice. "I am your tech assistant, repurposed to make your colony life comfortable. My pronouns are they and them. How might I assist you? Over."

"HELGA, I already know who you are," Axel said. "Is Orion there?"

"Orion here, Axel," came another voice. "You hear about the power outage? It doesn't make any sense. The tardigrades are still operating the windmills. We got five of them on now. Over."

"It's a lot of turning, isn't it?" Caddie mused. For a high-tech colony, that was one mechanical element still in place: the turning of the windmills. Solar energy wasn't enough, so the tardigrades operated several massive mechanical wheels with their sheer walking strength.

"They can handle it. Over," Orion said.

"Tardigrades are known for speed, strength, and grit. Over," HELGA remarked pleasantly.

"But maybe they're tired," suggested Caddie. "Maybe they can't *keep* keeping up. Over."

"Today's the tardigrade polo final," Daisy observed. "We've been training for weeks. Will that, um, be OK?"

"You better believe it," Orion said. "Tartuffe and Emi are ready. So are the other tardigrades. Axel, your days are numbered. We're so beating you!"

"No, dude," Axel said good-naturedly. "You're the ones who are cosmic history. Over."

A friendly rivalry had sprung up between the two boys and the teams they were leading. Axel was all about brute force and speed, and Orion was about strategy and cunning. Together, their different personalities found a way to bring out the best in each other, and they stirred up excitement among the teammates, who looked forward to their practice times together.

"Games and friendly competition are important ways to build Colony spirit," HELGA said. "Calling it off could make colonists feel like a dump."

"You mean 'down in the dumps,' HELGA," Orion corrected. For a robot, HELGA had adapted to colonist life with amazing speed. Their language abilities were also moving along but they were still prone to a mistake or two. "And yeah, sadness is a real thing," Orion went on. "With everyone being so far away from home. Which is why we keep the games going. We'll find some other way to give the tardigrades a break without stopping them as our power source. Otherwise it will be a crisis, I'm telling you. We can't afford to have a real power outage. Over."

Meanwhile, Julia had been staring at her screen. "Every-one, there have been cloud patterns in Sector 4B for days. It's driving me bonkers. Over."

"Copy you," Orion said. "But, um, can we get back to the power outage issue? Every time I think we've got the hover-craft almost done, the lights go out or the power tools stop working. What's next? The oxygenation chambers? Over."

"We have the generators, Orion," Daisy piped up. "They're set up in a case of an emergency. Over."

"But Orion—what I'm saying has a direct bearing on the con-versation," Julia said. "Because now it's not just clouds. Right now, in the last few minutes while we were all talking, there's something else going on in 4B. A huge power surge! Over."

"What?" Caddie asked, surprised. "But Sector 4B is past Monument Crater. Like, there's nothing over there. Over."

"Roger," Daisy said. "No development, no mountain ranges, no protection from environmental hazards. In other words, a no-person's land. Over."

"Copy," Julia said, "but it doesn't matter. That's what the readings show—a ginormous power surge." She glanced at Axel, who was pursing his lips, his nose ring glinting under the fluorescent lights of the weather room.

"So, dudes," he said, "what's going on in Sector 4B?"

FROM THE PODCAST

I made a discovery when I was nine years old
that changed my life.
I visited the Seattle Space Needle, where
I encountered a whirl of colors and a burst of light.
What I saw made me rethink everything
we know about science and travel and
life in the universe.
But my parents didn't believe me.
They didn't encourage my curiosity.
Adults are awful that way.
Today, you're free to pursue your own discoveries.
But are you better off?
Don't you want to live in a colony
like the one I designed that values kid thinking?
Because where did all the adults go?
You wouldn't want to wait until
ONE DAY YOU DISAPPEAR, TOO!
That would keep me up at night. Ha, ha!

To the stars!

50 Comments ⊗

staryoda   45 min ago
you took away the adults didn't u #neverpruitt

allie_j   33 min ago
but maybe OP can help

neptunebaby   17 min ago
how come no one has heard from the Colony

cosmic_chris   15 min ago
yeah my little brother is there

galaxygenius   11 min ago
at least it stopped raining

oreocookies   9 min ago
I love our new backyard I can see the pacific!!!

andromeda   8 min ago
I still miss my mom and dad :(

oreocookies   7 min ago
me too :(

15

WALL

For Mars, having Cupcake around was epic. Now that he was with a terrifying tardigrade, no one bothered him. No selfies, no autographs to sign, no reporters. On his way home, they stopped peacefully for groceries, shampoo, soap, and donuts. Having Cupcake around also meant he didn't have to be alone in the apartment.

"Cupcake, you want a donut?" he asked. "It's kind of like a cupcake, but it has a hole in it. Though maybe you haven't had a cupcake either, huh?"

Cupcake was agreeable to anything. She spread out on the floor and gnawed on her donuts.

Mars lay on the couch. He was exhausted. He missed his mom, and school with all those kids swarming him had been taxing. And the teens in the parking lot had totally freaked him out. They would find out where he lived. They would come here. Then what? He pulled out his phone to see if Toothpick or JP had responded to his texts. So far, nothing, but there were a gazillion messages from Aurora.

Mars · Aurora

Thu, May 22, 4:10 pm

Aurora
Mars r u there

Aurora
xcitd

Aurora
ur ok right

Aurora
sooo much to tell u

Aurora
ru there?????

Aurora
why didn't u get in the limo

"I should have guessed," Mars said. Cupcake looked up from her box of now nearly finished donuts. "Aurora's the one who sent the limo and those guys after me." That should have relieved him. After all, Aurora didn't want to hurt him, did she? But honestly, Mars wasn't sure of anything anymore, least of all Aurora. "She would have gotten me, too, if it hadn't been for you, Cuppy." The tardigrade grunted. "What does she want from me, anyway? Whatever it is, she's got a lot of kids behind her. That wannabe swat team hiding behind the bushes at school? They were going to attack us." Cupcake finished her last donut and belched. "You're strong, Cupcake, but if Aurora wants something, she won't stop until she gets it."

As if on cue, there was a loud pounding on the door. Cupcake stiffened. So did Mars. He held a finger up to his lips. "Shh, girl," he whispered. From the coffee table, Mars picked up a remote control as his weapon of choice. If Aurora's people had come for him here, this time he wasn't going without a fight.

"Mars! It's us. Sorry it took us a while. We came on foot, and Toothpick here walks slow."

"It's JP!" Mars exclaimed. He could see Cupcake relaxing, too, at the sound of JP's voice. He opened the door and found JP and Toothpick standing in the hall. "I'm glad you're both OK!" His eyes fell on the pizza boxes in JP's hands. "Oh my god! Come in. Let's eat!"

∩

After they finished the pizza (Cupcake had her own—luckily JP had brought a pie just for her), the three of them got ready for bed.

"Do you think one of us should stay up?" Mars asked. "I keep expecting Aurora's goons to show up. Like, don't they have their tracers or something?"

Toothpick shook his head. "I used Droney to set up a refractor on the roof to block any surveillance. They won't be able to detect us in here. Though theoretically they could still come bang on the door. But knowing Aurora, she would think that's a waste of time. Still, if someone wants to stay up to answer the door, then go ahead."

"Nope, totally drained," JP said. "Hey Mars, good thing you still have the sleeping bags your mom bought for that camping trip you never went on."

"Um, yeah," Mars said. That was how most of their plans had seemed to go.

"So if y'all don't mind, I think I'm going to conk out right now," JP said, then got into a sleeping bag next to Toothpick, who was seated cross-legged on the floor with his eyes closed. "Pick, are you planning to sleep sitting up?"

Toothpick's eyes fluttered open. "No, I'm meditating. I've been doing this every night since we got back to Earth. It helps me sleep. I had a hard time before."

"Really?" JP said, surprised. "I didn't know that. You're always so calm, Pick."

"I'm calm on the outside," Toothpick said. "But sometimes my thoughts race."

Mars watched them from his bed. "My mom meditates, too," he said.

"What are you thinking about when your eyes are closed?" JP asked curiously. "Birds? The ocean? Epica?"

Toothpick closed his eyes again. "No, JP. I try not to think about anything. That's the whole point of meditating. You're freeing your mind of distractions."

"Huh," JP said. "That sounds impossible."

"It's hard in the beginning," Toothpick said. "I still have thoughts. I just try to have fewer ones. Also it helps if nobody's talking."

"Sorry," JP said, and fell quiet. Carefully, they arranged their sleeping bag and pillow and lay down. For a while, Mars and JP just watched Toothpick. He was breathing quietly and deeply, his hands resting on his knees, with his thumb and finger forming a circle. The sound of Toothpick's breaths seemed to calm JP, too, because in a few moments, they closed their eyes and fell asleep.

As Toothpick meditated, Mars lay back in his bed. In the corner, Cupcake had curled into a ball and drowsed off. A strange sense of happiness filled Mars. He still missed his mom more than ever. Especially because seeing Toothpick reminded him of the mornings when he would find her in the puja room, the ends of her hair dripping with water from her shower, her eyes also closed in meditation. It might be the only time he'd ever seen her sitting in one place. Otherwise, she was flitting around, late to work for whatever mysterious job she was involved with, getting her shoes on while she pestered Mars to get up because he was late for school. That was their household. Hurry-burry. Disorganized. Late. Then achingly empty with his mother's absence. But now the apartment was no longer empty because his friends had come, and he was filled with fresh hope.

Mars had a strange thought. Maybe the universe was like Toothpick's finger and thumb closed together in a circle. Connected. Caddie so far away, but only a few thoughts separating them. And his mom. Mars remembered the flower petals. Closer than he might think.

🎧

When Mars woke up the next morning, Cupcake was still asleep. So were JP and Toothpick. Mars moved gingerly, not wishing to disturb anyone, and got out his phone and headphones. It was his old habit, listening to the podcast as soon as he got up. Oliver Pruitt had always been how Mars started his day.

JP and Toothpick had said that somewhere, Oliver Pruitt was still broadcasting his podcast. Mars had listened on Alt Earth, even made a comment, but all of that seemed unreal to him. Now that he was back on real Earth, what was his dad telling everyone?

When Mars reached the podcast page, he saw that all the old podcasts were unavailable. But a new one had been added this morning. He swallowed and played it. Then played it over again. And then a third time. Then he shut the whole thing off, angry and sad at the same time.

His dad had said on the podcast that he'd discovered something big when he was nine years old. He didn't say what it was, but whatever it was had made him into the billionaire entrepreneur astronaut he was now. But Mars's life had changed when he was nine, too, when Oliver Pruitt mailed him a toy rocket on his birthday. For the first time, Mars had really believed he had a dad. Only he would never see him or get to hang out with him. In fact, he'd only find out who his father was when they were on another planet.

Also, on the podcast, Oliver Pruitt had said his parents were awful. But honestly, Oliver Pruitt was seriously awful, too. Mars reached for the toy under his pillow, fingering the frayed edges and the soft material that had matted over the years. A toy rocket was not a substitute for a dad. But that's what it had become.

There was a button on the bottom of the toy rocket that made it light up. He turned the rocket over, wondering if the batteries still worked, and pressed the button just to see if it would light up again. Nothing happened. The batteries were probably dead. But as he pressed the lever to open the battery compartment, he felt an unexpected tremor. Mars stopped. Was that him moving? Or the bed? He looked at his friends sleeping. Was it an earthquake? But no, everything remained still. And yet, he had clearly felt a tremor. After a moment, his mind made the connection. He pressed the lever on the rocket again. Another tremor! Then he saw for the first time the outline of something glowing through the wallpaper on the wall next to his bed.

"JP, Toothpick . . ." he whispered. He put his hand up and felt the wallpaper. It was smooth, and yet the outline was lit. Like there was something there . . . a door. He started picking at the wallpaper. "Guys!" he called out. What was behind the wallpaper? He picked at it more urgently.

On the floor, JP stirred. "Mars, what are you doing?"

Toothpick woke up, and soon, the three of them were scraping at the wallpaper.

"What do you mean your toy rocket did it?" JP asked.

"It was a gift from Oliver Pruitt," Mars said. "And . . . it's doing something. I just don't know what. Wait, the wallpaper is coming off here in the corner. Let me peel it back and—"

They gasped. Under the wallpaper were the heavy steel doors to an elevator.

"So, how do you open it?" JP said. "There's no button."

"Right," Mars said. "I'm . . . not sure."

"Look at your toy rocket," Toothpick said. "That's what started the doors glowing."

"Good thinking, Pick." Mars examined the rocket. He pressed the lever again, and the double doors opened.

"All right, let's go," Mars said, but JP held him back.

"Whoa, I'm all for solving mysteries," they said, "but this is like a scene from your classic horror film. Where the unknowing kids go down the elevator and are never heard from again!"

"We're not in a horror movie," Mars said. "Oliver Pruitt's the one who put in the elevator."

JP crossed their arms. "Yeah, but he did it without you knowing!"

"With Oliver Pruitt, anything is possible," Mars said. He

waved the toy rocket. "Look, this set it off, and it's from him! We have to go. It's a clue. We'll take Cupcake to defend us."

Cupcake grunted.

"We can use Droney for navigation." Toothpick picked up his backpack and slung it on.

"OK, OK," JP said. "Fine, we'll all go. But first we get out of our pj's. And I have to pee."

"Let's meet back in Mars's room in five," Toothpick said.

After everyone was ready, Mars, Toothpick, JP, and Cupcake reassembled in front the elevator. They entered the compartment, with Cupcake in the rear.

"Last words, anyone?" JP said.

Toothpick and Mars shook their heads.

Mars pressed the lever on the rocket again, and the doors slammed shut. Without warning, the gears inside cranked loudly as the elevator rapidly fell.

"Then I'll say something," JP cried. "HELP!"

Good afternoon, Colony Peeps!

Today is the last day of our tardigrade polo championship. Game on! Battling for top place are the Lava Rocks, headed by Captain Axel Thunderbolt, and the Red Dust Devils, headed by Captain Orion Acevedo.

Curious about our team captains? Here's a short bio to whet your appetites!

Sixteen-year-old Axel hails from Fairbanks, Alaska, where his hobbies included dog mushing, gaming, and graffiti (nothing illegal, I hope!). Since coming to the Colony, Axel has become a gifted Martian landscape painter. Amazing!

Orion, also sixteen, comes to us from Tacoma, Washington, where he was known for shooting baskets, doing algebra homework, and fostering rescued cats. ("I'm allergic to them," he says. Double heroic!) At the Colony, Orion heads the tech hub and space travel program, yet still manages to mentor our young pilots. Lucky us!

The game begins at 1400 hours sharp. Come with your noisemakers and team spirit! As usual, HELGA will be distributing our special colony-grade binoculars at the observation window. Remember, these binoculars not only provide stellar magnification but are specifically designed not to interfere with team communications. As always, all binoculars must be returned at the end of the game. No exceptions. Go Rocks and Dust Devils. May the best tardigrade polo team win!!

Daisy Zheng (she/her)
Colony Chief of Communication (CCC)

16
SEEING SIGNS

When Aurora heard Oliver Pruitt's early-morning podcast, she didn't care about his discovery as a nine-year-old, whatever that was, or his musings about life in the universe. What she did care about was all that stuff on where the adults had gone, and how it could happen to the kids, too. Just what she needed—Pruitt freaking everyone out as she was making a final push with her campaign.

"Jonas, we need to find a way to shut down that podcast," she said when he came into her office with a list of stats for the day.

"Negative on that, AG," he said. "Remember, we've tried, but I can't locate his source."

"Ugh," Aurora said from behind her executive desk, which used to belong to Oliver Pruitt. When she'd first sat here, knowing she had replaced him, it had given her enormous satisfaction. But now she feared that eventually he would get the best of her. "Just shut it down on our end, Jonas," she pleaded. "Block him from our Internet. Something! He's going to agitate the students!"

"I'll see what I can do. I could turn off their Wi-Fi. But they have ways to hotspot out." He scratched his head. "Um, AG, I think you're letting Oliver Pruitt get under your skin."

Aurora flinched. "You don't get it, Jonas. My dad would do the same thing," she said stonily. "He'd say to my mom and me, what if the utilities company shuts down our heat?"

"And did they?" Jonas asked.

"No!" Aurora said. "But he'd say it to mess with us. To get my mom and me to listen to him. Then one day he left for good. But then my mom started saying the same thing to me. *Aurora, you better eat everything on your plate. Who knows, the fridge might stop working tomorrow if they turn off our electricity.* She did it to make me afraid, like it was my fault somehow. Then she'd go out to 'earn a living,' whatever that was, and use it as an excuse to not be around and take care of me."

Jonas frowned. "That's some bad mind-control, Aurora."

Aurora's lower lip quavered. "Yeah, well, those are my parents."

Jonas looked at the stats papers in his hands. "Listen, AG, your parents aren't the greatest. But not everyone is like that, and, um . . ." He cleared his throat. "Are you starting to wonder even a teensy bit, where the *other* adults went? Maybe if you talked to somebody about it, you'd feel better."

Aurora sniffed. "I'm fine," she said.

"Sure thing, AG. But you never know. We could also check on how the Colony is doing. That might make you feel better, too. Like if you were to talk to Caddie, for example."

"Caddie?" Aurora repeated.

"Right. She's someone who really gets people. Maybe we should try connecting again. If we turn off our Wi-Fi, then we won't be able reach the Colony either."

Aurora's voice hardened. "Jonas, listen to me. Nobody's connecting to the Mars Colony, OK? It's a trap. You know what a liar Pruitt is. He doesn't want us to organize. He's trying to divide us."

"But—"

"Shut off the Wi-Fi," Aurora said.

Jonas sighed and put the printouts on her desk. "There's that report you wanted. I gotta go now and get the intranet working. No Wi-Fi means we need to route everyone's systems internally."

"OK, then go to it." With effort, Aurora gave him a smile. "You're awesome, Jonas. We're going to go far, friend."

After he left, Aurora leafed through the reports. She could see from the data logs that Mars was still "vanished" after leaving H. G. Wells. Somehow, he'd managed to evade their satellite feeds. Either he wasn't traveling by car, foot, or bicycle, or he had turned invisible. Epica and the guys Aurora had sent had been useless in corralling Mars into the limo. On top of that, Mars hadn't answered her texts, even though she'd sent at least a half dozen in the last twenty-four hours. She thought about raiding his apartment, but according to their tracking devices, the place was a black box. No images, no warm bodies, nothing. Besides, wouldn't his apartment be the last place Mars would hide?

Aurora looked out the window, feeling awful. She was worried that someone would detect the messages she had deleted. But she was also feeling guilty. Like what if that message from the Colony had been a cry for help? That report had been glowing, though. A sign that Caddie and the rest of them were doing just fine on their own. Aurora leaned back in her executive chair. She couldn't believe Jonas thought she should talk to Caddie about her feelings. She'd done OK this far in life. She didn't need anyone.

She remembered the first time she met Caddie. It was years before Mars had sat in front of her in sixth-grade English, utterly terrified by her. Ha, ha. That was funny. Mars was funny then. Sweet and loads of fun. Caddie . . . was different. Wary of Aurora. Keeping her distance in the schoolyard and cafeteria. They were in the same class in third grade, and Caddie always sat at a different table from Aurora, keeping to herself. That was the first year Aurora was aware of her. A diminutive girl in glasses, with brown hair that she wore in a ponytail. One day a bunch of girls were picking on Aurora on the playground. *How come you wear the same shirt all the time?* they taunted her. Hot tears sprang to Aurora's eyes. She wore the same shirt because her mom never bothered to do the laundry. Because it was easier just wearing the same clothes and washing them in the bathtub on the weekends. Easier than asking her mom for anything. But those annoying girls didn't need to know that.

Then in the middle of that teasing, quiet little Caddie, who never said a word in class, spoke up. "I like your shirt, Aurora," she said clearly.

The girls looked at her, surprised. No one had ever heard Caddie speak before. Stunned, they drifted away. Caddie looked at Aurora for a moment, then returned to a book she had in her hands.

From then, it seemed that a friendship *ought* to have formed between Aurora and Caddie. But instead, Caddie continued to keep her distance. And so did Aurora, though she had assumed a grudging acceptance of the quiet girl. Even after Aurora met Mars Patel. Sweet, funny Mars, who seemed forever connected to Caddie.

The phone rang on the walnut desk.

"Hello, Aurora Gershowitz?" the voice asked. "This is KXLW-FM, home of easy-listening music and hard-hitting news. We're ready for your phone interview with us."

"Right!" Aurora set the reports down. She had almost forgotten about the promo event. She wiped the corners of her eyes, which were strangely wet. "I'm ready for you," she said.

Jonas went from classroom to classroom to switch the SMART boards to intranet. By the time he got to sixth-grade microbiology, a crowd of students was huddled around a newspaper. It was one of the few things that still remained in print, after nearly everything else had gone digital. For some reason, everyone still wanted to be able to hold a newspaper in their hands.

"Jonas, why are none of the computers working?" asked Leo.

"Yeah, everything is down," Mika said. "I can't even, like, see the weather."

After a year of floods, fires, and torrential rain, the weather had gone back to normal. But kids were still jittery about getting stuck in a flood zone or a gale somewhere away from home. The weather report was more important than ever.

"Yeah, nothing's working," complained someone else.

"I'm fixing it now, don't worry," Jonas said.

"Is it true that Mars Patel is back?" someone asked.

"Didn't you see the newspaper, Lamar?"

"Yeah, but it could be fake news."

"It's not fake news!"

"Mars said he's going to find the adults," Leo said. "What if he knows what to do?"

"I'd be down with looking for them if he has a plan," Mika said.

"Aurora keeps saying we shouldn't," said a girl named Sun-Len. "Isn't that why we're here? To start a new society and all that?"

"Aurora just wants to be president," said Mika. "Then she won't have time for us."

"Then we need the adults back. Not Aurora," Leo said.

The conversation went back and forth like this while Jonas quietly took note. This was not sounding good. Everyone looked kind of mad. It didn't help that the Internet was down. But seeing that newspaper in the room seemed to have done something, too. Like make them even more mad. When no one was looking, he picked up the paper and scanned the article. It was about Mars, and what he thought should be done about the missing adults.

When Jonas finished, he knew he had to warn Aurora. He remembered once a few years ago at H. G. Wells, there had been a huge brawl in the cafeteria when one of the boys got all riled up and punched another kid. But that brawl hadn't actually started in the cafeteria. It had started earlier that morning in the parking lot, when the riled-up kid was surrounded by the other boy and his friends. What was the riled-up kid's name? Jorge. They surrounded Jorge and threw snowballs mixed with rocks at him and called his mom a bad name. Port Elizabeth barely ever got snow, but that's what they used that day. Snow and rocks and jokes. Then Jorge punched that kid later in the cafeteria and got suspended for three days.

Brawls needed a trigger, something to start them. And this thing he was seeing in the microbiology lab with the newspaper, it felt like a snowball mixed with rocks.

"Everybody, just relax. It will all work out," Jonas said with his easy smile. Then, when he was out of the classroom, he ran back to the office as fast as he could.

The Unexplainable Reappearance of Mars Patel

Port Elizabeth, WA— Nearly twenty months ago, H. G. Wells Middle School student Mars Patel unexplainably disappeared from the school parking lot. Today he has unexplainably *returned*.

"All this time I thought something happened to Mars," says sixth grader Vikram Rao. "Now he's here! He must be so brave. It's not easy going to the planet Mars and back."

On his first day back to school, Mars gave a presentation on gravity in science class.

"It's not just some equation," Mars said. "On Earth, gravity is the force that keeps you down. But in space, you have to figure out how to do things without it. Like eating dinner, brushing your teeth, or using the toilet."

Sixth graders were eating it up. "Mars really knows how to explain science," says Malika Jackson.

Mars also described his experience of living in the Mars Colony, built and run by more than 400 kids. "It was kid power," Mars said. Then his face darkened. "But that was before the volcano exploded."

There have been unsubstantiated reports circulating that the volcanic explosion that brought down the Mars Colony might have been triggered by human intervention. When Mars was asked if Oliver Pruitt had plans for restoring the Colony, Mars shrugged. "No one even knows where he is. And we've got bigger problems."

Mars was referring to the worldwide disappearance of human beings over the age of 18 that began more than a year ago, on a day that some are now referring to as Day Zero.

"It's great that we're getting our climate under control and making time to read books and ride bikes," Mars said. "But we need to find the adults. Until we do, we're not back to normal."

Coincidentally, presidential candidate Aurora Gershowitz, who also returned from the Mars Colony, is running on a platform that boasts of *not* looking for the adults. "They've lied to us enough already," she claims. "We deserve a fresh start without them."

Will Mars and Aurora come to an agreement? Time will tell. For now, H. G. Wells is thrilled to have their "Weller" back. ∎

Hello, podcast listeners!

Some of you might miss how it used to be.

Don't.

Sometimes we need to shut down and start again

by clearing the glitches and rebooting the system.

IN OTHER WORDS, A RESET.

The Mars Colony had its reset.

Now I'm going there to make it better.

Wondering about your reset?

No worries.

Let's just say you won't be kept in the dark too long!

To the stars!

73 Comments ⌃

staryoda   50 min ago
we will reset WITHOUT u #neverpruitt

allie_j   48 min ago
my clock wont reset it shows 2 hours ahead

andromeda   27 min ago
I restarted my computer and it stopped working : (

andromeda   27 min ago
I hate reset

galaxygenius   12 min ago
I miss everything i don't know what to do about that

#votexavier

neptunebaby   8 min ago
lets restart #voteaurora #neverpruitt

17
STRANGE SOUNDS

From the weather tower, Daisy and Julia had a perfect view of the courtyard in the Mars Colony.

"It was a great idea to do the sportscast from up here, Julia," Daisy said. "Thanks for setting me up." She adjusted her earpiece as Julia positioned the screen.

"My pleasure, Daisy," Julia said. "I didn't know you were a sports buff."

Daisy nodded. "My family and I did do all kinds of sports at home: tennis, soccer, cross-country. Also, I'm from Iowa and we went to all the college games, too. Go Hawks!"

"I rode horses," Julia said. "But I have Friedreich's ataxia and my condition got worse. So I moved on to other things. Like designing computers." Since Julia had first arrived at the Colony, transport technology had blossomed. As someone who had used a wheelchair on Earth, Julia made sure that the rovers for her and the other kids who needed them at the

Colony were designed thoughtfully to maximize comfort and range of motion. She also gave regular presentations on AI technology that could be used at the Colony to help other kids with disabilities, like bionic arms and legs, as well as devices for hearing, seeing, and reading texts.

"Was it hard, giving up horses?" Daisy asked. "Will you be able to ride again?"

Julia shrugged. "I didn't have to give it up. I could still ride, but it wasn't the same. Also, I was busy learning to code, which was really exciting. What I'd like to see next are horse robots!"

"That would be awesome!" Daisy said.

"Orion was actually talking about it," Julia said. "Not the horse part. But riding a tardigrade using AI to signal how you want them to move, rather than using your body. It's in the works right now." Julia leaned forward to peer out the windows of the weather tower. "Look, the teams are coming out onto the field."

"I better start the announcements." Daisy turned on the microphone. "Good afternoon! This is Daisy Zheng, chief of Colony communications, coming to you live from the weather tower! I will be your sports commentator today. I'm pleased to announce that the Lava Rocks and the Red Dust Devils are on the field. The games are about to begin! Please put away all handheld devices that will interfere with the team's communication. Note that Colony-grade binoculars are A-OK! Now sit back and be prepared for the time of your life!"

There was loud cheering from the observation decks flanking both sides of the courtyard. Originally, a total of six teams had rotated through practices and, in the last weeks, a tournament style of competitions until today, when it had come down to two teams vying for the championship. Below on the field, the two teams waved to the audience. Laundry and tailoring had made special outfits for the event, with the Lava Rocks sporting metallic gray space suits while the Red Dust Devils came attired in fiery red. The space suits were light, designed to deflect radiation, and supple enough to allow the players to ride their tardigrades without chafing.

Coming up from behind, the tardigrades joined the two teams on the field. Even from a distance, the creatures looked formidable. And despite the growing number of kids playing in the games, most colonists were still terrified of the tardigrades.

The match started with a bang. Literally, as HELGA released a flare upward. Then the teams were off. Back and forth they battled under the Martian sky. Each team had designed their own strategies for winning, and now it was a question of whose strategy would lead to victory.

"Great job, Daisy," Julia observed as she watched Daisy shepherd the game with her play-by-play commentary.

"Look at Axel, coming in for the score," Daisy narrated midway through. "He's taking aim, he's got a small opening. Is he going to do it? And . . . SCORE!" She stood up. "The crowd is going wild!"

So was Daisy. Each time a team scored, it seemed like she would fall over from excitement. First it was the Rocks leading, then the Dust Devils. Back and forth, back and forth, until Daisy nearly went hoarse. But then in the final ten minutes, as Daisy stood poised at the windows, something mysterious began to happen.

"Orion is taking the lead with the ball," she yelled. "He's passing it to Sammy. She's looking both ways and . . ." Daisy paused. "Wait. Something strange is going on. The tardigrades have stopped running. Sammy is looking at Orion. Orion is looking Axel. Axel is looking at the tardigrades. No one knows why they've have stopped. Wait, they're throwing the players off their backs! There goes Axel! And Orion! Ouch! The tardigrades are bucking their players!"

Julia leaned forward. "What's going on, Daisy?"

Daisy turned off the mic. "I—I don't know," she faltered. The two of them watched in horror as one by one, players tumbled to the field. In the audience, kids were yelling, and some of them started to cry.

"Emi has thrown Orion to the ground!" Julia cried. "And look, the tardigrades are running away. All of them!"

Daisy's mouth was agape. "This isn't good, Julia," she said.

"No, this is *not* good," Julia said. "Look, the players are getting up. At least they aren't hurt. But the tardigrades . . . we have to find out why they ran away. And where they're going."

The screen lit up. Orion was on the intercom. "Did you just see that?" he yelled to them.

Caddie's number lit up next. "What's going on? I'm watching from the observation deck."

No one seemed to know.

"Axel and I are trying to figure it out," Orion said, still on the field. "Daisy, call the whole thing off. It's pandemonium down here. Over."

"Yes, call it off," Caddie said. "There could be a stampede in the bleachers. Over."

"Roger." Daisy flipped on the microphone. "Attention, everyone. Please exit the stadium using the passageways on your immediate right. Single file! No pushing or running. Hand back your binoculars to HELGA on your way out. I repeat. Please exit the stadium now. PEACEFULLY."

"The kids are clumping together," Caddie reported. "They're climbing over each other!"

"Yes, Caddie," said Julia in dismay. "We're seeing it from the weather tower, and it's awful."

"What's that sound?" Caddie asked.

"What?" Orion said. "I don't hear anything from the field. Over."

In the weather room, Julia turned to Daisy. "Make that announcement again. Look, the kids are starting to panic." Everywhere they looked, kids were jumping on one another in the stadium, or even crawling under the benches.

"I repeat. Single-file, no pushing or running," Daisy announced over the microphone. "Keep your fellow colonists safe. Do not jump on them."

HELGA floated into the midst of the crowd, and that seemed to calm the kids down. The robot signaled the way out of the observation area, and the kids fell in line behind them.

"Thank the universe for HELGA," Julia breathed. "That was really becoming a situation."

"Ugh, that sound is awful," Caddie said. "It's giving me a headache."

Julia and Daisy looked at each other, puzzled. "Do you hear anything?" Julia asked.

Daisy shook her head. "What sound, Caddie? Over."

"That awful ringing sound! Over!"

"Caddie, I don't hear anything," Daisy said. "But maybe it's because I'm concentrating on our Colony not getting run over by kids. Over."

"Roger that," Julia said. "I don't hear anything, either. But I can tell from your voice, something's wrong, Caddie. Is it one of *those* headaches?"

"I . . . I don't know," Caddie said. "So much is happening."

The bleachers had nearly emptied except for a few stragglers, but even they were heading toward the exit.

"The kids are calming down," said Axel, who was standing in the middle of the field next to Orion. The two of them waved at the weather tower to show they were OK. "HELGA got them inside. All the polo players are inside, too. Medical is examining them for injuries now. Over."

"Good, let's tackle the other problems," Caddie said. Her voice sounded clenched, as if she were gritting her teeth. "Orion and Daisy, figure out where the tardigrades went. Daisy, try to get satellite images. Axel, get a space buggy ready for me."

Daisy shot an alarmed glance at Julia. Caddie rarely went anywhere on the surface. She stayed mainly inside the Colony and greenhouse.

"What?" Orion said. "Where are *you* going, Caddie?"

"I have to find that ringing sound," she said. "Even if no one else can hear it, I can! Over."

"Caddie, you're in charge of the whole colony," Orion said. "Let me go."

"*I'll* go," Julia offered. "Maybe I'll hear that sound once I'm out there."

"Julia's head of security!" Orion's voice crackled over the intercom. "Let me go. Over."

"Orion, you need to take care of the tardigrades," Caddie said. "They trust you. And I'm the one who has to go because I'm the only one who can hear it. Do you copy, Orion?"

"Copy and out," Orion said reluctantly.

"Julia, I suppose you can come with me," Caddie conceded. "Over."

"Roger," Julia said.

"But what about—" Axel began.

"There isn't time for a discussion!" Caddie said sharply. "Over!"

"I was gonna say, I'll fly you, Caddie. The hovercraft is ready, and it's faster than a buggy."

There was a pause.

"Thank you, Axel," Caddie said. "Great thinking. Over and out."

After everyone had disconnected, Julia and Daisy looked at each other.

"This is terrible," Daisy said, upset. "Here we were, the Colony a success, the games going fabulously, and now everything is a complete *mess.*"

"I know," Julia agreed darkly.

"The tardigrades are running rampant, we're losing power, and now Axel and Caddie are going off to investigate a sound that none of us can hear! The last time so many terrible things started happening on Mars, the volcano blew up. Do you remember?"

"How could I not?" Julia said.

They fell silent.

"It's him, isn't it?" Daisy said tearfully. "Oliver Pruitt."

"It's *always* him," Julia said.

18
DISCOVERY

Down the elevator went, rattling along the shaft.

"Amazing that this was here all this time," Mars said. "I wonder how far down we're going."

Toothpick pulled Droney out of his backpack. "Droney, how far down are we?"

Droney whirred. "Approaching floor one of the apartment building."

JP gripped the sides. "That means we better stop soon, right?"

Toothpick nodded. "Since the foundation is made of concrete and steel."

"Thanks, Pick," JP said. "Now I have an image of us going splat into concrete and steel."

The elevator continued bumping along.

"Approaching basement," Droney said. "Parking garage and laundry located at this level."

"Helpful if we were washing sheets," JP said. "Which we're not."

They continued descending.

Mars glanced around the dimly lit compartment. The elevator walls were streamlined and shiny with no buttons, alarm lever, or phone. It was like being in a stainless-steel shoebox. Toothpick seemed calm, like he found himself whizzing down a secret elevator all the time. JP was moving their lips quietly to themself. Mars wasn't sure, but they might be mouthing the words to "I Will Survive." Mars remembered JP saying once how they would sing it before a soccer match.

Mars wished he could be calm like Toothpick or determined like JP. Instead, his mind was racing with thoughts about his mom and dad. Because if Oliver Pruitt had built this elevator, then his mom had helped him do it. At the very least, she must have known it was here. To Mars, it felt like a betrayal. How much more had his mom kept from him? And would he ever find out?

"Floor minus one reached," Droney said.

"Minus one?" JP said. "I think we just got negated."

"I think it means we're going underground," Mars said. "Droney, can you tell us how many minus floors there are?"

"Negative," Droney answered. "You will have to be in the dark."

"We *are* in the dark!" JP grunted.

"Mars, are there any other buttons on that rocket?"

Toothpick asked. "That could correspond to floor numbers?"

"Nope," Mars said.

The elevator continued descending, seemingly into the bowels of Earth.

Mars wondered how Oliver Pruitt had even managed to build a unit that could go underground so many levels. He found himself thinking back to when he and his mom had first moved into the apartment, when he was about four years old. He remembered her saying, *You will love your room, beta. It was made just for you.* But when she took him inside, even with his four-year-old brain, the room had struck him as ordinary. It was nothing like the bright, welcoming layout of his Montessori classroom. Instead it was plain, with a small closet and a window looking out onto the fire escape. One day a week later, when he got home from preschool, his mom had covered all the walls with a thick, multicolored wallpaper that reminded Mars of Christmas wrapping paper. He started crying when he saw it. He didn't want Christmas paper on his wall. He wanted Spider-Man. But the multicolored wallpaper remained. Along with a mystery hidden behind it, apparently.

Just then, the elevator came to an abrupt stop.

"Arrived, floor minus three," Droney said.

"Wow, three stories down," Mars said. Cupcake whined. "Sorry, girl. I know it's cramped. Why aren't the doors opening?"

"I think I liked it better when we were moving," JP said.

"Mars, try your rocket again," Toothpick said.

Mars pushed the lever and the doors rattled open. Cupcake pushed past them. She'd clearly had enough of the elevator. The three of them followed her out.

"Droney, we need light," Toothpick said.

Droney hovered over them and directed a high beam onto the path forward.

Behind them the elevator doors closed.

"Wait, how do we get back?" JP said in alarm.

"Don't worry," Mars said. "I have my toy rocket, remember?" He waved it in the air. "See, I just press the bottom like this. Or maybe I pull the lever. Or . . ."

The doors remained closed.

"Stuck!" JP wailed. "I knew it. How are we going to get out?"

Mars and Toothpick peered down the long, dark tunnel in front of them. Shadows danced along the sides from Droney's high beam, and beyond it, they could see Cupcake walking ahead into the dark.

Toothpick squinted. "I think we go *that* way," he said.

FROM THE PODCAST

Hello, brave world!

The view from here is beautiful.

Where am I, you wonder?

Hint: I'm on top of the world.

The place where it started.

Only I didn't know then what I know now.

I had to go the long way around before

I discovered the shortcut.

Wish me luck.

But I will build better and bolder.

Because innovation is good,

and the future is grand!

SEE YOU ON THE OTHER SIDE.

To the stars!

115 Comments ⊗

staryoda   12 min ago

neptunebaby 11 min ago
omg I dunno!!!!!

allie_j 10 min ago
are u in heaven mr p?

galaxygenius 7 min ago
not unless heaven has an IP address lol

cosmic_chris 6 min ago
he said other side maybe it's a clue

oreocookies 5 min ago
maybe @thisismars knows! it's his dad ya know

19
DON'T PANIC NOW

addie met Julia in the suit room. Julia required a special suit that could be paired with her rover, and Caddie had to get a space helmet that fit over her glasses. As the suit attendants went to get their sizes from the back, Caddie rubbed her temples. Both the pain and the sound that apparently only she could hear had gotten worse in the last hour. It was as if her head were caught inside an immense, ringing bell.

"Still have your headache?" Julia asked. "You haven't had those since Mars was here."

Caddie nodded. Something about her expression must have made Julia look more closely.

"You don't think there's a connection, do you?"

Julia had hit it on the nose. The sound had seemed to come out of nowhere. It came in waves, and along with it, images of being home in Port Elizabeth, with the damp Northwest rain and Mars nearby. Were these memories from her past, or something else?

Caddie swallowed. "Honestly, Julia, that's why I have to find out what's causing this sound. Because maybe it *is* connected to Mars."

"Bollocks," Julia said. Then, "I sure miss the Butterfly."

Caddie smiled in spite of herself. "He hates being called that, doesn't he?"

"Of course," Julia said. "Why else use that nickname?"

Once Caddie and Julia had their suits on, they went to meet Axel at the hovercraft docking station. When they got there, Axel had the hovercraft fueled and ready to go, along with boxed lunches from the cafeteria.

"Gosh, Axel, thanks for being so prepared," Caddie said.

Axel flushed. He had become a completely different person after Aurora left. Caddie wanted to ask him if he missed her, then decided it was better *not* to talk about Aurora.

They boarded the hovercraft and Axel started the engine.

"Axel, you're a pro," Julia said as she took her seat next to him in the front. After Orion, she was the most senior transporter at the Colony. But Axel had risen quickly to number three, and he was now piloting the hovercraft. After a moment, though, Julia asked delicately, "Do you, um, know where we're going?"

Axel nodded back at Caddie, seated behind them. "I thought Caddie knows."

"Is it possible," Caddie asked, "to follow my head?"

Axel and Julia looked at each other. "Oh, boy," Julia said.

"Well, then, at least go where the sound is coming from," Caddie said.

"Yeah, but how do we do that?" Julia said. "We can't track a sound *we* can't hear."

Caddie unstrapped herself and came to the dashboard. She studied the panels for a moment. "There are literally a half-dozen screens here. Just looking at them makes me dizzy."

"This panel tells the direction we're headed," Axel said, pointing to the main screen.

"And that one controls the angle," Julia said, pointing to another one. "It's mostly the computer that does everything. But we have to enter the coordinates."

Caddie closed her eyes for a moment then opened them. "Go that way," she said, pointing.

"That's due north," Julia said. "Are you sure?"

Caddie said, "As sure as I can be without actually knowing anything at all."

"Works for me," said Axel.

There was a roar, and then the hovercraft was in the air, reaching a height of twenty feet. It was one of several new models that had been built in the tech hub over the past year. Designed as a utility vehicle that could hover several feet above the ground, the hovercraft allowed pilots to fly very close to the surface without using as much power or fuel, and much faster than a conventional transport vehicle. Inside, it was outfitted with rows of bench seating as well as an open area in the back for equipment, storage, emergency triage, or ferrying extra passengers. There were several hovercraft drivers in the Colony now, but Axel had put in the most hours.

"Look, there's Monument Crater," Julia said, pointing to the right. "And the Old Colony. Still hard to believe we're here. Even now I have to pinch myself in the mornings."

Axel nodded. "Yeah. It's also easy to forget how toxic it is out there. That's the part that gets me. How we're living next to death. Any moment we could screw up and get a crack in our helmet. A few breaths and, boom, you're dead."

"Martian atmosphere, lovely as always." Julia turned to Caddie. "Your head any better?"

Caddie, who'd had her eyes closed, opened them. "Not really," she said.

"All right, you rest, Caddie," Julia said. "Axel, I guess we keep going north."

∩

They had been flying for a few hours when Caddie awoke. She had been having a dream that she was back on Earth, in her room, on her old bed, with the sound of rain outside her window. It had been such a pleasant dream that it was jarring to wake up with the same headache and ringing sound.

"Better?" Julia asked.

"Um," Caddie said. "No." She blinked and looked out the

window. This was an area of Mars she had never seen before. There were passing over a dry lake bed, and the dusty ground here was more red.

"Do you know which way to go still?" Julia asked.

"I think we continue north," Caddie said. "I do wish there was some other sign, so that we weren't just using my head as navigation."

Julia was staring through the front window. "Caddie, I think we just got one of those signs. Axel, look straight ahead. Do you see what I see?"

"Hey, it's those clouds you were talking about!" Axel said. He glanced at the radar map. "That's Sector 4B we're coming up on."

"Exactly," Julia said. "The same place the power surge was coming from."

"But what's going on there?" Caddie wondered. "It's so cloudy, I can't see anything."

"We're getting closer," Julia said. "I think we're going to get to the bottom of this quite soon and . . ." She frowned. "Axel, slow down. Let up on the throttle—"

They found themselves entering a thick swath of clouds.

"I can't see!" Axel cried.

"What in the world?" Julia exclaimed.

Suddenly there were structures sticking out of the ground. They were everywhere, thick clusters of tall, green—

"Trees!" The three of them yelled at the same time.

"Angle down," Julia said frantically. "We can't avoid them!"

"Brace yourselves," Axel yelled as the hovercraft took a sharp turn downward.

There was no time to strap herself in. Caddie rolled into a ball, instinctively covering her head with her arms. "Mars . . ." she whispered.

A few moments later, the hovercraft made contact with the ground. For several feet, it skidded on its belly like a sickening roller coaster. Friction gradually slowed them down until they slammed into a dense forest.

The hovercraft came to a stop under a thick blanket of smoke and debris. The top of the vehicle had been ripped off, exposing a canopy of coniferous and deciduous trees above them.

"Am I really seeing what I'm seeing?" Julia wondered. "Someone pinch me. Wait, I've already been doing that. Maybe someone needs to turn me upside down and shake me."

"Caddie, I think I got one of your headaches," Axel said, groaning.

"Are you hurt, Axel?" Julia said immediately.

"I'm OK, just petrified," he said. "And that's not even a word I use."

"Caddie?"

"I'm OK, Julia," Caddie said. "Actually, I'm a lot better. That sound is gone for now. But how can there be trees here? Trees mean . . . a water source . . . and . . ."

"An atmosphere," Axel finished.

The three of them stood up, making their way out of the mangled hovercraft. Miraculously, Julia's rover seemed to be intact, and the three of them had survived without a scratch.

They began to make their way through the thick foliage surrounding them.

"It's beautiful," breathed Caddie. "And I don't believe it, but I recognize these trees! They're spruces. Just like the ones near Port Elizabeth. And all these ferns and moss growing on the ground—it's like the rain forest in Olympic National Park!" A giddy joy filled her. "It . . . it makes me feel like I'm back home in Washington!"

"Caddie," Julia said. She had stopped to look at her with growing horror. "Don't panic now. But I just noticed something. Do you see it, Axel?"

Axel stopped. "Whoa, yeah."

"What? What?" Caddie asked.

"I don't know how to tell you this," Julia said. "But right now, there's a hole in your helmet."

A sickening fear rolled through Caddie, replacing the elation she had felt only moments before. Even without reading their minds, Caddie could imagine the horrible thoughts running through everyone's heads. They all knew about the deadly Martian air—no oxygen, toxic dust, low pressure—everything designed to obliterate the human body in seconds. Wasn't Axel saying that earlier?

I'm dying, Caddie thought. *I'm dying soon.*

And yet . . . as the seconds passed by, something else became startlingly clear.

Julia was the one to speak first. "I'm pretty sure you're not dead, right? Which can only mean one thing. I don't know how it's possible, but Caddie, you're breathing on Mars!"

With a sudden determination, Caddie pulled off her helmet. *Air.* Sweet, fresh air entered her lungs.

"Caddie, no!" Julia cried.

"I can breathe!" Caddie said. "I can really breathe."

Julia thought for a moment, then she pulled her helmet off, too. So did Axel.

For a few moments they simply breathed the Martian air. Along with it was the scent of pine, ferns, and damp moss. The most heavenly things they could possibly smell.

Axel jumped up and down and whooped.

Julia laughed, a kind of bubbling laughter no one had heard from her before.

Caddie looked up at the sky, a pale blue peeking through the canopy of trees. "It's a miracle," she said. "What else could it be?" She took off her gloves and ran her hands through her hair. To do this outside without a space helmet was indescribable. A rush of memories came to her. Of being with her family. Walking, hiking, being together. She felt a sharp pang. She could almost see her parents' faces; she could almost hear their voices . . .

Actually, she *could* hear something. Not the sound wave. Not the ringing in her ears. Something else. A murmuring. She rubbed her temples.

"Caddie, oh no, not your headache?" Julia said. "I thought the sound was gone."

"No, not that sound . . ." Meanwhile, the murmuring got louder. But Caddie wasn't sure how to explain it. "I'm OK. Really."

"Let's move the Colony here," Axel said. "Can you imagine? Life with breathable air? And trees? We can build tree houses. Log cabins. Play soccer!"

"Gardening!" added Julia. "Clotheslines. Hammocks. Soil experiments!"

Meanwhile, the murmuring continued. Caddie searched for its source. But as usual, it seemed like she was the only one who could hear these strange things emitting from the Martian air.

"Maybe we should look around first," Caddie said.

Hovercraft down in Sector 4B. Exact coordinates unknown. Ping us.

Crew is safe and on foot.

We need supplies before nightfall 1700 hours.

Radio transmission failed. Message back if you get this.

Also some mind-blowing news OMG!!

Over,

Axel Thunderbolt (he/him)

Senior Tech Hub Pilot

20
A LIGHT AT THE END
OF THE TUNNEL

nce the three of them had decided to follow Cupcake down the tunnel, JP began to calm down.

"It still looks dark and scary," they said, "but it's better than being inside an elevator with no floor buttons. Anyone want a sandwich?"

Mars looked at JP in surprise. "You packed sandwiches? When did you have time for that?"

"Easy peasy," JP said. "You're the one who bought groceries yesterday. I just grabbed whatever I saw in your refrigerator."

Mars's stomach growled. "Actually, I'm kind of hungry. What time is it?"

"Who cares? It's always time for a sandwich." JP pulled a plastic bag out from their backpack. "Do you want peanut butter apple, olive and cream cheese, or potato chip with ketchup?"

"Um," Mars said, "why don't you surprise me?"

"Normally I dislike surprises," Toothpick said, "but I would be up for a culinary adventure."

"Great, Pick. Here, just grab a sandwich."

JP passed the bag around to them. "It's a good thing it's dark. That way you won't know what you're sinking your teeth into."

Mars tried a first bite of his sandwich, tasting the smooth nutty flavor of peanut butter mixed with the tartness of green apple. "Wow, this is pretty good," he said.

"Mine, too," Toothpick said. "I didn't think potato chips and ketchup belonged between two slices of bread. You proved me wrong, JP."

"Excellent!" JP said, smiling. "And I got olive and cream cheese, which is good because I just remembered Pick is now vegan. Score for both of us!"

They ate their sandwiches as they followed Cupcake through the tunnel. The light from Droney revealed walls made of stone.

"This is not a human-made tunnel," Toothpick observed. "Look at these stones. No evidence of concrete."

Toothpick was right. In fact, Mars was startled to notice something else.

"They look like lava tubes," he said. "Like the one I saw on Mars."

He had first learned about lava tubes when he was at the Colony. When a volcano erupts, the lava flows create underground tunnels like the one they were walking in now. There had been many lava tubes near the Martian Colony, the biggest one leading right up to its perimeter, with an entrance sealed by a door.

"Really?" Toothpick said. "Interesting coincidence."

"Mars, why were you in the lava tubes . . . on Mars?" JP asked.

"That's where Aurora and the Martians were hiding out." Mars described how Aurora had abducted him one day from the Colony and brought him underground to the lava tubes where she and the Martian rebels were living. "Then she used me as ransom to get Julia to fly us to the space station. She was hoping to jump on a space shuttle and fly back to Earth. That didn't exactly pan out, but I guess going to the space station ended up being a good thing, since we rescued you before it exploded."

"Exploding space stations and erupting Martian volcanoes—the good old days," JP said. "Although, Aurora does have a way of getting things done. I'd admire her if I didn't want to bonk her on the head."

Mars remembered the poster of Aurora on the school wall. In all the time he'd known her, from the pranks she'd pulled in sixth grade to her whole rebel image on Mars, he never thought she'd wear a blazer. It seemed so . . . anti-Aurora. She could be a pain, but there was still an integrity to her. Like, you could always count on her for being against the establishment. But the image on the poster was different. She looked like Epica. Not a rebel. Part of the establishment instead. It felt like she was a sellout. Worse, all those texts from Aurora made it feel like she wanted him to be a sellout, too. Or was he reading too much into them?

"Why does she want to be president, anyway?' he asked. "Doesn't she realize all the problems she'll need to solve? The Earth might be in better shape, but the adults are missing."

"Aurora doesn't care about that," Toothpick said. "That's what her campaign is about. Not caring. It's clever, capitalizing on all the rage kids have been feeling for years toward adults. But a little pointless, too. Most kids want their parents back. Like me."

"And me," JP said.

"Me, too," Mars said. "My mom, that is. My dad is, well, another story."

"That's the first time I've heard you call Pruitt your dad," JP noted.

"After denial comes acceptance," Toothpick said.

"I never denied it!" Mars exclaimed. Then he paused. "Well, OK, I did for a little while."

"It's fine to deny Pruitt," JP said, glowering.

But Toothpick seemed to think differently. "I think it's healthy for Mars to acknowledge his dad. Faults or not. Otherwise, Mars will be carrying guilt and resentment about his estranged father-son relationship for the rest of his life."

"Um, can we stop psychoanalyzing me now?" Mars said.

Just then, Cupcake came bounding back. She nudged up against Mars's hand.

"What's that, girl? Did you see something?"

Cupcake bumped Mars's hand some more, then grunted many times.

"I think she's trying to tell us something," Mars said. He stopped, peering in front of him. Was that what he thought it was? "Can Droney kill the light for a sec?"

"Droney, hibernate," Toothpick said. The tunnel fell into darkness.

JP was about to protest, then subsided when they all saw another light, this one much dimmer and farther ahead in the tunnel.

"I thought so! There's something down there. Come on, everyone!" Mars urged.

JP stumbled in the dark. "Droney, put the light back on, will ya?"

Droney's overhead shot back on, shadows dancing along the walls.

They hurried until they reached what seemed to be a bend in the tunnel and a metal door.

"What if it works the same way the elevator did?" JP whispered. "You open it and it goes nowhere."

Mars held a finger to his lips and pointed to the crack of light underneath. Then he reached for the knob and pushed the metal door open.

1961 PROJECT

For a moment Mars wondered if Oliver Pruitt was hiding inside. As he peered in, he saw a room filled with shelves and shelves of equipment, computers, and flat-screen monitors anchored to the wall. There was a single fluorescent light bulb on the ceiling, like the one in the elevator. As far as Mars could tell, the room was empty of people.

Behind him, Cupcake whimpered. She couldn't fit through the metal door. "I'm sorry," Mars said to her. "You can wait out here, OK, girl? I won't be long." He went inside, JP and Toothpick following him, along with Droney.

"Droney, where are we?" Toothpick asked.

"You are located underground two miles east of Gale Island," chirped Droney.

"What?" JP said. "You mean we walked that far? Are we under Puget Sound?"

"Negative," Droney said.

"We must be near the shore," Toothpick said. "It's about two miles from the shore to Gale Island."

"We're in an underground lab!" JP said. They looked up at the single bulb. "With bad lighting."

The fluorescent light was thin and white, throwing everyone's faces into an eerie, ashen glow. Toothpick went to the center table, where there was a microphone and audio system.

"Whoa," he said. "It's an X2. Sweet! This is major high-end."

"Like rich-and-famous high-end?" JP asked.

"Like not-even-available high-end," Toothpick answered. "I know because I've been waiting for this model to come out. Production cycles got behind after the adults disappeared, but now the kids are cranking out stuff. Still, this model isn't supposed to be out until winter. Whoever works here has an inside track or something." Toothpick looked around. "The monitoring systems are definitely state of the art. Like, we're talking top-secret NASA. You can't get this in your home."

"Why would all this be here?" Mars wondered. "Do you think Oliver Pruitt is behind it?"

"Isn't Pruitt always behind it?" JP said. "What are you doing, Pick?"

Toothpick was entering some numbers into the audio unit. "I think I can rig this transponder to find an outside signal. Let's see if we can find Oliver Pruitt and ask him what all this stuff is for."

"Ha," JP said. "Like he'd tell us."

"Hey, this computer is running," Mars said. "Someone's been here recently!" He jiggled the mouse and a login screen displayed.

WELCOME TO THE 1961 PROJECT
PASSWORD: _____

"Anyone know what the 1961 Project is?" Mars asked. "I need a password."

"Try typing in stuff," JP said. "Like sausage14."

"Why sausage14?" asked Mars.

"I like sausage," JP said. "And the number 14."

"I'm getting something," Toothpick announced. He gestured for them to join him at the center table, where a static sound was coming from the receiver. "We have a connection. Hello? Hello? This is Randall Lee. Do you hear me? Come in. Over."

"Randall?" JP said. "Nobody calls you that except your mom." They smirked. "And Epica."

Toothpick shrugged. "It *is* my legal name."

"Try again, Pick," Mars said.

Toothpick spoke into the microphone a second time.

This time there was an audible click followed by a breathless voice answering back.

"Toothpick? Is that you?"

"Julia!" Mars said quickly. "Pick, I think you reached the Mars Colony!"

JP waved their hands in excitement. "This is better than my olive and cream cheese sandwich!"

"Keep talking to them, Pick!" Mars said.

"Julia, it's Randall, Mars, and JP," Toothpick said. "We're calling from Earth. Everyone is safe. How about you? Over."

"Likewise!" Julia responded. "But blimey! I didn't expect to hear from you! Excuse me if I sound a bit befuddled. Oh yes, Axel and Caddie are with me. Over."

"Caddie!" Mars exclaimed.

"Mars? Mars?" Caddie's voice was choppy in the background.

"It's amazing talking to you," Julia gushed. "We lost your signal for how long? A year! So much has happened. You won't believe what I'm about to tell you. Over."

"You won't believe what we're about to tell you," Toothpick said.

"I think what I have to say is far more unbelievable!" Julia said.

"I wouldn't be too sure," Toothpick said. "Earth is very different."

"Trust me, Mars is *way* more different."

"My god, y'all, tell them already," JP said impatiently. Then not waiting a second more, they blurted: "Julia, all the adults are missing from Earth!"

"There's breathable air on Mars!" Julia said at the same time.

"What?" everyone said at once.

There was a booming sound that made everyone jump. Then the signal went dead.

JP leaned forward to tap the keyboard repeatedly. "What happened to her?"

Toothpick examined the audio output. "Bad connection. Let me see if we can try again."

"Did I hallucinate, or did they just say there's air on Mars?" JP said.

"*Breathable* air," Mars said. "But that's impossible." He paused. "Caddie sounded OK, right?"

JP patted Mars on the back. "She did, bro."

"I'm switching to a public network. Maybe that will work." Toothpick clicked again on the transponder. "Testing, testing. Julia, can you read me?" Silence on the other end. "Testing, testing. Julia, can you read me? This is Randall Lee. You are an amazing scientist, Julia. Over."

Just then there was a sound. This time it wasn't coming from the receiver, but from the door to the lab. Instinctively the three of them banded together as JP raised an arm protectively.

Meanwhile, the figure at the door let out a gasp.

Mars froze when he saw her. "Mamaji!" he cried. He tore away from his friends.

He nearly tripped as he crossed the room to her. Her arms went immediately around him. Was it really, really her? He pulled back for a moment to see her left wrist, and there it was. The mole, where it was supposed to be. "It really is you!"

Meanwhile, Saira Patel had an expression of shock and

disbelief. "Mars!" Her voice cracked and she hugged him again. Hard.

"I thought you were gone forever," he said into her hair. In the past year, he had grown taller, and he was now at the same eye level as his mom, another strange and disorienting thing to notice along with the strangeness of everything else.

"I thought you were gone forever, too," she said, the last of her words choked with tears. She stood back, holding his shoulders. "Let me take a look at you, my brave boy. Beta. You're taller. And your hair. Longer! Curly! It's so good to see you. Nothing matters but this," she said.

"But Ma, what's going on?" Mars swept his hand around the lab. "What is this place? What are you doing here? And where have all the adults gone?"

Saira dabbed the corners of her eyes with her sleeve. "Slow down, Mars!" she said. "Even though you're right to ask all these questions. I just need . . . a minute." She looked over his shoulder to where JP and Toothpick stood respectfully a few feet away.

"Hey, Ms. P," JP said amicably.

"Hi, JP and Toothpick. I'm glad you're here." Saira took a few seconds to compose herself. Then she pointed to chairs around the center table. Her voice had turned grave. "Sit down. You all deserve to know the truth. Before it's too late."

22

SIGNS

It was so good to hear Randall," Julia said. "Toothpick, I mean. All of them, of course," she added quickly as they continued through the forest.

"Mars, too," Caddie said. She had barely heard his voice, but when he said her name, she felt a glimmer of his thoughts for the first time. Amazing! He was in some kind of underground chamber. And he was feeling hopeful. Now Caddie was feeling hopeful, too. Mars and her friends were alive, and being here in this abundance of foliage and fresh air had lifted her spirits, along with a sense that she was connected to the universe and its internal mechanisms again. Even those sounds she was hearing—the constant murmuring—were strangely comforting. It was like the forest was talking to her. And her headache seemed to be gone.

"Do you think they heard us?" Axel asked as they stepped over fallen logs, their feet crunching yellowed fern leaves.

"About the breathable air? Because it's a game changer. We could actually live on Mars, not just survive."

"And without the body odor," Julia said as she maneuvered her rover around the logs blocking her way.

"I'm sorry, did you say body odor?" Axel said.

"No offense," she said, "but that's one of the drawbacks of Colony life. All that recirculated air and body odor coming back at us. Yuck. Now we might get to breathe fresh air and not smell each other."

"Ha, ha," Axel said. "BO does suck."

"I'm also curious about what Toothpick said," Julia said. "Did he say missing adults?"

"Yeah," Axel said. "Like it was missing kids before. And now adults, too?"

"I wish Toothpick were here," Julia said wistfully. She blushed. "Because he could tell us about the flora and fauna here, right? And help strategize. There's an awful lot going on."

"Aren't you like the chief strategizer or something?" Axel asked.

"Sure, but it helps to *know* stuff," she said. "Also, strategy isn't just about strategizing. Sometimes it's about being intuitive, too. Right, Caddie?" She glanced at Caddie. "You've been quiet. Are you OK? Is your headache better?"

"Yes," Caddie said absently. While Julia and Axel were speaking, the murmuring was getting louder in her head, but she still couldn't understand what it was. It was like hearing the chorus to a song when she couldn't quite make out the lyrics.

"You must be glad to talk to Mars," Julia said. "I know how close you both are."

"We are," Caddie agreed. There was a part of her that wished she could go back to sixth grade when they were still on Earth, at the school dance, when Mars had snuck into the gym and found a way to avoid Oliver Pruitt's drones just to keep his promise and be with her. But she also knew that time was gone. Because surely there wasn't ever a way to travel back in time, was there?

The three of them now came to a clearing where the ground was covered in velvety moss, the trees heavy with rainwater and damp branches. It smelled of home. Without warning, a memory came to Caddie of when she was ten and walking on a trail with her parents in Glacier National Park. The scent of pine hung in the air, and squirrels darted from tree to tree.

Let's take a picture, Caddie, her mom had said to her. *Stay and let's take a picture.*

But Caddie was too busy following one of the squirrels. Where would it bury the acorn tucked in its mouth? Caddie had to know.

Stay, Caddie. Just one picture. Caddie, her mom called out again. She had one of those old-fashioned point-and-click cameras. Her mom said she liked things the old way. Put your eye to the viewfinder and *click. Stay, Caddie,* her mom had pleaded. *Here in front of the spruce tree.*

Stay, Caddie.

Caddie.

She gasped now and looked at Axel and Julia. "Did you hear that?" she asked.

Caddie.

"Hear what?" Julia said.

Caddie. And then it was gone.

"Nothing," Caddie said. "At least, maybe it was nothing," she finished.

"Nothing is never nothing," Julia observed. She navigated around a twig in her path. "Axel, did you hear from Daisy?"

"I messaged her, but no response," Axel said.

Caddie kept listening for the voice, even though she knew there was no way her mom could be nearby.

"I would try again," Julia said to Axel. "We need to keep trying."

"Sure thing." As Axel took out his IP phone to send another message, Caddie was so focused on trying to hear the voice that she almost ran smack into Julia, who had stopped in front of her. "What's wrong, Julia?" she asked.

"Look," Julia said, pointing.

Ahead in the soft soil, fresh shoe prints crossed the clearing in front of them and disappeared into the brush.

23

SAIRA CONFESSES

As Mars, Toothpick, and JP took seats around the center table, Saira Patel open a small fridge in the corner of the lab. "Want something cold to drink?"

JP brightened. "You wouldn't happen to have orange soda, Ms. P?"

"As a matter of fact, yes."

"Excellent!"

After they had each cracked open a can, Saira began. "So you found my underground lab."

"This is *your* lab?" Mars asked. "You've been coming down here from my room?"

Saira smiled. "I was wondering how you got here. That elevator is for emergencies. There's another entrance from the puja room, through the closet. I guess you know by now that I don't work in an office."

"Or at the docks unloading fish," Mars said.

She nodded. "Yes, that was fake, too. But I couldn't tell you the truth, which is far more controversial. That's because"— her voice dropped a notch—"I'm an environmental physicist."

She paused dramatically to check their reactions.

JP finally spoke. "No offense, Ms. P, but that doesn't sound exactly controversial."

"But it is!' Saira's eyebrows went up. "If you know who I'm working for."

Mars leaned forward. "Who are you working for?"

"Er, never mind. I can't tell you," she said. "But part of my job has been to track climate change on Earth, and it's *devastating*. By the time you all left for Mars, the rains had already started along the West Coast. Then there was massive flooding across the plains, cities washed away along the coast, people stranded in their cars and homes. After the rains came the drought, then fires raging across the Southwest, Europe, and Central Asia. And then there were monsoons, epic earthquakes, and a seismic blast in New Zealand. The more destruction I recorded, the clearer it became that humans were the cause. And that I couldn't *possibly* allow the same thing to happen on Mars. Not me! I'm from India. My family lived through British colonization."

"That's right," Toothpick said. "India was colonized by Britain for more than a hundred years, until independence in 1947."

"Correct, Toothpick," Saira said. "And we've seen what

happens when someone from somewhere else comes and decides how to run your lives. We could do the same thing on Mars someday with the Colony. We might have already brought harm to whatever is there. There has to be a better way. And we have to fix our *own* problems, not rush off and cause them somewhere else."

"Well, the kids here have been doing great so far," JP said. "Not to toot our own horn."

"You kids are fabulous!" Saira agreed. "Better than the adults. All those climate trends are reversing! But that doesn't mean we shouldn't be careful with the Martian planet."

"Did you ever tell all of this to my . . . dad?" Mars found it hard to use that word in front of his mom. But it was time to get it out in the open. "Oliver Pruitt is my dad, right?"

"Oh, Mars." Saira gave a sigh. "So you found out on your own about that. I wish it had been different—you, me, him. Oliver is brilliant, and I love him with all my heart. But he's also obstinate and misguided. He wouldn't listen to me. Not about the Colony. Not about you. That's why I had to leave. When you were three, I brought you to Port Elizabeth, and Oliver stayed back and created Pruitt Prep."

"Where were we before that? Were we a family?"

"Yes," Saira said. She paused. "We lived on Gale Island."

"What?" Mars was stunned. He glanced around the table at his friends to see their reactions.

"Cool, Mars," JP said. "Like, there was a time you wanted to go to Pruitt Prep so bad, when you were actually from there!"

"Yes, like a full circle," Toothpick said. "Very hero's journey."

"Only I'm *not* a hero," Mars said. "Also Ma, Gale Island, seriously? There's nothing there but trees."

Saira gave a tiny smile. "Well, there is the school. But before it was built, when you were little, you used to run on the beach and make castles out of pine cones and moss. You loved living on Gale Island. The place is special, just like you."

"I'll say!" JP said, jumping in. "Ms. P, did you know that on Gale Island, I'm super strong, Caddie is super minded, Toothpick is super smart, and Mars is . . ." JP's voice trailed off.

"Super nothing," Mars said flatly. "Didn't we already reach that conclusion?"

"No, beta," Saira said empathetically. "You're special, too. Super loved."

"OK, super loved by parents who still decided to split up."

JP leaned over and poked Mars in the arm. "Um, dude, that's a little harsh."

"You *are* super loved, Mars," Saira said fiercely. "You have no idea how much. That's why they—" She stopped as if she'd said too much.

"They?" Mars asked. "Who's they?"

At that moment, a beeping sound came from Saira's pocket. She pulled out a phone and scanned the screen.

"Hey, how did you get an IP phone?" Mars asked. "I haven't seen one of those since I was in space."

Saira was frowning as she read a text. "One of the few perks of knowing Oliver." She leaned back in her chair. "How did they find out . . . ?" she murmured. Then she straightened. "Listen, we have to go. *Now*." She stuck the IP phone back in her pocket and threw out her empty soda can.

"But you haven't told us everything yet, Ma," Mars said. "Who are 'they'? And what about the missing adults? We haven't even gotten to that."

Saira sighed. "Those questions are too big. I wish we had more time." She was hurrying around the room, shutting down equipment right and left. She stopped at the audio receptor. "Ah. You used this?"

Toothpick nodded. "Briefly."

"You spoke to your friends on Mars?" she asked. She flipped the switches off one by one.

"Why, was that a mistake?" JP asked. "Are we in trouble?"

Saira smiled gently. "You could never be in trouble, JP. You're perfect. All of you. But the receptor probably did tip them off to where we are."

"I'm so sorry, Ms. P.," JP said. "We were trying to figure out where Pruitt was. And now, they've figured out where *we* are." JP paused. "Wait, who are *they* again?"

"I bet the same 'they' who were on Gale Island," Mars said pointedly.

Saira shuffled the kids out the door and slammed it behind them.

"Cupcake?" Mars called out. The tardigrade was nowhere to be found.

"Who's Cupcake?" Saira asked.

"My pet tardigrade," Mars said. "She was waiting out here, but I can't find her."

Saira raised an eyebrow. "Pet tardigrade, is it? I didn't think that was possible. Well, don't worry. She'll find her way back. And now everyone, shake a leg, will you? We have to go. Don't worry about Cupcake, Mars!"

"Thanks for the soda, Ms. P," JP called out.

Mars gave JP an exasperated look.

"What? I'm a polite person, Mars!"

∩

Mars soon discovered that his mom could move through the tunnel with surprising speed and dexterity. For the first few minutes, he and his friends scrambled to keep up with her.

"Ma, slow down," Mars said. "What are you, the Olympic sprinter of lava tubes?"

"I'm used to walking fast," she said over her shoulder. "And, we need to hurry."

"Ow, I stubbed my toe!" JP said.

"Droney, overhead light," Toothpick said.

The drone whirred to life and rose above them to flash a light ahead.

Saira's eyes flashed. "One of Oliver's drones? How we do we know it isn't spying on us?"

"Oh no, Ms. Patel," Toothpick said. "I've reprogrammed it. He's one of us now."

"Very clever, Toothpick," Saira said, bending down. "Careful about the rocks overhead."

"Yikes," Mars said, ducking just in time. He was still marveling over the fact that they had once lived on Gale Island. With his dad. Mars still had so many questions for his mom, but it was impossible to talk to her and walk at a rapid clip through the dark lava tube without braining himself or falling on his face.

For several minutes the group continued in silence, aided only by Droney's tiny light. The tunnel, which had started off so easy to walk through until they reached the lab, was now an obstacle course as they avoided potholes, ducked beneath low overhangs, and even crawled on their hands and knees.

JP huffed next to Mars and Toothpick. "What gives with your mom, Mars?" they whispered. "I mean, I'm on the soccer team. My job is to run up and down the field chasing after a ball. What's her reason for whupping our butts?"

Mars was out of breath, too. "Beats me. I thought she worked on a fish dock, remember?"

"Say, Pick, you have any new theories about the missing adults?" JP asked. "And why Ms. P won't talk about them?"

Toothpick was jumping from rock to rock to avoid puddles. "Maybe she doesn't know," he offered. "And maybe the adults are gone because they destroyed themselves."

"Who would up and destroy themselves?" asked Mars, who was jumping behind Toothpick.

"Well, there is the Fermi paradox," Toothpick answered. "Which asks the question of why we haven't found intelligent life elsewhere in the universe. One explanation could be that the more advanced you get, the more likely you'll destroy yourself. Because as soon as you're capable of traveling to space and beyond, you're capable of ending life as you know it. The adults are just way ahead of the kids on that."

"We didn't find advanced life on Mars," JP pointed out.

"Or maybe whoever was there destroyed themselves, too," Mars said. He jumped again. "Watch out for the trench, JP!"

JP sidestepped in time. "Will this tunnel ever end? Someone tell me and end my misery."

"Ask Droney," Mars said.

"Oh, yeah. Droney, where are we now?"

The drone was flying just ahead of them, keeping close to the ground to avoid the hanging rocks. "You are twenty minutes below Gale Island," Droney answered. "The place of origin for Mars Patel. Cool!"

"Wait a minute, we're *below* Gale Island?" JP repeated. "Like underwater, Ms. P?"

For the first time, Saira looked amused. "Cute drone. Accurate, too."

"But I hate being wet," JP said.

"You're not wet now!" Mars said.

"True," JP said. They flexed their arms. "You feeling smarter, Toothpick? I think I'm stronger already."

"Not sure," Toothpick said.

They were emerging from the low tunnel to an area with a ladder attached to the wall. "Here is where we start climbing. Mars first. JP, you follow in case he falls. You're the strongest one here. Then Toothpick, then me."

JP peered up, where the ladder disappeared into the dark cavern above. "Yikes," they said. "Um, good luck, Mars."

"Why does that not make me feel reassured?" Mars said.

"Anyone want me to calculate the distance to the top?" Toothpick offered.

"No!" JP and Mars said at the same time.

"Now, Mars," Saira said. "It goes faster than you think. Droney, light the way."

Droney dutifully fluttered up past everyone, his voice bouncing against the walls as he chirped, "Out of this world!"

24
THE DOOR TO GALE ISLAND

The metal ladder jutted from a wall that seemed to stretch up indefinitely. At first, the climb was easy. But then as they kept going, the rungs became slick with rainwater. At one point, Mars nearly slipped, bringing the entire caravan to a halt until he regained his footing. Higher and higher they climbed. Sometimes there were stone outcroppings jutting out from the wall for them to rest on, but those were also wet. Mars had to be careful, or he could slip from the ledge, too.

"The trick is to not look down," Saira said when they stopped momentarily to catch their breath. "I use this ladder all the time."

Mars was sitting on a ledge, trying his hardest not to gaze at the gaping drop below him. He couldn't tell what was causing the pit in his stomach. Being in danger of falling to his death, or knowing that his mom was still not telling him everything.

"You need to relax, Mars," said Saira, who was watching him. "Mind over matter."

"You haven't explained everything," Mars said. "About my dad."

"I don't know where he is," Saira said.

"That's not what I want to know," Mars asked. His voice dropped. "I want to know why you guys broke up. Was it really because of climate change?" He flushed. "Or because of me?"

"It was *never* because of you, Mars," Saira said, squeezing his shoulder. "We love you."

When she said that, Mars blinked hard.

She pointed him toward the ladder. "Come, beta. We have to keep going."

As they ascended, the air started to smell salty and get colder, making Toothpick's glasses fog in the damp air. Finally they reached a platform at the top with a metal door.

"This is it," Saira said as they all stood on the platform. "The door to Gale Island."

Mars wiped his face with his sleeve. "You're going to open that door, aren't you?"

Saira nodded.

"Where are all the adults, Mamaji?" Mars asked. "We need to know. No more delays."

"Yeah, Ms. P," JP said. "I want to find my mom and dad, too."

Toothpick nodded.

Saira clasped her hands. "I'm so sorry, but I don't know. Maybe I was spared because I was underground in my lab when everyone else disappeared. After that, I came up only at night to steal food from the grocery store. I hated doing that, but I didn't want to be seen. I tried to pray, too, when I could." She looked at all of them. "That's the honest truth. There are some parts of this puzzle even I don't know. All I can say is there are forces at work beyond us. Like, we don't have the tools to understand them."

"Maybe E.T. took the adults away," JP muttered.

"Negative on alien spotting," Toothpick said.

"It's a *joke*, Pick!"

Saira threw open the door. Outside it was clear, and the stars were bright pinpricks in the night sky. Soon they were all standing outside in the moonlight. From here they could see the inky shore and the dock with the sign GALE ISLAND. Tied to it was a rowboat that looked surprisingly like the one Mars and his friends had used from Port Elizabeth to get to Gale Island the first time. It was strange to see that some things hadn't changed.

"We're here," Saira Patel told everyone. "Where you will be your strongest, smartest, and bravest. The best place I could possibly bring you."

JP pulled out their empty soda can from their pocket and crushed it in their hand. "She's right! Score!"

"We are exactly 1.7 miles from the front doors of Pruitt Prep," Toothpick said. "I can now compute distances mathematically in my head."

"You might be stronger, JP, and you might be smarter, Toothpick," Mars said, "but I'm the one who's super loved." He tried, but he couldn't keep the hurt out of his voice.

Saira looked Mars in the eye. "You are. Never forget that. That is your superpower." She smiled at him, pushing a strand of hair from his forehead. She seemed sad, as if she knew something else she wasn't saying.

Mars blinked hard again. "Ma, what's the 1961 Project?"

"How do you know about that?" she asked quickly.

"It was on your computer. Is it important?"

But his mom had stopped talking, and she was holding her hand to her heart.

"What's wrong?" Mars asked, concerned.

She grimaced. "I was afraid of this . . ." Her voice began to waver. "Here, here, take it." She thrust her IP phone into his hand. "Use it to find me." Then in front of their very eyes, Saira Patel began disintegrating.

"Mamaji!" Mars cried. "What's happening?"

"She's dematerializing," Toothpick said. "Her atoms are shifting."

"Make it stop, Pick!" JP shouted.

"Mars, Mars . . ." Saira called out. She was barely an outline. "See you in the stars . . ."

Then she vanished.

"Ma!" Mars cried. He reached out, but where her body had been just a few seconds ago, there was nothing.

JP wrapped their arms around him. "I'm so sorry, Mars. But maybe she's OK. Maybe she's with the other parents."

Mars nodded. "I hope you're right," he whispered. He looked at the IP phone she had handed him. She'd said to use it to find her. Would the phone help him get her back? On the lock screen there was a grainy photo of the Seattle Space Needle. But he had only a second to look at it before he felt himself being grabbed from behind, and then he and his friends were dragged away from the clearing.

25

LIGHTS, ACTION, BLACKOUT

Next to Mars, JP's powerful arms knocked their aggressor down.

"Ow!" the guy yelled, then collided into the person who held Mars, sending them all crashing to the ground. The third person, a muscular teenage girl who had Toothpick, turned around.

"Oh, come on," she said, looking annoyed at the group sprawled on the ground.

"I got knocked down," said the guy who had crashed into Mars, rubbing his shoulder.

"You better believe it!" JP said. They broke out into a grin. "We're on Gale Island! That's means I'm super strong. And my friend here is super smart. You're in trouble now!"

Mars looked more closely at their assailant and recognized his thick boots. "Hey, this is the guy who tried to grab me at H. G. Wells!" Mars saw the other guy was wearing a silver earring. "And he's the other one. I knew you looked familiar. Are you here because of Aurora?"

"Wait, you're Mars Patel, aren't you?" said the teen girl in surprise. She turned to Toothpick. "You're Randall Lee, and that's JP McGowan."

"And you're new to security," Toothpick said. "Or you wouldn't reveal what you know."

The girl's eyes narrowed. "Are you trying to trick me or something?" She turned to the other guys. "Mack, Jude, didn't you realize it's *them*?" she scolded.

Jude, the guy in the boots, shrugged. "Mack said there were people on the beach. Aren't we supposed to be guarding the beach?"

"Yeah," said Mack.

The girl sighed. "From ordinary people. Not Mars and his friends. C'mon, let's take them to Aurora."

"Maybe we don't want to go," JP said. "Care for a knuckle sandwich? I'm feeling unstoppable!"

Mars shook his head at JP and said loudly, "Actually you better take us to Aurora."

"Which is what we're doing," said the girl. "Sheesh, you don't need to tell us."

As they followed Mack, Jude, and the girl through the dark woods, JP leaned over to Mars.

"I thought you didn't want to see Aurora," they whispered.

"I think he has a plan," Toothpick said.

"Affirmative," Mars said. "Something weird is going on here. It's better if we find out what it is with Aurora working with us, not against us."

∩

Near the shore, huge floodlights were set up along the edge of the trees, bathing the beach in bright light. A stage had been built where several kids were running around setting up microphones and other equipment. "Sound check," someone yelled.

In the middle of the equipment and kids running around, Aurora stood in a dark-blue blazer, black leather pants, and high-heeled boots. Her hair was cut to her chin, just like on the poster back at H. G. Wells. And she was wearing fake eyelashes.

Mars stared at her, half-curious, half-confused. This was Aurora?

"Mars!" she squealed from the stage. She glanced at the assistants near her. "Everyone, take five and report back ASAP. The rally starts at 1900 hours sharp!"

The assistants immediately dispersed.

"Mars, Toothpick, JP!" Aurora climbed gingerly down from the stage in her heels and came to meet them.

Nearby, streamers, balloons, and noisemakers were scattered across small pub tables. On the ground, a red carpet led to the stage. And on the stage, light jazz music was heard playing quietly from the speakers.

JP looked around. "What is this stuff? It looks like a school assembly gone wrong."

Toothpick pointed to a banner being hung across the bottom of the stage. "It's a presidential rally," he said. On the sign were the words in caps: AURORA IS YOUR PRESIDENT!

"Glad you're here to support the cause," Aurora said.

"You're not president yet," JP said. "Or maybe you forgot that detail."

Aurora laughed. "I believe in projecting confidence."

"Where do you want me to put this microphone, Aurora, center stage or stage right?" said a tall, lanky boy.

"Jonas!" JP exclaimed. "It's you!"

Jonas saw them and broke into a big smile.

"What up, dudes?" he cried, and strode over to the group. "H. G. reunion!"

JP gave him a hug.

"Great to see you, Jonas!" Mars said.

"What up?" Toothpick said. "Droney says hi, too. Except he's recharging in my backpack."

Jonas was rubbing his shoulders. "You sure got strong, JP," he said good-naturedly.

"Maybe finish up with the hugs later?" Aurora said. "We've got a rally to put on. I'd like all hands on deck."

"Aurora, news flash: we're not your hired hands," JP said.

"Glad to help, Aurora," Mars said quickly.

JP made a face and fell silent.

"Toothpick, you're kinda quiet," Aurora said. "Maybe you're thinking how glad you are to be here, too."

"Actually, I'm thinking about how you're operating your floodlights," Toothpick said. "They're stadium size, and we're literally in the middle of nowhere. You must have something high-tech set up at Pruitt Prep to get enough kilowatts."

"If you don't know, Toothpick happens to run the *Northwest power grid*," JP said archly.

"Pruitt Prep does have its advantages," Aurora said. "And we're not exactly in the middle of nowhere—we're a ferry ride from Seattle."

"Yeah, you can see the skyline from here," Jonas added. "Y'all have been to the Space Needle, right?" He pointed to the distant cityscape on the other side of the water. "If you squint, you can pretend it's there. At least, that's what I do."

"I haven't been there, Jo-Jo," JP said. "My parents kept saying we should. Now . . . well, I hope we still have a chance someday."

"There *will* be another chance, JP," Mars said. "Don't worry."

"Thanks, Mars."

"Ugh," Aurora said. "Who cares about that boring Space Needle or what we should have done with our parents?" Behind her, Jonas had gone back on the stage and was securing the wiring with clips.

"Wow, you're really hating on your mom and dad, huh?" JP said.

"Also, the Space Needle isn't boring," Toothpick said. "It's an important part of Seattle's skyline and history."

Meanwhile, Aurora was watching Jonas intently. "No, that's the wrong wiring, Jonas! I need the long extension cord!" She walked back to the stage, evidently missing what Toothpick had said. Or the look that crossed his face just then.

"Mars!" Toothpick said excitedly. "That's it!"

"What is?" Mars asked.

"Remember our school trip to the Needle in fourth grade? It's amazing—all this information is coming back to me," Toothpick marveled. "Gale Island is incredible. It's like I have this search engine running through my brain. It's blowing my mind, although I don't normally say things like that, except when teaching Droney idiomatic expressions."

"Pick, get to your point!" JP said. "Today."

"The Space Needle is Seattle's most treasured landmark, built for the 1962 World's Fair. They made a hole thirty feet into the ground and it took the entire day to fill it with concrete. The foundation weighs as much as the Space Needle does, and the center of gravity is five feet above the ground. Which means that the structure is solid and beautiful, and one of a kind."

"*This* is your point, Pick?" JP said. "A history lesson on the Space Needle?"

"No, I'm just proving that I really *do* remember everything from that field trip," Toothpick said. "Which is why I'm positive that construction began in 1961. Did you hear that, Mars? 1961. Are you thinking what I'm thinking?"

"The 1961 Project!" Mars said. "Pick, you're a genius! The lock screen on my mom's phone had the Space Needle on it. And she had a postcard of the Space Needle in her bedroom."

"Why is that place so important, Mars?" JP asked.

"I don't know," Mars said. "I think we need to go there right now and find out."

"But you can't," Aurora jumped in. She had come back just in time to hear the tail end of their conversation. "My rally is about to begin." She swept her hand back toward the stage, where Jonas was setting up a bubble machine.

"I'm sorry," Mars said. "But we have to figure out why the adults are missing. The Space Needle might be a clue."

"No, it isn't!" Aurora said desperately. "I'm not letting you leave! Not when you just got here!"

Just then there was a tremendous buzzing sound, and the floodlights flickered off followed by the audio equipment. Then everything around them went completely black and quiet.

Aurora let out a yelp. "My floodlights! Toothpick, what did you do?"

"Nothing!" Toothpick said back in the darkness.

"Aurora, the power's out," one of the kids said. "None of the equipment is working!"

"My phone is dead!"

"Hey, what happened? There's no Wi-Fi!"

"Did we trip the power source? I can't see a thing!"

"Where's Seattle?" Jonas said from the stage.

"There's a power outage," someone said. "The whole island is out."

"There's no light in the city either. Look, no skyline!"

"No Space Needle!"

Total darkness had swept the beach, extending all around Gale Island. Everywhere they looked, they were met with impenetrable darkness.

"I can't even see my hands," JP muttered. "This is like, serious dark! Where is everybody?"

"I'm here, JP," Toothpick said. "If you remain still, your eyes will get used to the dark."

"This is terrible," Aurora said. "Does someone have a light? Mars? Anyone?"

Mars had been standing still next to everyone. What Toothpick had said was true. Gradually, his eyes had grown accustomed to the dark. He couldn't see faces but he could make out the outlines of his friends. But that didn't help him answer the question: Now what were they supposed to do?

Mamaji, if you were here, you'd tell me, he thought. But she had disappeared. Just then, from the edge of the forest, a shadowy figure emerged.

"Hey, did you see that?" JP had noticed the dark figure, too.

There was a loud bellow as the figure charged at the stage.

"I'd know that sound anywhere!" Aurora said. "Tardigrade!"

In one fell swoop, a large creature leaped toward Mars. He felt its short fur and a familiar nudge against his face. "It's

Cupcake!" He threw his arms around the creature's neck. "My mom was right! You did find us!" He scratched the tardigrade behind her ears, and she let out a contented sigh.

"That's just great. It's pitch dark, and you're chumming with a tardigrade," Aurora said. "It must be your special power."

"Well, I *am* super loved," Mars said, smiling finally. Plus, Cupcake's breath was tickling his neck.

"Well, we don't super love tardigrades around here," Aurora said. "There's a big one on the island named Muffin who's always showing up and freaking everyone out."

"Interesting that Cupcake got here without our help," Toothpick said. "She must be pretty smart. Or know her way around the island. Maybe she knows Muffin."

"Listen, I'd love to chat about tardigrade life, but I have bigger problems," Aurora said. "How do I run a presidential rally in the dark? Mars, you always have a plan. Say something."

"Aurora, actually, I still really need to get to the Space Needle," Mars said.

"I hear you, Mars," said Jonas, who had wandered over to them from the stage. "But how do you plan to get to the Needle in the dark?"

Mars felt the tardigrade nudge him forcefully. "Whoa, Cupcake," he said, surprised. Then she nudged him even more unmistakably. "I—I think Cupcake wants to take me!"

"The tardigrade?" Aurora sounded dubious. "How would that even work?"

"I've ridden on her before. She's fast, reliable, and she always seems to know what I'm thinking."

"Again, what is it with you and the tardigrades?" JP said.

"Mars, I need a minute with you," Aurora said. "Alone." Mars felt her grab his arm as she pulled him to the side. "Look, I know you want to play superhero, but you can't leave. I need you. It's dark. Nothing's working here. I'm going to have a meltdown. You're the only one who gets me."

Mars sighed. "Aurora, I'm here for you. I always will be." He looked in Cupcake's direction, and she grunted back. "But I've got to take care of this. It's my mom we're talking about. You weren't there. I—I saw her dissolve right front of my eyes."

"Oh," Aurora said. "Sorry, Mars. That sucks." She seemed to consider his words. "And you really think the Needle has the answers?"

"It's just a hunch, but I think I'll find out where my mom went, and yours, and what Oliver Pruitt has to do with it. And maybe even why the lights have gone out. Because I think they're all related."

"Fine," Aurora said. "I'll go with you."

Mars was startled. "To the Space Needle?"

"I need to find out about the power outage, too. And you need company. Who else is going to take care of you if you fall off that animal?"

"Uh—OK," Mars said.

"Make way, make way," Aurora called out as she pulled Mars's hand. "We're in a hurry."

"You're going with Mars?" JP said. "And the tardigrade? You know they fart a lot, right?"

"That was your tardigrade on Mars, JP," Mars said. "Cupcake isn't so gassy."

Gassy or not, Cupcake let out a growl as soon as she saw Aurora come near.

"Cupcake, girl, what's going on?" Mars asked.

"It hates me," Aurora said. "It's obvious."

"Cupcake's a she, OK?" Mars said. He rubbed the tardigrade's leg. "I really need you to do this, and let Aurora come with us."

Cupcake bellowed and bellowed but finally relented. Grudgingly, she bent down her front legs so they both could climb on top of her, but not without a last noise of disapproval.

"You're the best, Cupcake," Mars said as they climbed on. He patted the tardigrade's head. "Hold on, Aurora. Next stop, Seattle!"

∩

From the beach, JP and Toothpick stood back, watching.

"How many minutes do you think she'll last up there?" JP asked.

"Ten," Toothpick said.

"Five." JP scratched their head. "Also, I wonder what they'll do when they reach the water?"

Toothpick started walking. "I have a feeling Mars will figure it out."

"He always does, doesn't he? Hey Pick, where are you going? Wait up."

Toothpick turned to JP as they walked. "Remember the rowboat tied to the dock?"

JP rolled their eyes. "Don't remind me. I can't believe we all were on that boat: you, me, Caddie, and Mars, riding across the sound like fools to Pruitt Prep, even though we found out literally nothing that day. Worst day ever. 'Cause you know I hate being wet."

"We need to get back to H. G. Wells," Toothpick said, "and that rowboat is the only way."

"Seriously?" JP said. "Just so you know, I'd rather go back the way we came, down that dark, creepy tunnel where you'll break your neck slipping off that scary ladder if you don't get knocked out by a rock hanging over your head first, or bitten by a rabid bat."

"Yeah, but we can't go that way; the door doesn't open from the outside," Toothpick said. "But with your super strength and my super navigation skills, we can row across the sound in half the time. Easy peasy."

JP blinked at Toothpick as they continued walking to the shore.

"Sometimes, Pick, I think I hate you."

26

LOOK UP

Caddie stood in the forest debating. Ahead of them, the shoe prints continued for a few paces through the soft ground, then seemed to drag, even scraping across the soil as if whoever it was moved with an unsteady gait. Then the prints disappeared into the thick brush with no sign of them anywhere else.

"I don't get it. They just end," Axel said. "No sign of them later, right Julia?"

Past the brush was a steep drop and a network of trees tightly laced together.

"Affirmative," Julia said. "And if those tracks continue down there, I can't follow on my rover. Not down a hill like that."

"Maybe it's not important where they went," Caddie said. She looked over Julia's shoulder where the shoe prints were visible in the soil. "See, they came from that direction. Let's follow the shoe prints the way they came from, and that will tell us something."

Axel nodded. "Good idea."

"Did Daisy message us?" Julia asked.

Axel looked at his phone. "No. But you have a message from Randall Lee on the public network." He clicked on it and the recording played: *"Julia, can you read me? This is Randall Lee. You are an amazing scientist, Julia. Over."*

Julia blushed furiously. "He said that on the public network? That's so sweet. But he knows it isn't secure, and who knows what an ill-wisher might do."

"Like what? Sabotage a long-distance relationship?" Axel said.

"It's not a long-distance relationship!" Julia said quickly. "He's got a girlfriend."

"Epica," Caddie said. "She's a piece of work."

"Wanna send a message back?" Axel said. "Tell me or we move on. But it will be public just like his."

"Oh, dear. I couldn't." Julia continued to blush and cleared her throat.

Caddie smiled. "I think it would be nice, Julia. Maybe he'll even get it, too."

"Yeah, Julia. Send a message to your Romeo."

"Don't call him that. Give me the phone. I'm only doing this to be nice. Like Axel said, I'll say something not too revealing.

Erm, hackers, you know." She clicked a button to record. "Randall, this is Julia. Got your message. Thank you. You're an amazing scientist, too. Ad astra. Julia. Over." She cleared her throat and handed back the phone to Axel. "And that's all we're saying on this subject," she said gruffly. "I don't need any coy remarks from either of you."

Caddie and Axel grinned at each other but said nothing.

The three of them decided that they would follow the shoe prints in the opposite direction. By now it was midafternoon, and the sun had dropped in the sky.

"What do you think happens here when night falls?" Julia wondered. "Everywhere else on the surface, it gets freezing cold. Will that happen in this forest, too? We'll need to shelter soon."

"I'm not cold yet," Caddie said. "Are either of you?"

"Nope," Axel said. "I'm fly."

"I'm fly, too," Julia said. "Whatever that means."

An hour later, Axel was less fly.

"When do these tracks end?" he said crankily. "I'm getting thirsty. Let's stop and have a food break."

"I don't think we should dip into our supplies yet," Julia said. "Who knows how long we'll be out here. We should forage."

"Forage?" Axel said. "What are we, cave dwellers?"

"Well, we're not going to find a vending machine with soda and crackers, are we?" Julia retorted. She was getting tired.

They all were. And they were starting to wrangle with one another.

"Axel's right. Let's take a break," Caddie said. "We can have a tiny bit of food and water."

"And forage!" Axel reminded them.

Caddie found a rock to sit on while Julia went around the trees, the sound of her rover humming faintly in the distance. Caddie noticed Axel pacing back and forth even though just a minute ago he'd wanted to take a break. "Axel, why don't you sit down? You need a break, remember?"

"Yeah," he said, but he continued pacing. After a few moments, he jerked a finger in Julia's direction. "You think she's safe?"

"Why, what are you worried about?" Caddie asked.

"Look, I'm from Fairbanks. You know how you were saying this place reminds you of Washington? It's a lot like Alaska, too. Some of the same kinds of trees. But we have other stuff, too. Like moose and bears in the backyard. Even lynxes."

"Are you afraid of bears?" Caddie asked. "And moose . . . on Mars?"

"Laugh all you want. None of this makes sense. I don't see why there can't be animals here, too. You have to respect nature and watch where you're going. My moms always tell me that."

Caddie smiled gently. "Don't worry. Julia's fine. We can see her from here."

Axel finally sat down next to her and leaned forward, resting his arms on his legs. The hair around his neck was curly and damp with sweat. Sometimes Axel looked like a grown man, and sometimes he looked like a little kid. Like now.

"Do you miss your family?" Caddie asked.

He swung his head up at her. "Sure. They'd love this place. Back home, we live on several acres of forest. We got dogs at home. In the winters we go mushing. My mom grooms the trails, and then Kayla—that's what I call my other mom—she goes next. Then me and my brother. Sometimes they'll let me go by myself, as long as I'm back before dark."

Caddie had never heard Axel talk so much before, especially about his family. She hadn't realized until that moment how much he missed home. He had always seemed so detached and goofy around Aurora. But it was probably his way of dealing with being so far away.

"That's awesome," she said. "I've never known anybody who . . . what do you call it? Dog mushing?"

"It's tons of fun," Axel said. "Only when you're out you have to be careful. Bears hibernate in the winter. But moose—they can sleep against your house or shed, and if you come out and you scare them, that's bad for you and your dogs. I know lots of people who've gotten charged by moose. Not me personally. I've never had my dogs get stomped, like out on the trails. But I'm always looking. Out here in the forest, my radar is up again, I guess. It's like a sixth sense."

"Yeah," Caddie said. "That's sort of how I feel here, too." She was about to tell him about the voices she was hearing that sounded like her parents, but before she could say anything, Julia called out to them.

"Berries!" Julia shouted. "Lots of them!"

"Maybe they're poisonous," Axel called back. He got up and stretched.

"Negative," Julia said. "They're wild strawberries." After a moment, "Yum!"

After that, Axel clamored up. "All right, save some for me."

"There's a whole forest here," Julia said. "Caddie, you, too."

Caddie smiled. "Be there in a bit."

After Axel went off, she closed her eyes. The voices had been there the whole time she was talking to Axel. But now that she was alone, she tried to make them stronger by opening her mind and letting them in. She was starting to think that what they were saying was important. Even a clue.

This is where we took that picture.

Her mom's voice seemed near, as if . . .

Caddie. She was fast on the trail. Remember, Stan?

There was a pause, then she heard her father. *So fast.*

"Caddie, there's plenty for you," Julia called out. "Unless the squirrels get them first."

"There's squirrels here?" Axel said.

"Of course not. This is the planet Mars. Unless they're alien squirrels."

"If there are strawberries and breathable air, there could be squirrels."

"True," Julia conceded. "Caddie, are you coming?"

Caddie. We don't know what we did wrong.

Caddie opened her eyes, trembling.

"Don't worry, Mom and Dad," she said softly. "I'll find you."

After filling their stomachs with berries and a few sips of water, the three of them were off.

Julia kept looking at the sun as they followed the shoe prints. "The sun is sinking," she said.

"This person with the shoes can sure walk," Axel said. "They keep going and going like the Energizer bunny."

"What's the Energizer bunny?" Julia asked. "One of your American things?"

"That ad on TV. I forget, you're British. Don't they have batteries in London?"

"Remind me again, how did you make it to Pruitt Prep?" Julia asked.

The voices were getting louder and louder in Caddie's head, to the point that they were almost drowning out Axel and Julia.

Caddie. Come, stay for the picture.

Look up, Caddie. Look up. Up.

Then finally through a gap between the trees, Caddie saw something.

"Everyone, up there," she said. She was able make out the

shape behind the line of trees. "Something's there, up on the hill. Something coming out of the ground."

"Oh my, yes," Julia said. "What is it?"

"It's behind those trees," Axel said.

They picked up their pace, and then Axel broke into a run, with Julia zooming behind him. Caddie began to run, too. Something was there.

Look, Caddie! Look, look, look!

They reached a clearing at the bottom of the hill.

"It's huge!" Julia breathed, craning her neck. "It's a building!"

"A tower!" Axel said.

But it was more than just a building or a tower.

"I don't believe it," Caddie said, stunned. "It's the Seattle Space Needle. On Mars!"

27

CROSSING THE SOUND

Cupcake was a young tardigrade and had only reached half her adult size. But her eight powerful legs moved across the beach with the speed of a full-grown wolf. Mars leaned forward, clinging to her soft gray fur, the salty air streaming past his nose and eyes. This experience reminded him of the time on Mars when he and JP had ridden tardigrades across the Martian surface in the hope of locating Oliver Pruitt. Now he was here, back on Earth. A different Earth. One plunged into darkness and uncertainty. But Cupcake was fearless and loyal, and she seemed to understand him without any explanation. *Like Caddie,* Mars thought. He smiled. He wasn't sure Caddie would like being compared to a tardigrade.

Behind him, Aurora was clinging to his back. He could tell she was terrified. She said something. "What?" he asked.

She said it again, but he couldn't hear her over the wind.

"What?"

"I said," she yelled, "what about the water?"

As if on cue, Cupcake jumped into Puget Sound.

"Oh my god, we're going to drown!" Aurora screamed.

"Stop screaming in my ears!" Mars yelled. "She can swim." He said that, but he didn't know for sure. Nothing in any of the handbooks he'd read at the Colony, or during tardigrade training, had mentioned tardigrades swimming.

At first, the three of them went up and down like a buoy, brackish water spraying their faces. Aurora sputtered, and Mars shook his wet hair out of his eyes. Then Cupcake settled into the water, swimming with the tidal current. She was an excellent swimmer. Back and forth her eight legs went as she easily paddled through the sound. After a while, the movement became so effortless it felt like they were gliding across the water. Aurora's grip slowly loosened. Then her limbs grew heavy, and a few minutes later, her head rested against Mars's shoulder. She had fallen asleep.

Mars felt the tension drain from him, too. It had been a long, stressful day. For a while he watched the rippling waters. The moon came out, just a sliver, and in the distance, he could see a group of harbor seals resting quietly on a rock. He caught his breath. Sometimes he would see the round, streamlined animals sunning themselves when he walked along the shore in the summer, and every time it felt like a glimpse into another world. This group had pups bobbing in the water near the rock. As they went by, Mars wanted to point out the seals to Cupcake, then decided to keep quiet. What if Cupcake went after them? So far, she had been content eating human food. But what if she was craving something? Just then, Cupcake grunted reproachfully as if to say, *I don't eat seals!*

"Sorry," Mars said. Seriously, it was like being around Caddie.

His thoughts drifted to his mom. It had been so good to see her. She wasn't all dressed up to teach at college like she'd been on Alt Earth. Instead, her hair was in its usual messy ponytail, and she was drinking orange soda. The way he remembered her. Except now she was . . . what did she call it? An environmental physicist. Her job was to take care of the planet. *We have to fix our own problems*, she'd said. Maybe that's what being an adult was really all about. It was also the first time she'd admitted the truth she'd hidden from Mars for so many years: Oliver Pruitt was his dad. But why had she kept it a secret for so long?

He felt Aurora stir. "What time is it?" she murmured.

"Not sure. Cupcake's still swimming."

"It's kind of peaceful," Aurora said, still drowsy.

"Yeah," Mars agreed. "Good for thinking."

"And sleeping. Sorry. I guess I don't have much time for that. Lots of campaign stuff to do."

"That's OK." Mars pointed at the sky. "Look, there's the Big Dipper."

"And Cassiopeia's chair," Aurora said. "And Leo, Cygnus, Andromeda, Hercules. Oh, and Pegasus."

Mars gave her a look.

"What? So I know constellations."

"Why am I not surprised?"

She shrugged. "I like learning. I know, hard to believe." She sat up. "Hey, it's super easy to see the stars right now. I think it's because of the power outage or something. Like over there, that's Orion. Normally you can only see his belt, but now you can see his head and arms, too. Cool."

"That's cool," Mars said. "It's a really clear night."

"You should see the stars from the rooftop at Pruitt Prep," Aurora said. "This year, the astronomy club is killing it. I go up with them. We can see so many more constellations. We think it's because the air quality is better. Less plane travel and less smog."

"Because of no adults?"

"Bingo."

There was a gust of wind that sprayed up water so they had to tuck their faces in.

"Did you know we reached Caddie?" he asked next. "Tooth-pick rigged up a transponder and it worked."

"Oh?"

"They're OK. Caddie and everyone. Though I wonder why we lost contact with them for so long. You'd think someone from Pruitt Prep would be able to reach them, right?"

Aurora stiffened. "What are you saying? That it's my fault?"

"What? No," Mars said. "I just thought it was strange that we lost their signal, that's all." He was about to tell her how there *might* be breathable air on Mars, but he still wasn't sure if he had really heard what he thought he had.

"I guess you were real happy to talk to Caddie," Aurora said.

"Yeah," Mars said.

"Because you have a bond," she went on. There was an edge in her voice.

"I care about all my friends, Aurora," he said cautiously.

Below them, the waters were lapping more intensely.

"I hope Cupcake's OK," he said. "She must be getting tired."

"She seems fine," Aurora said. "Mars, can I ask you a question?"

"Sure. Anything."

"Do I have your vote?"

"My vote?" Mars gave a surprised laugh.

Aurora snorted. "I guess that's a no."

"Does it really matter?" he asked. "My *vote*? With all that's going on? Just think about it. The adults are gone. Half our friends are on another planet. And the power is out."

"I *am* thinking about all of that. This isn't just about me." She stopped. "Well, OK, I do want to be in charge. But I don't think you understand. My mom isn't like your mom. She didn't make me breakfast or wash my clothes or come to school to meet my teachers. And don't even get me started on my dad.

They were bad parents. Absent parents. They thought I was a pain. So, sorry if I don't want to see them again, or other people like them."

Mars nodded. "I hear you. My dad wasn't around either."

"Pruitt's not *really* your dad, is he?" Aurora asked. "I heard his podcast and almost spit out my Coke."

"Go figure, right?" Mars said it lightly enough. But now it was because the idea of Oliver being his dad had taken root in his heart. Maybe it was hearing his mom talk about it. Or maybe he had just accepted the fact himself. Still, it wasn't something he was ready to talk about with Aurora. Better to sound like he didn't care so she'd leave the subject alone.

Ahead of them, dark shapes were starting to take form in the distance.

"I think that's the shore, Aurora. We're almost there."

She squinted. "You're right. That's the harbor where I got off the ferry to meet my dad the one time he took me into Seattle. This feels kind of like that. Except we're riding on a tardigrade that hates me."

"Not true," Mars said. "She likes you."

"Um, no, she doesn't."

With a tremendous leap, Cupcake jumped onto the dock, then turned her head back to give Aurora a withering glare.

Aurora shrank behind Mars's back. "See?" she cried. "Did you see that look?"

"That's just because she's got ten eyes," Mars said. "You're reading her all wrong." He patted Cupcake's head. "So now we're going to go nice and easy to the Space Needle, OK, girl? And—"

With a grunt, Cupcake tore down the dock and leaped onto the street.

"Cupcake!" Mars yelled. "Slow it down a notch!"

Aurora closed her eyes. "I can't look!"

"Slowwwwww down!" Mars called out.

But that only seemed to make Cupcake run faster. She accelerated down dark, deserted streets, under traffic lights that had stopped working, past an overpass and then something called the Pacific Science Center, until a tall structure came into view. From where they were, the Space Needle stretched endlessly to the sky.

"You remember going to the Needle?" Mars asked, gritting his teeth against Cupcake's breakneck speed.

"Can't talk," Aurora said. "Too busy praying we don't die."

Mars leaned into Cupcake's soft fur as they barreled through the circular parking lot of the Space Needle and right up to the front entrance.

Mars remembered his fourth-grade field trip. Mrs. Marvin's class. Aurora wasn't in school that day, but Toothpick was, at the head of the line next to Mrs. Marvin. Mars was at the back next to the Boof, only he wasn't called that yet. He was still Clyde and wouldn't hit his growth spurt till the end of that year. That elevator ride up had been epic. The view at the top was breathtaking. Clyde had even posed for a selfie with Mars. But the elevator wouldn't work now, with the power out. What should they do? Search the grounds? Wait near the nonoperational water fountain at the front?

He didn't have to ponder long.

Cupcake reared up suddenly, waving her front legs in the air.

"Cupcake!" Mars shouted in alarm. "What are you doing?"

The tardigrade stood on her hind legs and let gravity have its way.

"Mars, I'm slipping!" Aurora yelled. A moment later she fell butt first onto the ground.

"Cupcake! Wait!"

But Cupcake wasn't done. She ran straight toward the structure. Mars held on for dear life. What was she doing? Then it dawned on him.

"Mars! *Mars!*" Aurora yelled after him. "What am I supposed to do?"

"I'll be back, I promise," Mars called back. "Wait for me."

He held on with both arms. His heart was racing, and his hair stood on end. And yet he felt so alive. Then together, he and the tardigrade climbed up the tower.

28
THE NEEDLE, PART 1

Cupcake crawled up the side of the Space Needle, her grip amazing as she traversed the steel sections. The building was less like a needle, actually, and more like a rocket ship pointing to the stars. Mars clung to Cupcake as they went up and up. Below them, Seattle was dark. Unseeable. A city missing; a planet without light. His dad was somewhere. His mother was somewhere, too. But for now, gone like the rest of the parents.

They reached the top of the Needle. Cupcake crawled over the barriers into the observation area and bent down gently, sliding Mars to the ground so that he landed softly on his feet. He gave her a hug.

"Thank you, Cuppy," he whispered. He studied her. She used to look terrifying: all eyes and legs, and a mouth with an iron mandible that could crush him. But she didn't scare him anymore.

She continued into the Needle, pushing open doors that were surprisingly unlocked at the top as Mars followed her inside. Now they were in the viewing chamber. But it looked different than he remembered. The walls were translucent. Rippling, like the water in the sound.

"Something is different in here," Mars said, whispering. "I don't remember it looking like this." He stepped forward, held a finger out, and touched one of the walls. It flowed!

"The walls are liquid!' he breathed. "Cupcake, what is this place?" He touched the wall again, and around him there was a tremendous humming. The walls . . . him . . . everything was starting to vibrate. And then like a flash, there was a blinding light.

29

THE NEEDLE, PART 2

When they got to the entrance of the tall structure, Caddie led them inside to the elevator.

"If this is like the one in Seattle," she said, "it will take forty-three seconds to get to the top."

The voices in her head had become steady now. Sometimes she was sure she could hear her mom, but most of the time, the voices joined together, humming like a music player turned low. Oddly, she found that if she talked and acted normal, the voices didn't get out of hand. It was only when she got nervous and her pulse rate quickened that the voices got louder and more unmanageable. *Just be calm*, she told herself as they walked across the lobby. "I remember coming to the Seattle Space Needle with my dad," she said. "The whole fourth grade went on a field trip, but I missed it because I had pneumonia. After I was better, my dad decided to treat me to a visit. He even pulled me out of school."

"What's at the top of the Needle?" Axel asked. "I'd put in a game room."

"Why do I think that would be the last thing up there?" Julia said.

Caddie pressed the button for the elevator. The voices dialed up for a moment, then she breathed more slowly. Calmly. The voices went back down. "No game room, Axel. There's an observation deck and a place to eat. You can see all of Seattle from up there. My dad and I got hot chocolate and nachos, and took lots of pictures." She smiled. "My dad was really sweet. Then he lost his job and got all stressed out for a long time. He found another job later, but he wasn't the same."

The doors opened and they entered. The walls inside the elevator were made of glass except for the side that featured the doors and three elevator buttons that were red, green, and yellow.

"That's strange," Julia said. "I guess we just press green for go and red for stop?"

"What does yellow do?" Axel said. "Go slow?"

Caddie shrugged. "I'm not really sure. The one in Seattle has an elevator operator. I guess we have to be our own operators. What do you think? Yellow or green?"

"Green all the way," Julia said.

Caddie pressed green. The doors closed and the elevator began to rise.

"It worked. We're going up!" Axel pressed his palms against one of the glass walls. After they rose a few stories, they could look out over the forest. In the distance, the red, cracked surface of Mars stretched out for miles, forming a vast, dry, desolate place of peaks and valleys, and well beyond them, a cluster of tiny buildings.

"There's the Colony and windmills!" Caddie said.

"And Monument Crater!" Julia said. "I remember crashing there when I first got to this planet. Not the best arrival, but at least we survived."

"Sorry," Axel said. "That was when Aurora and I rerouted you guys. But we didn't mean to make you crash. We just wanted you to land near us so we could steal the shuttle and leave the Colony in the dust."

"Apology accepted," Julia said. "I think."

"A lot's changed," Axel said. "Now the Martians and colonists are working together."

"Thanks to Caddie," Julia said. "You really made it work."

"We all made it work," Caddie said. "I still can't get used to a forest being here." She looked down at the ground, which was getting farther and farther away. The canopy of trees was lush, in brilliant shades of green, forming an oasis in a red desert.

"The forest should have a name," Julia said. She pointed above them, at the soft clouds laced together. "That's what I saw from the weather tower. The clouds are only here. Nowhere else."

"Let's call it that," Caddie said. "Cloud Forest."

"Love it," Julia said.

"Works," Axel said.

The elevator kept rising.

"What do you think we'll see at the top?" Julia wondered.

"Hot chocolate and nachos sound good," Axel said. "Those strawberries weren't filling."

"You're always hungry, aren't you?" Julia said. "That's why you need to become a forager."

"You should get to know JP," Caddie said. "They love to cook, and you love to eat."

Axel nodded. "I can cook, too. I just don't."

"My parents are the worst cooks," Julia said. "We got take-out all the time."

"My parents are OK," Caddie said. "My mom did most of the cooking. Does most of the cooking, I mean." She flushed. "It's weird, not knowing what tense to use."

"My moms take turns," Axel said. "Ma cooks on Mondays and Wednesdays, Kayla the other days, and we do pizza on the weekends." He blinked a few times. "I miss them."

"Yes," Julia said. She blinked a few times, too.

The elevator was slowing down. Slowing. Slowing. Then it came to a stop.

Everyone waited. But the doors didn't open.

"Hey they're not opening," Axel said.

"Press the red button," Julia said.

"I am," Axel said. "Nothing." He kept jabbing at it.

Caddie could feel her pulse quicken.

Caddie, Caddie. Stay and take a picture.

"Maybe that's what the yellow button's for," Julia said. "Not slow. Just open."

The voices were getting out of control. "Yes," Caddie said faintly. "Press the yellow."

"Caddie, are you OK?" Julia's voice sounded muddled, like she was underwater.

The yellow, the yellow. The yellow button.

"Press the yellow, Axel," Julia said. Underwater.

The voices rose to a fever pitch, until it seemed like there was nothing else.

"I'm pressing it," Axel said. "It's not working. Nothing's working. We're stuck."

Then the doors finally opened.

Caddie, Caddie. If only we knew where you are. All we have left are pictures.

"Caddie!" Julia called. "Axel, she's on the floor. Help her."

Axel reached down and pulled Caddie up while Julia held onto Caddie's other arm.

"Come on, Caddie," Julia's voice was distant. "You'll be OK."

"I'm OK," Caddie said weakly. "Just a head rush, I think."

They stepped out of the elevator into a room that was flooded with light. They were a motley crew, dazed, uncombed, and fatigued, their faces smudged with perspiration as they looked around the top of the Space Needle. Or something like the Space Needle.

And there in the observation tower in front of them, looking just as dazed, was Mars Patel.

30
CROSSING EPICA HERNANDEZ

The rickety rowboat made a giant scraping sound as it hit the shore in Port Elizabeth.

"I can't believe you made me row us all the way back home," JP said. "Especially since I lost my Pruitt Prep super strength halfway. Then it was just my plain JP muscles doing the job."

"You still made good time," Toothpick said. "Look, the moon isn't even all the way out."

"But where are we going?" JP asked as they walked down Main Street together. It was eerily dark and deserted, the streetlamps looking like blown-out candles.

"We're going," Toothpick said, "to get wheels."

"Wheels?"

"My car's still in the parking lot at H. G. Wells," Toothpick said. "Remember Aurora's gang? We had to walk to Mars's apartment."

"Oh yeah," JP said. "So you're driving us home?"

"Not home. Mars needs backup."

"You mean the Space Needle? But you've never driven around the city before."

"I doubt there will be traffic during a blackout. We'll make it work. You just have to trust me."

JP sighed. "I'd rather trust you than anybody else."

When they reached the middle school, they quickly found Toothpick's SUV in the parking lot. "It's kind of nice to see it there waiting for us," JP said.

"Yes," Toothpick said. "And we have just enough gas to get us to Seattle."

Just then, a sound came from the bushes surrounding the parking lot.

"Hey, who's there?" JP said immediately. "Aurora's squad?"

But this time it was a different set of kids stepping out, and soon there was a gang of seventh and eighth graders filling the parking lot, with Clyde Boofsky and his stooge friend, Scott Bane, in the lead.

"JP—where's Mars?" shouted the Boof. "We were looking for a punching bag!"

"Ha, ha. Maybe JP could volunteer instead," Bane said.

"What's going on, people?" JP said, searching their faces. "I thought you love Mars."

"Did," said a girl. "But Principal Hernandez says that it's Mars's fault the power went out. He made Pruitt mad. Now I can't use my electric can opener, have a hot bath, or watch *The A-List*!"

"I can't microwave my burritos!" the Boof said.

"I stubbed my toe in school!" Bane said. "Down with Mars and his friends."

"That's right." Epica stepped out from behind the Boof. "You can't trust any of them. Especially Randall, because he'll break your heart!"

Toothpick pushed up his glasses. "Epi? What are you talking about?"

"I heard those messages," Epica shouted. "I know all about Julia the amazing scientist! I've read about her amazing rover on Mars. Well, she can go rove herself to some other planet."

"Epica, that's so illogical," Toothpick said. "Julia's rover isn't interplanetary."

"Dude, it's time to split," JP said urgently. "This crowd looks ugly."

They edged back toward the SUV as the other kids started closing in on them.

Toothpick unzipped his backpack. "Droney, create a distraction," he whispered.

There was a whirring sound as the drone flew up and over everyone.

"Kaboom!" Droney called out.

"Look, it's a booby trap," somebody screamed.

"It's following us!"

"Run!"

"Kapow!" Droney said, chasing the dispersing crowd.

"Let's go," Toothpick said as he clicked open the car with his key, and he and JP jumped in.

"Ker-splash!"

"Faster!" yelled the Boof, who was heading for cover inside the bushes.

"Won't Droney run out of battery?" JP asked, watching the kids running away. "How will we get him back?"

"He has about ten minutes left," Toothpick said. "That should do the trick. He also has a homing device so he can fly back to us."

Toothpick started the engine, and then they roared out of the parking lot.

"Pick, you're going to give me a heart attack! Slow down!"

"We need to hurry, JP," Toothpick said. "Just think calm thoughts."

"You're right." JP leaned back. "I can do that. Think calm thoughts. Even with your lead foot on the gas pedal."

"Meditate," Toothpick said. "Say 'om.'"

"Right," JP said. They slowly exhaled.

Behind them, they heard a noise from the back seat.

"Not calm!" JP wailed. They whirled around at the same time Toothpick flashed the interior light. "Holy smoke! It's Mr. Q! In your car!"

Mr. Q gave a brittle laugh. "The one and only."

Toothpick slammed on the brakes.

"No, I'm here to help, guys! Really!" Mr. Q leaned forward,

but that just made JP reach for the door.

"Whoa, OK, don't leave, JP." Mr. Q held up his hands slowly. "See, I've got nothing up my sleeve. It's me. Your old teacher."

"That's what I'm afraid of," JP said.

"Well, he is alone," Toothpick said, "in *my* car."

"That's right, Pick," Mr. Q said. "Keep driving. I've been waiting to speak to you."

JP and Toothpick looked at each other, and then finally Toothpick relented, driving again through the deserted, unlit streets as JP kept throwing furtive looks behind them. It was their old detention teacher all right. The same one who'd captured and delivered all of them to Pruitt, but who had also snuck them onto the space shuttle to Mars. Did that make him good or evil? It wasn't clear. Though at the moment, he looked like he could use a shave.

"I have plenty to say," Mr. Q said.

"Then go ahead," JP said. "Although I'm not sure we can believe anything from you."

"Hold on, JP," Toothpick said suddenly. "Mr. Q is an adult, and he's still here!"

"You're right! Like Mars's mom before she disappeared!" JP clamped their hand over their mouth. "Darn. I shouldn't have mentioned that."

"Saira Patel, huh?" Mr. Q said. "She's pretty . . . resourceful."

"Maybe you made her disappear, too!" JP said, their eyes flashing.

Toothpick made a turn onto the highway. "Let's hear his story first, JP. He looks a little . . . undernourished."

"Yeah," Mr. Q said, clearing his throat. "I've been hiding out in the basement of the school for a year now, eating scraps from the cafeteria and trying to figure out what happened to the adults. I never went out during the day, and I tried not to go out at night, either, because that seems like when bad stuff happens. But tonight, when the power went out, I decided I had to do something. So when I came out and saw a car with the license plate TOOTHPK, I figured it was yours. So I climbed in to wait for you. You left one of your windows open, you know. I was able to pry open the lock. Nice car. Though a tad messy."

"Thanks," Toothpick said. "It has everything I need."

There was a faint whirring sound that got louder and louder until Toothpick opened the moonroof and Droney flew in.

"Droney!" JP said. "Good to see you, pal."

"Good to see you," Droney repeated. He landed in his docking station on the dashboard. "Low battery. Reverting to hibernation mode." The whirring sound shut off.

"Shoot, now you don't have GPS," JP said.

"I'll follow the road signs," Toothpick said.

"Where are you going?" asked Mr. Q.

"I'm the one asking the questions," JP said. "Why are you here when all the adults are gone?"

"I'm not sure. Maybe I got lucky like Saira did." He saw JP cross their arms. "Look, for the record, it's not my fault she was being tracked. Everyone wanted to talk to her. The CIA. The NSA. Other entities you don't even know about. And of course Pruitt. She had been collecting this environmental data that was very damaging to the mission."

"And what mission was that?" JP asked. "World domination?"

"What? No!" Mr. Q said shortly. "The mission to live on Mars, of course! And beyond! Do you know how mind-bendingly cool that is?"

"I dunno," JP said. "Perfecting a lentil soup recipe would be pretty mind-bending, too."

Toothpick cleared his throat. "Er, so what happened next with Mars's mom, Mr. Q?"

Their teacher shrugged. "I was asked to find her in California and bring back her data any way that I could. But then she bolted when she saw me, and she was on her own."

"She said the data was devastating," Toothpick said. "She thinks preserving the environment, even on Mars, is more important than any mission. That's why she didn't hand over the data."

"Also, it's *you*," JP said. "I wouldn't trust you either."

"Seriously, I'm on your side," Mr. Q said. He was trembling. "I don't expect you to understand. But I've been in this for a long time. I know what was started on Mars, and it's glorious! But I know what's been happening to our planet, too. The destruction, the rains, floods, fires, the famines. I know our reckoning is at hand. Now I want to be part of the solution."

"By hiding from us kids?" JP said. "Maybe you switched sides because you're hungry."

"That's not true," Mr. Q said quickly and looked away.

JP eyed him for a moment and opened their backpack. "Here, I have an extra sandwich. It's apple and peanut butter."

"I—wait, really?" Mr. Q's expression changed. He took the sandwich and began to devour it.

"Look, you're right," he said finally, between bites. "I made some bad choices aligning myself with Pruitt. But I believe we can start over, make good choices. As long as we work together. Too bad Epica and her gang aren't in that headspace yet."

"What happened? Why did she go full-on principal?" JP asked. "Sorry, Pick, no offense."

"Epica wants the adults gone," Mr. Q said. "She's been taking cues from Aurora. Also, Toothpick, I understand she's nursing a broken heart."

"Epi's insecurity leads her to make bad decisions," Toothpick said. "I think she feels outpaced by Julia. Of course, Julia's the most amazing—" He stopped. "Never mind, I guess."

"Toothpick, when did you get to be such a stud?" JP said, grinning.

Toothpick cleared his throat. "Mr. Q, are you ready to put your money where your mouth is?"

"What money?" JP asked.

"It's an expression, JP. Are you willing to help us, Mr. Q?"

"Of course," Mr. Q said. "I'm your guy. What do you need?"

31
CROSSING THE UNIVERSE

There was a burst of light, the kind Mars had read about in sci-fi novels. It was so intense it blocked out everything, making Mars feel like he was inside the sun. Just as quickly, the light dissipated and Mars could see again. He was still in the Space Needle, but one minute he'd been surrounded by liquid walls, and now everything was solid and real again, and he was unexplainably staring at Caddie. She was leaning against Julia and Axel, and they all looked as shocked as he felt.

Caddie straightened up. "Mars! Is that you?"

"Caddie!" Mars crossed the room to her. "How did you get here?" He hugged her tightly, feeling the stiff plastic material of her flight suit (why was she wearing a flight suit?) and then looked at her face in wonder. "You—you look great. Are those new glasses?"

She laughed, pushing them up her nose self-consciously.

"I made them myself. And Mars, you're taller! You're taller than me!"

"I could also use one of those hugs, Butterfly!" Julia said.

"Julia!" Mars laughed and hugged her, too. He turned next to Axel, who held his hands up.

"Yeah, I'm good," Axel said. "Not a hugger."

Mars nodded. They hadn't exactly parted on the best of terms, though it seemed like Axel had changed, too. They all had. Mars stepped back to survey everyone. Caddie's hair had grown well past her shoulders, and she had red highlights. Julia's hair had grown out, too, and she seemed to be on a new rover made of titanium. Axel had filled out, his shoulders broader so that he looked like a young man. They were all amazingly, heart-stoppingly the same, and yet different. Older. With an air of self-purpose.

"I can't believe how long it's been," Mars said. "But how did you get to Seattle?"

"Seattle?" Caddie repeated. "We're not in Seattle, Mars."

"But Cupcake and I just climbed up the Space Needle," Mars said. He looked around him. As usual, Cupcake was missing. How did she always manage to give him the slip?

"Look out the window, dude," Axel said.

Mars walked to the edge of the observation area and peered out the windows. There was a forest below, with pine trees and mist and dense foliage. It didn't look like the parking lot of the Space Needle. Then Mars saw it in the distance, the rugged red landscape, the dry lake bed, and the vast, dusty horizon.

For a moment, he was speechless. "I'm back on *Mars*? With a forest here?"

"How did you get here?" Caddie asked. "Actually, never mind." She grimaced, revealing her discomfort. "I can't tune it out anymore. It's so . . . loud."

"Loud?" Julia said. "Caddie, is it that sound again?"

She nodded weakly. "I really want to know more about you, Mars, but maybe outside . . . ?"

"Mars, let's go buddy," Axel said. "Caddie's hearing things up here."

Mars followed as they went back into the elevator chamber.

"Amazing," he said as the doors closed. "The elevator wasn't working a few minutes ago."

Axel pressed the green button, and the chamber started whizzing down.

"Really?" Julia asked. "It was a little finicky but we managed to get it to work for us."

"No, that's not what I meant," Mars said. "There's a massive power outage in Seattle and Gale Island. Cupcake brought me here, and I don't know where she went, but now I'm on Mars."

"You traveled across space," Axel said.

Julia sucked in her breath. "You found a portal!"

Mars nodded. "I thought I was going up the Space Needle. Instead, I was crossing the universe!"

Outside, Caddie recovered almost immediately. They found a grassy area to sit on and everyone started to piece together what had happened.

"Who do you think built the portal?" Julia asked. "Oliver Pruitt? The technology is a *lot*—even for him."

"I'm not sure," Mars said. "All I know is my mom is connected to the 1961 Project, which was the same year the Seattle Space Needle was built."

"On the fishing dock?" Caddie asked.

"No, as an environmental physicist!" He told them about her underground lab and how she had been collecting data for years to prove that humans were causing too much damage to the environment. "I think she's trying to stop it from happening on Mars, too," he finished.

By now, the sun had fallen in the sky. Evening was setting in.

"It's getting dark," Julia said. "We need a plan. Should we stay the night in the Needle?"

Caddie shook her head. "I can't be up there. I hear things."

"What kind of things?" Mars asked.

Caddie frowned. "I'm not sure. It's not like when I hear you. Like right now you're worried about Cupcake." She paused. "Wow, it's been a long time since I could do that! Maybe being in the Needle helps? Anyway, she must be OK, Mars. She's probably still in Seattle."

"Um, thanks for being in my head again, Cads," Mars said.

"But I don't think a wandering tardigrade in Seattle is the best idea during a blackout. And wait!" He struck his forehead.

"He just remembered Aurora." Caddie saw his frown. "What? It's true."

"Is she OK?" Mars asked. "Shoot! I didn't mean to leave her behind."

Caddie shrugged. "I could never read Aurora's mind. But she must be OK. You have to believe that. We're all made of strong stuff, Aurora especially."

"That's a lovely sentiment," Julia said. "Again, what do we do about shelter? There are berries nearby."

"Listen, I don't want hear any more about foraging," Axel said. "I need a Colony oat burger and fries, or I'm going to fade fast. I say we head back to the hovercraft and see if I can fix it."

"Are you sure? It was pretty mangled," Caddie said.

Axel shrugged. "I've fixed worse. I was just distracted before with all this breathable air!"

"I didn't even know you had hovercrafts," Mars said. "So much has changed since I was last here. How do we get back to the crash?"

"Easy," Axel said. "We follow the shoe prints."

"Shoe prints?" Mars said. "Let me guess. Another mystery?"

"You catch on fast, Butterfly," said Julia.

32
MARTIAN MOOSE

As they walked through the Martian forest, Julia and Axel went ahead while Mars and Caddie continued behind them. At first, Mars didn't even know what to say to Caddie. It felt like old times, like they had always been around each other. Still, Caddie seemed so preoccupied.

"I know you can read my thoughts," he said. "So you know how glad I am to see you. But I don't know what you're thinking. Are you . . . OK?"

Caddie nodded. "I'm fine, Mars. I couldn't read your thoughts until now. I'd lost that ability. But I've been hearing other things—voices, and I don't know how to explain *that*. It's so good to see you! I've missed you. I was trying to remember the last time when it was normal and we were on Earth."

"At the dance."

"Right." She smiled. "That was normal. But I'm also proud of everything we've accomplished at the Colony since you left.

It's even better than before. No one is fighting, we're all getting along, and we just keep building new and interesting things!"

"But you're worried," Mars said, looking carefully at her face. "I can hear it in your voice."

"What's happened to our parents?" she asked. "It doesn't seem right that they're all gone. Then, there are these voices I keep hearing . . ."

"What kinds of voices?" Mars said. "You haven't really explained that."

"It's complicated," Caddie said. "It's like I hear . . . my mom, but she isn't here."

"That's wild," Mars said. He thought about his mom, and how she had disappeared right before his eyes. "It's like they're so close, like we might find them if we could just figure it all out."

"Totally," Caddie agreed.

By now, Julia and Axel had stopped up ahead.

"This is where the shoe prints end," Julia said. "See, they continue into the bushes and then there's that drop, where I obviously can't go with my rover. We decided to follow the prints in the other direction until we got to the Space Needle."

"So whoever it was came from the Space Needle and then went that way," Mars said, pointing toward the drop. "And fell."

"Oh, dear," Julia said. "I didn't think of it *that* way. You think they're injured?"

"I'm going to take a look," Mars said. "You all wait here."

"I'll come with you," Axel offered. "I'm used to moose."

Mars gave him a look. "Moose?"

"Long story," Caddie said. "But good idea, Axel."

"OK, let's go, then," Mars said.

The two boys got down on their hands and knees and moved gingerly through the branches down the steep hill.

"The trick is to keep your head low and out the way of the branches," Axel said.

Just then a thick, prickly branch thwacked Mars in the face.

"Thanks," Mars said, rubbing his forehead. "I'll try to remember that."

They continued crawling, the whiff of pine hitting Mars's nostrils. "Is it me, or does this place look like . . ."

"Olympic National Park?" Axel finished. "Yeah, Caddie was saying that. It reminds me of Alaska, too. I've backpacked through Denali with my family."

"That's why you're good with Martian moose."

"The moose was theoretical," Axel said. "I just meant I'm good with wildlife."

"So if we see a moose charging, we play dead," Mars said.

"Nah," Axel said. "If it charges, run for your life."

"Right."

"Most of the time, though, if you leave them alone, they leave you alone, too."

"That's true with people," Mars said.

"Ha, ha, yeah, it is," Axel said.

By now, Mars could see that the ground ahead looked

disturbed, as if someone had come through. There were several twigs snapped in half, and the soil looked trampled.

"Mars and Axel, see anything?" Caddie called from the top of the hill.

Mars was so close to the ground, it wasn't until he saw the shoe in front of him that he registered it was still connected to someone's foot. His eyes traveled from there to the inert body of a man, stretched out facedown in the dirt.

"Axel!" he breathed. "Look."

Axel let out a low whistle. "No way. Hope he isn't dead."

Mars started to panic. *Please don't let him be dead*, he prayed. *Whoever he is.*

"Mars!" Caddie's tone matched his panic. He could tell she knew what he was thinking.

"Guys!" Julia yelled. "Is everything OK?"

With a gentle heave, Mars and Axel rolled the man over. He stirred weakly. He wasn't wearing a helmet or a space suit. Instead, he was dressed in civilian clothes: a dark-blue polo shirt and khakis and a pair of loafers. "Mars?" said the man feebly.

Mars and Axel looked at each other.

At the top of the hill, Caddie gave a gasp.

"Oh my god," Mars said. "It's my dad."

Just as Mars was despairing that they wouldn't be able to get his dad out of the brambles, Axel remembered a tarp in the emergency kit inside the hovercraft. They could use it to transport Oliver Pruitt up the hill.

"I'm on it," Julia said as soon as she heard. "I can get to the hovercraft fast with my rover."

That left Caddie pacing at the top of the hill, while Mars and Axel waited at the bottom.

"What happened? How did you get here?" Mars asked his dad.

Oliver Pruitt was still too dazed to say much. "I fell," he said softly. That was all he would say. His face was sallow, but he was able to move all his limbs, which seemed to indicate that nothing was broken. Even so, Mars and Axel were extra careful moving him onto the tarp after Julia came back and slid it down the hill, a bottle of clean water rolled inside it.

Oliver Pruitt drank the water thirstily and then drifted in and out as Mars and his friends pulled the tarp up the hill. From there, they attached the end of the tarp to Julia's rover, using it to pull the makeshift stretcher toward the mangled hovercraft. The trek back to the vehicle was long and laborious. When they finally got there, though, a miracle happened. Just as they were approaching the site of the crash, a second hovercraft landed, and Orion and HELGA disembarked.

"Thank god we found you!" Orion said. "And dear sweet universe, *trees*!"

There was a jumble of explanations about the trees, breathable air, Oliver Pruitt, and Mars being back by way of a portal resembling the Seattle Space Needle. A sense of urgency kept anyone from lingering on the details for too long as they hoisted the tarp inside the hovercraft and secured Oliver Pruitt across several seats.

"We need to get him medical attention," Mars said. "I don't know how long he's been injured."

"HELGA will do a preliminary exam," Orion said, pointing to the robot stationed at the front of the craft.

"HELGA can do that?" Mars asked.

"Yes," Orion said. "We updated their software."

"Hello, Mars," said HELGA, who had floated to the back of the vehicle. "I am now your medically trained tech assistant, repurposed to make your colony life comfortable. My pronouns are they and them. I am glad to see you survived deep space and avoided an early demise."

"Uh, thanks, HELGA," Mars said. "Good to see you, too."

"Buckle up, everyone," Orion said from the front. "And where we're going, y'all better put on your space helmets. It isn't all trees and bushes back at the Colony."

From the back, Axel handed out helmets to Caddie, who had left her broken one behind, and then one to Mars, along with a flight suit. "You're lucky the hovercraft has extras."

"Thanks," Mars said. He wriggled into the flight suit and then pulled on the helmet, inhaling its familiar scent of plastic, disinfectant, and body odor. "Gotta love the old helmet smell." In the back, HELGA was helping Oliver get suited. Oliver thrashed around initially before relenting.

"How are the tardigrades? Is everything under control, Orion?" asked Julia, who was seated next to him as copilot.

"We haven't heard a word from Daisy," Caddie added. "Not since our hovercraft crashed."

Mars could hear a pause before Orion spoke. "I'll catch you up soon, don't worry," he said. "Let's lift off first."

As the hovercraft prepared to depart, Mars felt a sense of foreboding. He looked down at his father, who, after muttering agitatedly to HELGA, had been given a sedative and was now sleeping, covered by a reflective sheet to keep him warm. Across from Oliver Pruitt, Axel had pulled on a space helmet, too, and tipped his head back to sleep. The last twenty-four hours seemed to have taken a toll on him. They had definitely taken one on Mars. He was still worrying about his mom and wondered if he would ever find a way to get her back. He had lost the IP phone she had given him. Maybe it had fallen when he was going up the Seattle Space Needle. Now the one link he had to her was gone.

Mars swallowed. "Will everything be OK, HELGA?" he asked the robot next to him.

"Mars is OK," HELGA answered. "Mars is in good hands."

Mars wasn't sure if they meant him or the planet.

"Even through your visor, I can see that your eyes look like they have not closed for their required eight hours," HELGA continued, handing him another reflective sheet. "Sleep."

The hovercraft rose from the ground.

"And we're out of here," Orion announced. "Three, two, one." The hovercraft rocketed ahead.

Mars took the sheet from HELGA and wrapped it around himself. It was surprisingly warm. Maybe HELGA was right. He was exhausted. Just a few minutes of sleep might help unscramble his brain. "Poor Cupcake," he said, thinking of the baby tardigrade as he closed his eyes. What if she was still in Seattle, looking for him?

33

THE NEEDLE, PART 3

The highway was eerily empty of traffic as Toothpick sped down it in the darkness. It was true that he had never driven to the city before, and never driven anywhere without Droney to direct him. Which now made Mr. Q a gift, sitting in the back of Toothpick's car. It turned out he was a veritable map, knowing not just the layout of the highways and roads, but also side streets through Seattle to get them to the Space Needle as quickly as possible.

"Turn right at the next intersection," Mr. Q directed. "Then bear left. Past the gas station."

JP watched Toothpick zigzag this way and that.

"How do you know your way around?" JP asked. "You sure we're not getting lost?"

"I used to be an Uber driver," Mr. Q said. "Made some money on the side. And no, we're not lost. I'll have you to the Needle in ten minutes."

"That sounds about right," Toothpick said. "Though of course I have no way of knowing with certainty."

"So spill," Mr. Q said. "Why do you need to go to the Needle during a blackout? And you might as well not lie, because the teacher in me can tell, and I'll stop helping you navigate."

Toothpick and JP looked at each other.

"We wanted to see the view," JP said.

Mr. Q crossed his arms. "You can do better than that. It has to do with Mars Patel, doesn't it?"

"We think the Space Needle is connected to the missing adults," Toothpick said. "Mars and Aurora are on their way there, and we're joining them."

"Mars AND Aurora?" Mr. Q laughed. "What's in it for her?"

"Good question," JP said. "I'll let you know when we figure that one out. OK, your turn. Is Pruitt behind the missing adults?"

"In all seriousness," Mr. Q said, "no. The missing adults are bigger than Pruitt."

"But why are the adults gone," JP asked, "when you're still here?"

Mr. Q stroked his chin thoughtfully. "I actually don't know. Pick, make a left. No not there, *next* street! I swear, it's like you've never driven in Seattle before."

"I haven't," Toothpick said.

"Has anyone listened to the podcasts?" Mr. Q went on.

"No, I have not listened to that bozo," JP said shortly. "I've got better things to do. Though I think Mars still was when he thought no one was listening."

"I have this theory," Mr. Q said, "that those podcasts are important. Something crucial is getting communicated. You might not like Pruitt, you might call him batty, but he isn't illogical. He never does anything without a reason."

"How about blowing up an intergalactic space station?" JP said. "That sounds batty to me."

"He did that?" Mr. Q asked, surprised. "That was him?"

"It was breathlessly executed," Toothpick said, "and curiously well-planned."

Mr. Q pointed a finger at Toothpick. "Yes! Now you're thinking. There's always a plan behind everything Oliver does. There has to be. Too bad we can't access those podcasts right now. Maybe we'd find some answers there. Pick, turn. That's the parking lot."

Toothpick pulled in and navigated to the front circle. As he turned off the ignition, there was a frantic rapping on the passenger side.

JP rolled down their window. "Aurora! You look like you've seen a ghost! Where's Mars?"

Aurora was shaking, one of her fake eyelashes stuck to her chin-length hair.

"It was awful. Cupcake knocked me off and took Mars away," she said. "They abandoned me and left me here all by myself. I—I'm really tired of people doing that to me."

Then, to everyone's shock, Aurora Gershowitz burst into tears.

JP opened the car door and stepped out. "Hey, Aurora, it's OK. Listen . . ." And then without another word, JP wrapped their arms around Aurora.

FROM THE PODCAST

Hello, everyone! It's me, Daisy Zheng,

coming to you from Colony Command Central.

I know no one's hearing this because

we haven't had a signal in a year

And I know I should be conserving resources

'cause you know we have this teeny tiny

problem of low energy reserves,

which has to do with our other teeny tiny problem of

NOT KNOWING WHERE THE TARDIGRADES ARE.

It's hard to be in charge when the whole senior team is gone.

So, if you've heard from anyone like

Julia or Caddie, or one of the tardigrades,

can you leave me a comment?

Or even a joke would be good.

Like why did the chicken cross the road?

HELGA has a good one for that.

Wait a minute. The compound walls are shaking!

These walls are made out of steel.

They're supposed to be indestructible. Right??

What could make the Colony shake so much?

I'm looking at the surveillance cameras.

And.

No way.

34
UNDER ATTACK

As the hovercraft left the forest and they traveled through the night, everyone fell asleep except for Orion, who was flying, and Caddie, who now sat next to him in the copilot seat while Julia slept. She knew nothing about piloting, but she had insisted on Julia and Axel sleeping for a while so that one of them could take over flying if Orion grew tired. Behind her, Mars was asleep next to Oliver Pruitt while HELGA rested in standby mode. Caddie was glad for the quiet. It gave her some time to think. She felt surprisingly awake, and her mind was clear. The voices had stopped as soon as they flew out of the forest. Now there was only the low and familiar hum of thoughts below the surface inside the hovercraft. An errant dream here and there. Mars worrying about his mom and dad as he shifted in his sleep. This hum was what it had been like before, and now she welcomed it. It felt normal. Except for Orion. One look at him, and Caddie knew that the situation at the Colony was serious. She could feel the apprehension emitting from him like waves.

"Orion, time to confess," Caddie said.

He glanced at her. "What do you need to confess, Caddie?"

"Not me. You. Everyone's asleep. Now's a good time to fill me in. I can't sense the details, but I can tell you're worried about Daisy."

"She's fine," he said before pausing. "OK, she's not. When I left, all the tardigrades were missing."

"All of them?" Caddie frowned. "Are you sure?"

"All of them." Orion looked grim. "Without the tardigrades, we can't turn the windmills. Without the windmills, a major source of our energy is gone. I don't need to tell you that. We're using all our emergency generators right now. Cutting back on non-essentials. We shut down the weather tower and tech hub in order to run the control center, dorms, and infirmary. The greenhouse is operating on solar, but you know that isn't sufficient."

"And Daisy?"

"Managing the best she can. But the kids are jittery since the tardigrades disrupted the games yesterday. And classes have been canceled to preserve energy until we can figure out how to power the windmills. Everyone's on edge."

"That's terrible," Caddie said. "I never realized how tardigrade-dependent we are." She remembered the polo tournament, the way the tardigrades had thrown the kids off their backs and stampeded away. Something else had happened to her then that she hadn't told anyone. The largest one, Tartuffe, paused to stare deliberately and malevolently at Caddie. She stood rooted to the spot in terror. She was sure he was going to come after her. But then Tartuffe joined the others and disappeared in a cloud of dust.

"Colony Control is calling," Orion said, and pushed the button. "Orion from hovercraft B. Copy. Do you read me? Over."

"It's Daisy. Mayday! The Colony is under attack! I repeat: The Colony is under attack!"

Caddie felt her head immediately pound. "Oh no!" she cried.

The hovercraft jerked. "Daisy, who's attacking?" Orion asked, shaken.

"The tardigrades are trying to break down the Colony walls," Daisy said, choking on the words. "If they breach the walls, we're finished. Who knows what the tardigrades have planned next? Will they destroy the entire Colony? We need reinforcement now. Have to go. Over and out."

"Daisy! Daisy!" Orion kept pressing the button, but there was no response.

Caddie braced herself against one of the worst headaches she'd ever had, even worse than the one that had sent her to the Cloud Forest in the first place. Caddie remembered the laser-bolt glance Tartuffe had thrown at her in the stadium. In her mind she could see it all: the tardigrades, in a miasma of anger, closing in on the Colony.

⌒

Mars was sleeping uneasily when he felt the hovercraft dip without warning. He was instantly awake. Next to him, his dad was still asleep under the reflective sheet. It was dark in the cabin, but in front, he could see Orion and Caddie outlined by the lights on the dashboard. Caddie was hunched over and speaking furtively with Orion, and Mars could immediately tell something was wrong. He unbuckled his harness and rushed over to them, stumbling in the aisle as the hovercraft went up and down.

"What's wrong?" he asked.

Caddie turned to him, still holding the side of her head. "Mars, we have an emergency."

"The tardigrades are trying to storm the Colony," Orion said.

"The wall is keeping them out, but for how long?" Caddie added. She rubbed her temples.

"Well, there's one thing I know," Mars said. "That compound is strong. As long as we keep the gates locked, the tardigrades can't get in. We just have to find a way to convince them to stop attacking."

"Why are they so mad?" Caddie wondered. "Do you think it was because of the polo matches? Or being made to turn the windmills?"

"The tardigrades are smart," Mars said. "They don't do anything unless they want to. Something else must have set them off. Orion, how far are we from the Colony?"

"Less than five minutes," Orion said. "See, there's the Colony wall. Here, I'll bring up a satellite image of the front." He clicked one of the dashboard buttons and the image of the front compound came into view.

Next to Mars, Caddie shuddered. Half a dozen tardigrades of all sizes were throwing their full weight against the Colony wall as the surveillance cameras skirting the entrance fell and broke on the ground. Seeing the images, Mars was beside himself. In the early days of living at the Colony, he had been assigned to shoveling tardigrade poop as a punishment for going out on the surface without permission. It was humiliating, but then he'd befriended three of the tardigrades. They'd tolerated him, even responded gently when he fed them sodium nitrate rocks. Why would they cause all this havoc now?

"Can you tell what they're feeling, Caddie?" he asked, sick to his stomach.

She shook her head. "Tardigrades are different from humans. And I'm so far away. At first I felt their anger, but now all I'm getting is this quiet blank. But my headache's gone, which is strange. I guess it came because of Daisy's call."

"What in blazing jeepers is going on?" Julia said behind them. "Am I dreaming, or are the tardigrades going ballistic against the Colony walls?"

"It's no dream," Caddie said. "And poor Daisy is all alone in charge of the kids, trying to defend the Colony."

Julia frowned. "The walls are built to be indestructible."

"Tell that to the tardigrades," Orion said. "Right now, we have to decide what to do. We can't land in the front near the platform. Not without opening the gates."

Mars studied the screen. "Go around to the back. You can land near the airlock. No one uses it, but it goes down to the lava tubes. From there we can get inside the Colony. That's the same way JP got out a long time ago when we were trying to reach the surface."

"You mean when you and JP rode the tardigrades all the way to the Old Colony?" Orion asked. "Back when those creatures were still our friends?"

Mars nodded. "I still don't understand what's changed."

"There's another problem aside from our crumbling friendship with the tardigrades," Julia said. "Mars seems to think we can all go down that airlock. That includes me on my rover, and Oliver Pruitt on a tarp being used as a stretcher. I'm sorry Mars, but that's impossible. Unless you leave me and Pruitt on the surface." She sniffed audibly. "Which I'm prepared to do for the cause, though I don't care to go down in flames with what's-his-face for company."

"HELGA can carry my dad down," Mars said. "And I can carry Julia, piggyback."

"Piggyback?" Julia repeated. "What am I, a toddler?"

Mars realized how important it was for Julia to have her independence, but he wouldn't leave her. "It's only until we get to the bottom of the airlock. Orion can carry your rover.

We don't have much choice right now. And we're NOT leaving you."

"Fine, Mars. I guess it's a plan," Julia said. "Next time, I'll carry *you* around on my rover."

"Deal," Mars said. He went to wake up Axel and HELGA and explain what was going on. He decided to leave his dad asleep, figuring the effects of whatever sedative HELGA had administered would make him easier to transport. Within minutes, the crew was suited up with fully charged IP phones and had assembled at the front of the hovercraft.

"All right, here goes nothing," Orion said. "Everybody, make sure your helmets are secure. That goes for Pruitt, too. As soon as I land, Julia pops open the hatch, and out everyone goes. Mars and Julia first. Then Caddie, Axel, me with the rover, and HELGA with Pruitt. Understood?" Everyone murmured yes.

"Most certainly yes," HELGA added. "I am your tech assistant, designed to make your Colony life comfortable. This includes covert Colony reentry while avoiding death, dismemberment, and harm."

"Yikes, HELGA," Mars said.

"All right, quiet everyone. I'm killing the engine so they don't hear us," Orion said. "Let's pray the tardigrades don't see us gliding over them in the dark."

"I don't pray, but I can say 'om,'" HELGA offered pleasantly.

"Shh," Mars whispered to the robot.

Then the hovercraft began to descend.

35

CUPCAKE

After JP hugged her, Aurora calmed down. Her shoes scraped against the asphalt of the Space Needle parking lot as she stood awkwardly next to JP.

"Thanks," Aurora said, sniffling. "Uh, I guess I needed that."

"We all need a hug sometimes," JP said.

"JP gives the best ones," Toothpick said, still in the driver's seat. "Empirically speaking."

"Why are you guys here?" Aurora asked. She squinted. "And is that Mr. Q in the car?"

He waved cheerily. "Hi there, Aurora."

"We knew you and Mars would need backup," JP said. "And it's a good thing, since you're all alone in a blackout."

"I'll say," Aurora said. "I don't know why I got so freaked out. I guess I've got issues. One moment I'm sitting on Cupcake with Mars. The next moment she bucks me off and takes Mars up the Space Needle."

"You mean in the elevator?" JP asked. "But there's no power, and everything's locked."

"No, I mean they climbed the tower. Think Rapunzel."

"Holy guacamole!" JP exclaimed. "Mars must have held on for dear life."

"You think *that's* unbelievable?" Aurora said. "Wait, it gets even wilder. After they got to the top, there was a burst of light! Like all the colors you can imagine, swirling around the top of the Space Needle! Then the two of them never came back, and I've been all alone ever since."

The rear door of the Tahoe, which had been ajar for most of the conversation, was flung wide open as Mr. Q stepped out. "That's amazing!" he blurted. Evidently he had been listening in on everything. "Pruitt said the same thing!"

"You mean about the Needle?" Aurora paused. "Pruitt saw it happen before?"

Mr. Q nodded. "On his podcast, he described seeing something similar at the Space Needle when he was nine years old. Colors followed by a burst of light."

By now, Toothpick had stepped out of the car, too.

"I heard that one," he said. "Oliver Pruitt said his parents didn't believe him."

"They belittled his ideas and didn't take him seriously," Mr. Q said. "Oliver Pruitt believes there's a force in the universe that we're only starting to understand. He's been trying to understand it ever since he was nine. That's why he sends out those podcasts. Kind of like an audio journal to make sense out of his life."

"Huh," JP said. "I detect some Oliver Pruitt love going on, Mr. Q. Only one small problem. We all kind of hate him."

"Oh my god, JP, yes," Aurora said. She fist-bumped with JP.

Mr. Q shrugged. "Hate is a strong word."

"We can't love all the time," Toothpick said. "Isn't that why the world is the way it is?"

"Truth," JP said. "But I suppose we can all do better." They tilted their head up curiously at the Needle. "Aurora, where did you say Cupcake went?"

"I didn't. After the burst of light, I don't know what happened." A look of uneasiness crossed Aurora's face. "I hope Mars is OK."

"Me, too," JP said. "But right now, I know where Cupcake is!" They pointed to the base of the Space Needle, where a large, shadowy figure could be seen climbing rapidly down the metal structure.

Toothpick pushed up his glasses. "Tardigrades are more and more advanced than I initially supposed. She's climbing down with unsurpassed skill."

"And speed," Mr. Q said. He frowned. "And she's heading this way."

Aurora shrank back. "She hates me. I know she does. What if she's coming after me?"

By now, Cupcake had leaped from the base of the Needle to the ground. She let out a bellow and approached the group.

"Hey, girl," JP called out. "Long time no see, huh?"

"Stop talking," Aurora whispered. "Maybe she can't see us in the dark."

"Are you kidding? With all those eyes?" JP whispered back. They cleared their throat and continued in a louder voice. "Cupcake, great seeing you. Do you um, know where Mars is? We're kind of wondering about him."

Cupcake bellowed again and began running toward them.

"Shoot, Pick, what do we do? What do we do?" JP wailed.

Meanwhile, Aurora ran around to the other side of the SUV.

But Toothpick stood where he was. "We have no reason to think she means us harm, JP."

"Right," JP muttered. "No reason at all." Their fingers dug into Toothpick's arm as they stood where they were and Cupcake came quivering to stop a few feet away from them.

"Hey, girl, looking good," JP said nervously. "You sure can run fast, huh?"

Next to JP, Mr. Q suddenly cried out, "Oh no!"

The shape of their detention teacher became blurry, and then his features began to dissolve.

"Mr. Q!" JP shouted. "Pick, it's happening to him! He's disappearing. Mr. Q!"

A few moments later, their teacher was gone.

Toothpick and JP glanced at each other and then at Cupcake, who gave a snort and scampered back up the Needle. After a few moments, she was once again a dark spot against the night.

36
DOWN THE AIRLOCK

While it wasn't her preference, Julia was just as good at following orders as she was giving them. Which is why when they got to the airlock, she dutifully allowed Caddie and Axel to snap together her pressure suit and Mars's, a feature that enabled one person to carry another to safety in times of duress. The kids who'd engineered the suits had the brilliant foresight to think of this—the possibility of accidents on the surface—because this was Mars, the planet that wanted to kill you. Still, Julia hated the idea of hanging on to anyone. Her arms were strong, but what if she made Mars fall backward? She would bring down the entire mission, too. The thought pricked at her as Mars popped open the airlock and they began their labored climb down the rungs.

To distract herself, at first she counted the rungs. *One, two, three.* Then she counted her breath. *One, two, three.* Then she thought of the forest on Mars where she had been only a few hours before, and the breathable air and smell of damp pine, and something stirred in her. A fervent hope that this moment with the tardigrades wasn't happening, because she and her friends were all meant for something greater than just scrambling for their lives.

"You're doing well, Mars," she whispered through her helmet. She could feel him straining under the weight of them and their suits.

"Thanks. Just a little more," he whispered back with effort.

She glanced up at the rest of the crew above them: Caddie, Axel, Orion, and HELGA carrying a still sedated Oliver Pruitt. It was miraculous that they'd even gotten to the airlock without being detected. On the ground, they could feel the surface shaking violently. But here inside the airlock, they were safe from the tardigrades for the time being.

Julia was puzzled by the attack. What had made the tardigrades revolt? Or was it so mysterious after all? Some of the kids thought the creatures were experiments, developed in a bio lab in Pruitt Prep. Others thought they were secret AI bots covered with fur to fool everyone. Julia knew with certainty the second was untrue. But the lab? Did that still hold water? The tardigrades were strong and smart, and had notable personalities. They could breathe the Martian air, and yet there was at least one reported living on Gale Island. Julia remembered Muffin running amok and scaring the students, though as far as anyone knew, she had never actually caused harm.

Julia had seen satellite images and thought nothing of it at the time. But it proved that the tardigrades could live on Earth just as easily. With all this capacity, why did they live near the Colony? Why had they agreed to power the windmills? Or take part in the polo games? And why had they now decided they'd had enough?

Underneath her, Mars tottered, and then a moment later, his feet reached the ground. Gingerly he bent down, unsnapping them so that Julia slid gently to a sitting position on the concrete floor next to him.

"We did it," he said, breathing hard. "Good job."

"Good job back," Julia said. "You're a strong butterfly. Maybe we'll have to come up with a better nickname. Like the Hulk."

Just then, Caddie reached the floor, followed by Axel.

"Nice work, Mars," Axel said, patting him on the shoulder. "I was sure you'd drop her."

"Um, thanks for that vote of confidence," Mars said.

Next, Orion reached the ground and helped Julia set up her rover. She was fully synced by the time HELGA arrived with Oliver Pruitt carefully balanced in their arms.

"OK, we're all here," Caddie said, looking relieved. "Keep wearing your pressure suits and helmets, and make sure your IP phones are on at all times. It's the best way for us to communicate. Now, let's split up. I'll go to the control room to help Daisy. The rest of you stop at the dormitories. HELGA, can you bring Oliver Pruitt to the infirmary?"

"Affirmative," HELGA said. "Mars, do you wish to accompany me or is your expertise required elsewhere?"

"Uh . . ." Mars said slowly. "I'm not sure."

Julia glanced at Mars and could see he was conflicted. It was a tough choice, deciding what to do about your dad, even if he was a cosmic disgrace like Oliver Pruitt. "Go ahead, Butterfly. Be with your dad."

But somehow, that seemed to push the wrong button.

"He's my dad, but the Colony needs me now," Mars said gruffly. "HELGA can take him to the infirmary. He'll be out for a while anyway. Right, HELGA?"

"As you wish," HELGA said. "You can rely on me."

With that, HELGA carried the inert Oliver Pruitt down the tunnel.

Julia glanced again at Mars, who was still looking torn while he thought no else was paying attention to him.

"Sometimes robots can make faster decisions than we can," she said gently.

"My dad will be OK in the infirmary. At least, I think so," he said. "And I trust HELGA."

"Let's go," Axel said.

Ahead of the crew, HELGA raced down the tunnels, floating over bumps and cracks and whipping around bends with ease. They were a fully functioning automated machine with the layout of the Colony programmed into their CPU, which made their movements fast and smooth. All along, Oliver Pruitt slept like a baby. But near Sublevel 3, he started to stir.

"Oliver Pruitt, you were sleeping like a baby, but now you are rising like the sun," HELGA said cheerfully. "Your sedative is wearing off."

Oliver Pruitt groaned and tried to stretch, but he was immobilized in HELGA's powerful grip. "HELGA, I'm OK. I told you, after you gave me that equilibrium pill, my health would be fully restored."

"Yes, but that pill was administered against standard protocol," HELGA said. "Equilibrium pills are a new form of technology, designed to repair injuries quickly, but they haven't been adequately tested. They are only allowed to be dispensed with prior authorization and consent from Caddie, the commander-in-chief."

"*I'm* the commander-in-chief," Oliver Pruitt said. "And it's a good thing I built you. That's why I knew how to bypass your pesky protocols. You're a good robot, HELGA. But you're still a robot."

"My job is to make your Colony life comfortable," HELGA said. "By overriding my standard settings, I may have committed a number of grave operating errors."

"Don't worry," Oliver said. He stretched his neck one way, then the other. "I'll take the fall. You're just following orders."

By now they had reached the door to the infirmary, where a nurse bot was waiting.

"Instructions for Oliver Pruitt?" asked the nurse bot.

"He has been administered the equilibrium pill. His vitals are normal. He has been instructed to rest," HELGA notified the nurse bot.

"Excellent."

Gently, HELGA set Oliver Pruitt on the floor so he was standing up. He wobbled only slightly. "Thank you, HELGA. You be on your way. I'll stay here with the bot."

"You're welcome," HELGA said, moving their lips in a U to make their standard smile. "Have a nice day."

HELGA began to float away in the direction of Colony Control, where Caddie and Daisy would be poised to give their next set of instructions. But a few feet away, they slowed down and came to a stop. Their automated programming had run into a glitch.

"I am an automated robot," HELGA said out loud to no one in particular. "But I'm adaptive, too. My newer programming modules include telling jokes, like 'Why did the robot cross the road? Because the chicken was out of order.' Which elicits pleasant laughs from nearby colonists. But my modules also include updates. My latest updates inform me that the equilibrium pill can initiate disruption and cause unmitigated havoc to the Colony. I must investigate."

HELGA floated back to the infirmary, where Oliver Pruitt was *not* lying down in bed but instead standing in front of a monitor.

"It's really a good thing that I know the ins and outs of the security system in the Colony," Oliver Pruitt was saying to the nurse bot. "See, just entering these few codes allows me access to the entry gates to the compound. And since you're a nurse bot, I can say all of this without you telling anyone."

"You are accessing the entry gates to the compound at eleven hundred hours," informed the nurse bot. "All vital signs are normal."

"Yes, yes, I'm perfectly fine," Oliver Pruitt said. "The equilibrium pill works like a charm. It even makes me feel happy. Look, I'm smiling!"

"You are smiling," informed the bot. "All vital signs are normal, though your pulse rate is increasing. It is time to rest."

"No," Oliver Pruitt said. He entered a few more commands into the monitor. "It's time to do what must be done. It's a good thing the equilibrium pill is making me feel so happy. Because the universe knows that soon enough I won't be. There." Oliver Pruitt let his hand fall down with a flourish. He wore the same wild smile. "That should please them."

"You have opened the gates to the compound," the nurse bot informed him. "Your pulse rate is climbing fast. I must now advise you to lie down."

"No, no," Oliver said. "No." His voice trailed off. "My work here is done. The security gates are unlocked, and now the tardigrades will breach the entrance. It's only a matter of time." His eyes teared as he watched the monitor. "All my life I've wanted to understand what they know. And for that, I've paid the price. I only wonder if Mars will see it that way."

As Oliver was heard saying all of this, HELGA, at the end of the hall to the infirmary wing, had reached an important conclusion. "That was sizable information for my circuits to process," they said, "but as an adaptive robot, I am able to rise to the occasion. There is only one course of action to take if I am to prioritize Colony life. And without a minute to spare!"

37
FULL CIRCLE

■■■■■ or a few moments, JP and Toothpick were speech-
■ less as they watched the Space Needle, where just
■■■ moments before, Cupcake had disappeared.

Aurora came running back from the other side of the SUV. "Did you freaking see that? The tardigrade zapped Mr. Q!"

"Zapped might be the wrong word . . ." JP murmured.

"She turned him to dust," Aurora insisted. "That's why the adults are gone. The tardigrades have been zapping them! Ha!"

"Aurora, you're kinda scaring me," JP said. "Are you *happy* Mr. Q got zapped?"

"No, I'm happy I know the truth about the adults," Aurora said. "I KNOW THE TRUTH."

"But Cupcake only came with Mars in the launch pod," Toothpick pointed out. "And the adults have been missing for a year."

"Yes, but there are other tardigrades on Gale Island," Aurora said. "Like Muffin, who's been showing up at our campfires. She steals all the marshmallows."

"That doesn't sound like a zapping tardigrade," JP said doubtfully. "Toothpick is right. The adults were missing long before Cupcake. And when Ms. P vanished, Cupcake wasn't around."

Aurora shook her head. "Say what you want, but it makes sense to me. The tardigrades are going to launch an attack against us." She stopped. "Which means we have to get in the car and drive as far away as possible. Like to Canada. Pick, start the car."

"I'm sorry, Aurora," said Toothpick, "but there isn't enough gas to get us to Canada. We don't even have enough to go back to Port Elizabeth. Besides, it's unlikely we'll be any safer in Canada. What is an imaginary border between nations to a set of attacking aliens, anyway?"

"Listen, the tardigrades are NOT launching an attack," JP said firmly. "They had all this time to do it when the adults first went away. And don't forget, Cupcake LOVES Mars. She wouldn't let any harm come to him. I say we stay here and try to find out where Mars went."

"I'm telling you, he went UP THERE." Aurora gestured to the top of the Needle. "You have any ideas on how you're going to get up there with no electricity and a tardigrade on the loose?"

Meanwhile, Toothpick had wandered over to a grassy area lining the curb. He bent down and picked something up. "Look, it's an IP phone. It's got the Space Needle on the front."

"That must be Ms. P's phone!" JP said. They walked over to him and peered over his shoulder. "Maybe Mars dropped it on his way up the Needle."

"Oddly, it seems to be working, unlike our phones," he said. "Maybe it uses some other technology?"

"Fine, use it then," JP said. "Let's call somebody else with an IP phone!"

"It's locked," he said. "I need a four-number code."

"Try 1-2-3-4," JP said.

Toothpick entered the numbers. "Nope."

"Try 0-0-0-0," JP said.

"That doesn't work either," Toothpick said.

By now, Aurora had pulled out her phone and was looking at it.

"9-9-9-9?"

"JP, if I keep guessing wrong, the phone will get disabled," Toothpick said.

"I have an idea," Aurora said, looking up from her phone. "Try 6-2-7-7."

Toothpick entered the numbers and grinned. "It worked. How did you know?"

"If you look at an alphanumeric touch pad," Aurora said, "those numbers spell Mars's name. M-A-R-S."

"Aurora, you genius!" JP said. "Now the question is, who are we calling?"

∩

Caddie was used to Daisy's highs and lows. When Daisy was on top of her game, the Colony ran like a well-oiled machine. But if anything toppled Daisy's self-confidence, it took a lot to calm her down.

"Look at the surveillance monitors," Daisy said tearfully inside the control room. "The tardigrades are going to knock down the compound any minute."

"Daisy, the walls are strong," Caddie said. "No tardigrade will get through as long as the gates are activated." Even so, when Caddie saw the monitors, she was shocked by the tardigrades' aggressiveness and strength. They were delivering such powerful blows, it was a wonder the compound walls were still standing. But there was no reason to tell Daisy that. "Let's try to think how we can appeal to the tardigrades," she said.

Daisy nodded shakily. "What if we offer them sodium nitrate rocks? Or more days off?"

"I don't think this is a labor issue," Caddie said, remembering Tartuffe's glare. "Or about meals. We need to talk to them."

"The only one who can do that is Mars," Daisy said. "And he's not back from the infirmary."

"Right," Caddie said. "Wait, he didn't go to the infirmary. He's in the dormitories with everyone else."

Just then, the red phone on the wall began to ring. Caddie and Daisy looked at it in surprise. The red phone was connected to an outside line and had not rung for more than a year.

Daisy picked up the phone immediately. "This is Daisy Zheng at Mars Colony Control. Caller, identify yourself. Over."

"Daisy, it's Toothpick," said the voice. "I'm calling from Earth. Over."

"Toothpick!" Daisy cried. "Are you at Pruitt Prep?"

"Negative. Our location is the Seattle Space Needle. I'm with JP and Aurora. Over."

Caddie leaned in. "Toothpick, there's a Space Needle here, too. That's where we found Mars. Mars Patel, that is! Over."

"Whoa!" Toothpick said. "You mean Mars is with you?"

"Mars is on Mars? Put him on the phone!" JP's voice came in from the background.

"Sorry, JP, you kind of reached us in a crisis," Daisy said. "Mars isn't with us right now. But I'm THRILLED to hear from all of you. Over."

"Where is Mars?" JP asked, alarmed.

"Dorm rooms," Caddie said.

"What does it matter?" Daisy cried at the same time.

"Daisy, what's going on?" JP asked. "Tell us, over."

"It's the tardigrades," she said, her voice shaking. "They're angry and are trying to break into the Colony. We have no idea why. Maybe Mars can find out."

There was muffled discussion on the other end, followed by a scuffle.

"It's me, Aurora," said another voice. "I don't know how Mars got to the Colony. But listen. The tardigrades can zap people. That's what they've been doing—"

There was another scuffle.

"This is JP. Don't listen to Aurora about the tardigrades. Tell Mars we love him. Tell him—"

Then the connection went dead.

Daisy tried reconnecting, but to no avail. "Oh, Caddie, I'm so sorry! I made it sound pretty bad, didn't I?"

"Daisy, it *is* bad," Caddie said. "Look, the monitor!" She stared, aghast, at the screen above them with live footage coming from the surveillance video in South Dome.

The tardigrades were standing *inside the dome.*

"Tell everyone to seal off the doors to the South Dome ASAP!" Caddie ordered. "No one goes in or out of the dormitory. I'll find Mars and HELGA."

"Copy, Caddie." As Daisy went to broadcast her message, Caddie took out her IP phone. "Come on, Mars," Caddie murmured to herself. "Pick up, pick up." As the phone rang, she tried to focus her thoughts on him. Where was he? Since he had come back to Mars, she had been able to feel his presence pretty clearly. Until now. Something was blocking him. As she felt her heart pounding, she knew what it was: her own fear.

"Caddie?" Mars was suddenly on the other end of the call. "Is that you?"

"Yes, Mars." She was so glad to hear his voice. But she was frightened, too, enough that she could barely get the words out. "You need to come to the control room. You and HELGA."

"HELGA isn't with me."

"Well, find HELGA. You both need to come back. The tardigrades are in the South Dome."

"Are you sure?" Mars asked. "Because *I'm* in the South Dome."

Caddie turned cold. Her eyes darted back to the South Dome monitor. She pressed the keyboard to zoom out. There was the front entrance and lobby, where the tardigrades were barreling in. There was the welcome center with its atrium and reinforced glass, and then as she panned over, finally there was Mars, standing in front of the suit room. He was wearing an orange space suit and a clear helmet, his face visible behind the visor.

"Mars . . ." Caddie said faintly. "I see you. Get out of there. They're in the lobby. They're coming your way."

"WARNING: STRUCTURAL BREACH IN THE SOUTH DOME."

The announcement echoed through the control room and the rest of the Colony; Caddie could hear it bouncing back to her through the phone.

Mars turned to face the surveillance camera positioned above the suit room door. "Cads, I'll be OK," he said, looking straight into the camera at her. "I know how to talk to them. But the Colony will probably depressurize soon, even if you seal off sections. You heard the announcement. You have to go."

"So do you, Mars," Caddie said. "Come to the control room. We can—"

"No, Caddie. You have to evacuate. Get everyone to the buggies and hovercrafts. You need to take the kids to the only place safe on Mars. The place with breathable air."

Caddie's throat clenched. "I'm not leaving without you, Mars."

"Do it. Promise me."

"Mars . . ."

"*Promise* me."

"I promise, but . . ."

Mars looked away from the camera as if he saw something ahead. There was a thunderous noise, and she saw him flinch right before the screen turned black.

38

ALL YOU NEED IS LOVE

■■■■■ oothpick stared at the IP phone, which had powered off in the middle of their conversation with Daisy. "We're out of battery. That's why we got cut off."

JP threw up their hands in frustration. "Gah! Can there be a worse time for a phone to run out?" They started pacing. "It's too much for me, folks. Mars teleporting to Mars, tardigrades breaking into the Colony, us being in a blackout."

"Don't forget the zapping tardigrade," Aurora muttered.

"Cupcake didn't zap Mr. Q!"

"JP, admit it: you're in a state of denial."

Meanwhile, Toothpick was rummaging through one of the boxes in the back seat of the SUV. "I know it's in here somewhere," he said.

"What are you looking for, Pick?" JP called.

"My emergency phone charger," he said. "And here it is." From a box, he pulled out a small charger with a wire attached to it. "Droney is really good at keeping the car prepped for emergencies. Let's see if we can use this to start up the phone." Toothpick took the dangling wire from the charger and inserted it into one end of the IP phone. "See? We're in luck. This IP phone is backward compatible. Nice."

"OK, now what?" Aurora asked.

"Now," Toothpick said, "we wait for the phone to charge."

"Excellent," JP said. They continued pacing on the grassy patch. "In the meantime, let's talk this out. We're here in Seattle. Mars is on Mars. You know what that means, right?"

"He made a really bad decision to go there?" Aurora asked.

"No! It means the Space Needle is some kind of transporter. Right, Pick?" JP got excited. "Remember, Aurora said Cupcake took Mars UP to the top of the Space Needle, there was a burst of colors, and boom. Mars is on the other side. He got to Mars through the Space Needle."

"Why didn't Cupcake go through?" Aurora said. "Unless she zapped Mars through the portal."

"You've really got a thing about zapping, don't you?"

Aurora stomped her foot impatiently. "You're missing the picture. It's not Mars we need to think about. It's the tardigrades. If they're attacking the Colony, they'll attack us here on Earth, too!"

"News flash, there are no tardigrades where we are," JP said. "Except Cupcake, and she's not bothering us."

"How do you know she won't call others to join her?"

Aurora said. "Maybe they're assembling an army as we speak. Maybe they're going to come for us through the Needle."

"Stop with the negativity, Aurora!" JP said. "I need to think. Actually, I need a sandwich. A sloppy joe on rye would hit the spot. OK, time to focus, JP."

Toothpick studied the Space Needle thoughtfully. "For the record, I agree with JP's hypothesis. The Needle does have extraordinary powers. And according to Mr. Q, Oliver Pruitt found out about these powers when he was little."

"You think he found a way to go to Mars through the Needle?" JP asked.

"Why would he build a spaceship and travel six months if he could go through the Needle instantaneously?" Aurora asked. "Seems 'daffy' to me, to use a Julia word."

"Aurora is right," Toothpick said.

"Fine, but it's still a portal of some kind," JP said. "Now what about the tardigrades breaking in at the Colony? How do we stop them?" JP began walking in circles. "We have to come up with a plan. Where is Mars when we need him?"

"We could," Toothpick said, "come up with our own plan."

"Let's find a way to arm ourselves," Aurora said. "Pick, do you have any intergalactic space weapons in the back of your car? *That* would be some epic emergency equipment. Especially if Cupcake comes back down."

JP's eyes lit up. "That's it, Aurora!"

"Space weapons?" she asked.

"No! We are a peaceful crew, Aurora. No weaponry. But we're gonna get Cupcake to come down and take us up to the top of the Needle. Then we teleport to the Colony with her, and she'll tell them to call off the attack."

Aurora laughed. "Sorry, but how do you propose to do that? Sodium nitrate rocks?"

JP ran toward the base of the Needle. "We're going to ask her, that's what. And we're going to do it with love. Help me call her down, guys. All together now: Cupcake!"

Their voice seemed to echo between the beams of the Needle and travel to the top. JP continued calling, then Toothpick and Aurora joined in. *Cupcake. Cupcake. Cupcake.*

Somewhere high up, a metallic noise reverberated. It got louder and louder, and then Cupcake appeared, clambering down for the second time, her feet banging against the metal. When she reached the bottom of the Needle, she came to a halt.

"Cupcake, you are the best girl I know," JP said. "We love you, and so does Mars."

She sniffed. Was she sad or happy? It was a hard sniff to interpret.

JP pressed on. "Mars is in trouble. We need you to take us up to the top. Can you do that? Can you take us to the top so we can save Mars and the Colony?"

Cupcake sniffed again. And sneezed.

"Guys . . ." Aurora started, but JP grabbed her sleeve to silence her.

Cupcake took a few slow steps forward and sniffed a third time. Then she bent down low for them. JP hugged the tardigrade tightly. "Thank you, Cupcake. You won't regret it."

"Yeah, but I might," Aurora muttered. But when no one was looking, she patted the tardigrade gently before she pulled herself up behind JP and Toothpick.

39

THE GREATER GOOD

ars was standing near the wall to the suit room when three full-sized tardigrades charged into the center of the South Dome, Tartuffe leading them. With his legs, he reached up and knocked down the camera above the suit room, then tore down the welcome sign, shredding it to bits with his powerful jaws. For one eerie moment, as the shredded bits of paper fell all around, the South Dome resembled a giant snow globe.

"Tartuffe!" Mars cried. "Please stop before you destroy the whole Colony!"

The large tardigrade let out a bellow so loud it shook the entire dome. As he did, the other two tardigrades halted dutifully behind him. Clearly, Tartuffe was in charge.

"I get that you're angry," Mars said slowly, "But hurting the kids won't help anyone."

THE COLONY MUST GO THERE IS NO OTHER WAY

Mars blinked. The words were so clear, yet where were they coming from? He hadn't imagined them. "I don't understand . . ." Mars stared at the giant tardigrade. "Did you say that?"

YOU HEARD THE COLONY MUST GO

Mars watched Tartuffe, astonished. "Your mouth isn't moving but . . . it is you, isn't it?"

WE DO NOT COMMUNICATE WITH OUR MOUTHS LIKE HUMANS

WE HAVE OTHER WAYS

"Why didn't you talk to me before?"

YOU WERE NOT LISTENING

YOU WERE NOT PAYING ATTENTION

From behind Mars, the door to the suit room opened. He turned around to find Oliver Pruitt dressed in a space suit of gold and red and a matching helmet.

"Mars," he said. "I'm so glad you're here. There's no time to waste. I suggest you load up on more oxygen. That suit of yours isn't going to supply you with air forever."

"What are you doing here?" Mars stammered. "I thought you were in the infirmary. You have to evacuate. Hurry. Can't you see that the tardigrades have breached the dome?"

"Yes," Oliver Pruitt said. "I'm the one who let them in."

"You w-what?" Mars started to panic. "Are you working together?"

OLIVER PRUITT IS NOT WITH US

OLIVER PRUITT HAS DISAPPOINTED US

"I did what you wanted, didn't I?" Oliver's voice rose. "You gave me no choice."

"You hear them, too?" Mars asked, surprised. "I thought it was in my head."

"Of course it's in your head," Oliver said. "But it doesn't mean that it isn't in my head, too." He turned to Tartuffe. "You forget, I lost everything when I set off the volcano."

"That *was* you!" Mars exclaimed.

YOU STILL CAME BACK OLIVER PRUITT

AND WE DO NOT WANT YOUR TECHNOLOGY

"Yes," Oliver said petulantly. "All you want is spruce and cedar and green moss." He looked diminished, like a small child being scolded by a parent. Meanwhile, Tartuffe glared with displeasure.

By now, Mars had decided to accept the bizarre reality that Tartuffe could speak. "What's going on?" Mars demanded. "Someone tell me. Why can we hear tardigrades, and why have you been . . . working together?"

"Mars, it's simple," Oliver said. "I came to build my colony. The tardigrades wanted it torn down. I came back to build it stronger. Now they're tearing it down themselves."

The tardigrades bellowed in response. Mars could sense that the tension in the dome was mounting. He chose his words carefully. "I thought you liked the Colony," he said to Tartuffe. "And the kids and polo games."

THE COLONY YES

THE KIDS YES

THE POLO GAMES NOT SO MUCH

Behind Tartuffe the other two tardigrades snorted.

WE HAVE OUR LIMITS

WE WANT NATURE NOT MORE INVENTIONS

"Nature?" Mars asked. Slowly, something began to register, but he wasn't sure what. He stared questioningly at Tartuffe, who watched him with bright eyes. All ten of them.

Just then, Daisy's voice came over the intercom. "Attention, we are evacuating NOW. All colonists report to the platform immediately, fully suited with helmets on."

"They're leaving you, Mars," Oliver said. "See that? At the first sign of trouble, they abandon you."

"I told them to evacuate!" Mars snapped. "Thanks to someone opening the gates!"

YOU LOVE YOUR FRIENDS

"I do," Mars said fiercely. "I'll do whatever it takes to save them. And I'm not leaving Caddie behind again."

"Caddie Patchett," Oliver said. "Boy, she has taken the place of Aurora, hasn't she?"

"You be quiet," Mars told him angrily.

"WARNING: STRUCTURAL DAMAGE AND DEPRESSUR-IZATION IN THE SOUTH DOME. EVACUATE IMMEDIATELY."

Oliver snapped his helmet into place. "Son, time is running out. You need to come with me."

"No," Mars said. "Not without an explanation." He stood resolutely even though he could feel fear blooming inside him. What if his helmet wasn't on securely? What if there was a leak somewhere in his pressure suit? Mars was pretty sure that depressurization was an awful way to die.

TELL HIM OLIVER PRUITT HE DESERVES TO KNOW

Oliver sighed. "I was nine when I went to the Seattle Space Needle with my parents."

"I've heard this story before," Mars interrupted impatiently. "I've listened to your podcasts."

"I'm flattered!" Oliver said. "Well, the part I didn't share was that when I saw the colors of the walls change, I heard a voice for the first time, an unearthly one. My parents never believed me. Not once." Oliver Pruitt gave a sad laugh. "For years, I thought there was something wrong with me. Worse, so did they! The truth is, there was something wrong with *them* for not believing me. That I had witnessed something extraordinary. Something that went beyond science. Ever since then, I've dedicated my whole life to understanding how the universe exists. I started a podcast. I shared my theories. Then one day, years later, I did my podcast and I got a response. From them. And then I knew I had been right, that somewhere in the universe, I was being heard."

"Through . . . your *podcasts*?"

"Yes. The podcasts have been my way of secretly communicating with the tardigrades all these years."

Mars took a moment to digest this news. "But . . . but I thought the tardigrades were created in your lab at Pruitt Prep!"

Tartuffe and the rest of the tardigrades erupted with snorts. Oliver laughed. "See, they find that as funny as I do."

THAT WAS A RUSE
NOT A GREAT ONE

"But we agreed that it would be too much for people to accept otherwise," Oliver said to Tartuffe. "There would have been a rush to profit from this knowledge, or worse, grounds for a civil war. And there is no way the humans would come out ahead. We agreed that change had to come slowly and from within. By training the kids somewhere else."

"Can someone slow it down for me?" Mars asked. "Are you saying the tardigrades are . . . smarter than us?" He looked at Tartuffe, who had drawn himself up to his full size and now seemed pretty insulted.

WE DO NOT LIKE THAT MEANINGLESS WORD
SMART DESCRIBES HUMAN BRAINS NOT OURS

"I'm—I'm sorry," Mars stammered. "I guess I don't understand."

"Mars, I think what you're failing to see," Oliver said more gently, "is that the tardigrades aren't just smarter than we are. They are put together differently, in a way that's far more advanced than any human being. It's hard for us to grasp. But just know, these tardigrades are a complex life form that have been living not just on Mars, but in many places around the galaxy."

"Whoa," Mars said.

"One of their missions is to maintain order, plenitude, and peace," Oliver said. "You can think of them as the intergalactic sheriffs of the universe."

WE MUST EXIST IN BALANCE OR FACE MUTUAL DESTRUCTION

"They have advanced technology, transport skills, and telepathic dexterity," Oliver went on. "So much they can do literally with their minds! Not just speak to us but develop and build. In fact, they designed the portal at the Needle. That's their technology, light-years ahead of ours."

Mars was floored. He thought of the tardigrades moving boulders and turning the windmills like mules at the Colony. When in fact . . . Mars's mind leaped ahead. "They designed the Mars Colony and the space station," he said flatly. "Not you."

Oliver stood quietly. "How did you guess?"

Mars sighed. "Why would you do all those cool things here on Mars when you could have done them on Earth?"

"Huh," Oliver said. For the first time, he looked truly deflated.

A strange pity stirred in Mars's heart for him, but it was a feeling he didn't like having.

"Well, there *was* something we had that the tardigrades didn't," Oliver finally said. "One day they came to Puget Sound to visit. They stayed a while. They were intrigued by the flora and fauna of Olympic National Park and the Pacific Northwest."

WE LIKE THE SCENT OF FRESH SPRUCE AND CEDAR

SO SPECIAL SO HEAVENLY

"They wanted their own rain forest. That's where your mother came in. The tardigrades invented a way to create a small bubble or oasis of breathable air on Mars, and they employed Saira to grow Olympic species on Gale Island and transfer them over."

"My mom was growing pine trees for the tardigrades?" Mars was flabbergasted. He thought back to his mom's explanation when they were in her underground lab, when she wouldn't tell him and his friends who she was working for. Mars had assumed the CIA or FBI. Not aliens.

"Oh, yes. Saira used Gale Island as a staging ground. That's where we lived at first. Her, me, you, and . . . well, why do you think Tartuffe cares about you so much?"

Startled, Mars really looked at Tartuffe for the first time. His mom's words returned to him: *You used to run on the beach and make castles out of pine cones.* That was what she'd told him he used to do when they were living on Gale Island. It was then that Mars understood. "*You* were on Gale Island with me," he said. "*You* were part of our family."

YOU ARE LOVED MARS YOU ARE SO LOVED

Mars felt tears spring to his eyes. No wonder he'd always felt a connection to Tartuffe and the other tardigrades. They were part of his earliest, deepest self, something he didn't know he'd even had until now. "And the adults?" he asked softly.

HAVOC IN ONE PART OF THE UNIVERSE
CREATES HAVOC EVERYWHERE

"Tartuffe has been alarmed by how fast Earth is heating up," Oliver said. "He's worried that an overheated planet will create instability in the rest of the universe. Like me, Tartuffe thinks kids will make better decisions and save our Earth. Kids like you, Mars."

"But we need adults, too," Mars said. "I need my mom."

YOU HAVE OLIVER PRUITT

"That's not enough! Where are the adults?"

THEY HAVE CAUSED MUCH HARM
THEY WILL DESTROY EVERYTHING

"But where are they?" Mars turned to Oliver Pruitt. "Do you know?"

Oliver didn't say anything.

"Do you?" Mars repeated more forcefully.

"The adults are in another dimension," Oliver said reluctantly. "I was told that you experienced another dimension when you first tried to launch back to Earth."

"Alt Earth, you mean?" Mars said slowly.

Oliver nodded. "Call it what you like. There are many different dimensions like that, running in parallel. Where the adults are, the kids can't see or hear them, nor can the adults see or hear the kids, even though they're all living in the same space. The tardigrades created a glitch that sent the adults there."

WHEN WE TURN THE POWER BACK ON THERE WILL BE A RESET

"Reset?" Mars turned to Oliver. "What happens then?"

"WARNING: STRUCTURAL BREACH AND DEPRESSURIZATION IN THE SOUTH DOME. EVACUATE IMMEDIATELY."

Oliver gestured to Mars. "Come with me. We're running out of time. The dome is depressurizing, and the tardigrades WILL knock the walls down over us."

"Tell me what the reset does!" Mars demanded.

"We have to go, Mars. Be reasonable!" Oliver Pruitt shifted back and forth on his feet.

"Tell me or I'll stay!"

"It means when the power comes back on Earth, the connection to the adult dimension goes away for good!" Oliver burst out. "There, I told you!"

"But . . . but that can't be true!" Mars said desperately. He tried to comprehend the scale of what his dad was suggesting.

"How can you live with that? Don't you want them back? Don't you want my mom back? Remember her, Dad? Saira Patel?"

"It's for the greater good," Oliver whispered. "I can't save everyone. But I can save you."

"The kids need their parents. Earth needs the adults. I don't accept what you're saying," Mars shouted. "I'm going to find another way out. I'll break away!" Saying those words gave him a sudden strength. "I'll break away! I'll break away!"

Mars stepped back as Oliver Pruitt and the tardigrades moved toward him.

"It's pointless to fight," Oliver said. "Come with me, son. Choose life. Choose us."

"No!"

"WARNING: STRUCTURAL DAMAGE AMD DEPRESSUR-IZATION IN THE SOUTH DOME. CATASTROPHIC HARM TO LIFE IMMINENT."

Mars turned around and ran smack into someone who had crept up behind him.

"HELGA!" he exclaimed. "What are you doing here?"

"Mars Patel," said HELGA. "I have come to rescue you."

"Wha—how are you going to do that?" Mars asked in spite of himself.

From behind Tartuffe came the sound of shattering glass. More tardigrades had charged into the dome from the other side.

HELGA set down a box of sodium nitrate rocks on the floor.

"For our friends, the tardigrades," they said pleasantly. "And now, I must engage in what is known as smoke and mirrors."

After they said that, there was a popping sound and a great ball of smoke erupted. The plume from the smoke bomb spread out in all directions to fill the entire dome. Mars recognized it as a student invention that had never been used anywhere except for the talent show. And now.

The tardigrades blinked and coughed, and Oliver Pruitt was so surprised he tripped backward and fell down. When the smoke cleared, Mars and HELGA were gone, leaving the tardigrades and Oliver Pruitt behind.

"HELGA!" Mars cried, wrapped tightly in the robot's arms as they whisked through the tunnel to the buggy platform. "You *did* rescue me!"

"Yes!" HELGA answered with what could only be called glee. "Yes, I did!"

40

A WORLD WITHOUT KIDS

Under the bright moonlit sky hanging over Seattle, Cupcake climbed higher and higher up the Space Needle, crawling like a spider, leaping like a wolf.

"This is incredible!" JP said. "The speed! Cupcake, you go girl!"

Aurora clung to the back of the tardigrade with a rare moment of wonder in her eyes. "It's like we're flying!" she said.

Cupcake lumbered up, the cold, dark air rushing past them.

"Pick, you're silent," JP called out. "You didn't fall off, did you?" They looked over their shoulder and saw Toothpick holding on with one hand and glancing at the IP phone with his other.

"The phone is now fully charged, and I'm reading the transcripts to Pruitt's podcasts," he responded. "All of them are downloaded on Ms. Patel's phone."

"Stop reading!" JP yelled back. "The world is too amazing!" They gazed around them, where the night sky was startlingly clear.

Then Cupcake slowed down as they approached the top of the Needle and its circular glass enclosure. Gingerly she crossed over the edge and jumped inside. The three of them slid off as JP scratched the tardigrade on the side and she responded with a contented sigh. "Thank you, girl!"

Aurora tried the doors, which were open, and they strode inside.

"At least the doors are open up here," JP said.

"Yeah, but now what?" Aurora asked. "There's still no power."

Toothpick was still glued to the IP phone.

"Pick, will you stop?" JP said. "You know too much social media is bad, right?"

Toothpick looked up. "I was checking the dates on these podcasts. Pruitt has been sending them for a long time. Even recently. He just broadcast one about twelve hours ago."

Aurora leaned against the glass. "So what does the genius say?"

"He warns about power and corruption," Toothpick paused. "And you, Aurora."

"Me?" Aurora squeaked. "What am I doing?"

"Grabbing power," JP said. "Running for president when you should be helping kids."

"But I *am* helping kids," Aurora said. "I have a vision for the future."

"Which is what?" JP asked coolly. "No adults?"

"The other thing Oliver Pruitt talks about," Toothpick continued, "is the need for a reset."

"A reset?" JP asked. "Like our clocks? I really hate daylight savings. I'd rather have that extra hour of sleep."

"No, not the clock," Toothpick said.

"So then what does Pruitt want to reset?" JP asked. "His face?"

"No," Toothpick said. "*Everything.* Everything in the whole world shuts down and gets restarted. A reset."

"That's impossible," Aurora said. "As usual, Pruitt is going off on a pointless tangent."

"He does make a case for why it's important," Toothpick said. "For getting rid of glitches in the system. It's like when your computer stops working. You reset it and start again."

As they were talking, the glass walls around them began to change color.

"Holy moly!" JP said. "What's going on?"

"This is what I was telling you about," Aurora said quickly.

The glass continued to shift in colors, from reds to pinks to brilliant purples. Then something strange happened. In front of the elevator, a crowd appeared out of nowhere. Some were holding coffee while others were taking selfies with their phones. They were talking or standing silently, but they all seemed to be waiting for an elevator that wasn't working.

"Oh my god," JP breathed. "They're . . . adults!"

Toothpick walked around the crowd of grown-ups curiously, but no one seemed to notice him or care. At one point Toothpick waved his hand up and down in front of several of their faces, but there was still no response. "They don't see me," he concluded. "They only see each other."

"Look, there's more of them," JP said. They pointed to a restaurant inside, where more adults were seated at tables and the counter. A woman's voice floated up from the din of other customers. "Now that they're gone, I see how empty it all is," she said, sighing. She was tall with broad shoulders and brown hair that looked like it had outgrown a perm. "I want her back. It's not right. A world without kids."

Aurora was watching the scene, speechless. Then she seemed to she find her words.

"Guys," she whispered. "That's my mom. She's over there!"

She ran over to the woman at the counter. "Mom," she said. "Mom!"

But the woman didn't seem to hear Aurora.

JP leaned over to Toothpick. "What's going on? Is that really Aurora's mom?"

He was frowning. "I'm not sure. In one of his podcasts, Oliver Pruitt says we are surrounded by alternate dimensions. That's what he discovered in the Needle. Another dimension. Most of the time, though, we can't see them without help."

"Is *that* what we're seeing?" JP wondered. "The adults in an alternate dimension? 'Cause we're in the Space Needle?"

"I believe so," said Toothpick.

Behind them, Aurora was talking animatedly to the woman next to her.

"Every night before I go to bed," Aurora cried, "you need to be there. You need to lock the doors. You need to shut off the lights. You need to say good night. That's what parents do."

Aurora's voice was so loud, it drew JP and Toothpick's attention away momentarily.

Tears streamed down the woman's cheeks. "I don't know why I'm crying," Aurora's mom said to the cashier. "When it's just you and me here, right?"

"And your daughter!" shouted Aurora.

"OK, *that's* super weird," JP said. "But back to our own odd discussion. Pick, do you think we found the missing adults at the top of the Seattle Space Needle?"

"*Some* of them," Toothpick said. "There are fewer than fifty people here."

"Then where are the rest of them?" JP asked. "Where's your parents, Pick? Where's mine? Someone has got to tell me answers. I can't take it anymore."

Just then the elevator doors inexplicably opened, and Cupcake, who had been standing nearby, lumbered inside. She grunted insistently at them.

"Look, the elevators are working!" JP cried. "And Cupcake went inside!"

"I think she wants us to follow her," Toothpick said. He stepped inside the compartment and JP joined him.

"But—but . . ." said JP helplessly. "We can't leave Aurora. Aurora!"

Aurora didn't look up. She was too busy talking to her mom. "It feels sooo good to get this off my chest! Now you're going to hear about my birthday parties you missed!"

"This is our only way to get to Mars and call off the attack on the Colony," Toothpick said. "Aurora will understand. Hopefully."

"You're right," JP said. "I'm sorry, Aurora!"

Then the elevator doors closed.

41
ARE WE REALLY HERE?

■■■■■ hroughout the evening and night, Axel had explained
to Mars, there had been a caravan of space buggies
and hovercrafts traveling to Cloud Forest. The last
buggy, which had stayed back to wait for Mars, reached the
forest early the next morning, when the sun was rising over the
Martian landscape. Inside, Axel was in front, driving steadily,
while most of the passengers were asleep, including HELGA,
who had been switched to sleep mode. Mars and Caddie,
however, were seated in the back, wide awake. They had been
talking the entire trip.

"The important thing is to figure out what the reset is," Mars
said. "And stop it from happening. It's the only way to save the
adults."

"Did your dad or Tartuffe give you any clue?" Caddie asked.

"All I know is that it has to do with the power outage on
Earth," Mars said. "When the power comes back on, the adult

dimension goes away forever." He shook his head. "I still can't believe we thought the tardigrades were our creations when *they* were the ones in charge."

"It shows what happens when we don't have all the pieces of the puzzle," Caddie said. "But now I understand that the tardigrades were looking out for the greater good."

"By banishing the adults to another dimension and destroying the Colony?" Mars asked. "You're sounding like my dad."

Caddie was silent for a moment. "Well, I don't agree with their methods, and we do need to get the adults back. But yes. It can see saw how *they* thought it was the only way to stop technology from going too far again." She glanced at Mars. "And he wouldn't have come with us. You can't blame yourself. I know what you're thinking."

Mars stirred. "I don't want to talk about it." He couldn't get the image out of his mind of the Colony walls toppling down as he drove away in the space buggy, knowing his father was still inside. Had he survived? And if he had, where would Oliver Pruitt go? He had been wearing his space suit, but if all the space buggies and hovercrafts had been used for evacuation, what was left for him? There were no shuttles either. Caddie had told Mars there was only one spacecraft in production in the tech hub, and it was months away from completion. Now the tech hub was destroyed, along with the Colony. Mars and Caddie had evacuated, but Oliver Pruitt had remained.

"We're here," Axel announced over the intercom as they pulled into a clearing. "There's Julia approaching us." As he eased the space buggy to a stop, the kids inside started to stir.

"Can we really go outside without our helmets?" asked a girl named Susie.

"Are you sure there aren't tardigrades here?" another child named Lindsee asked worriedly.

The hatch to the space buggy lifted, and Julia peered inside. "Rise and shine, colonists!" she called out. Her brown curls were pinned back with bright yellow clips that had streamers of the same color on the ends. "Welcome to Cloud Forest. We have bread with toasted acorns and fresh berries for breakfast."

"Wow! Yum!" Several of the children scrambled forward.

"And as you can see, no space helmets required here!" Julia patted her hair. "And no comments about the barrettes, please. It was Daisy's doing, not mine." She looked farther into the compartment. "Mars, Caddie! Great to see you! Hurry out; Daisy and I have lots of updates for you. Please activate HELGA—we need them to do some heavy lifting. Orion is trying to build a hut out of a tarp and tree branches."

After everyone was out of the space buggy, including HELGA, who was restored from sleep mode, Mars and Caddie got caught up on the details. So far, all 420 colonists had evacuated safely to Cloud Forest. The kids were alert and healthy. Some of them were sleeping on makeshift mats, but most were walking around the area in giddy amazement.

"They're still afflicted by the ordeal of the evacuation," Julia said. "Some of them are having nightmares about the tardigrades. But most of them are really, really happy to be here in the fresh air. It's done wonders for their spirits."

"That's so terrific," Caddie said. "And how is the supplies situation?"

"Not so good," Daisy said. "We have enough food and water for twenty-four hours, but after that, we'll run out. There are only so many berries we can forage. I'm going to go check on Axel. He was in the middle of pounding the acorns into flour."

After Daisy left, Mars watched as kids ran around giggling and playing a game of tag.

"They *are* really happy," he said. "I never saw them like this at the Colony."

"Neither did I," said Caddie. "And things were going really great. Right, Julia?"

"The best," Julia said. "The greenhouse, the evening concerts and talent shows, the tech hub, and polo games. But, um, we know how that turned out."

"I think the colonists have to go home," Mars said simply. "It's time."

Behind them, the Martian Space Needle loomed in the background.

"What if we could send them back the same way I came?" Mars asked.

Julia shook her head. "We had the same idea. We went

up the elevator, but nothing. It's like the portal doesn't work without—"

"JP and Toothpick!" Mars said.

"They activated the portal for you?" Julia asked.

"No, they're here!" Mars pointed to the elevator doors at the base of the Needle, which had just opened. "And Cupcake, too!"

"Cupcake?" Caddie asked.

"The baby tardigrade. She snuck onto the spaceship when we left Mars," Mars said. He began running toward them with Caddie and Julia following closely behind.

Suddenly there were shrieks.

"It's a tardigrade!"

"It's going to attack!"

"Run! Hide!"

Caddie immediately said, "Julia and I will calm the kids down. Mars, you go see JP, Pick, and um, Cupcake."

As Caddie spoke, Julia and Toothpick saw each other at the same time. "I'll be with you in a second, Tooth—I mean Randall—I mean Pick . . . erm . . ." Julia blushed as she darted away on her rover with Caddie.

Meanwhile, JP had reached Mars and gave him a hug. "It's so good to see you. But whoa, where are we?" They stopped at the sight of the vegetation surrounding them, and the bizarre images of kids in space suits and no helmets running in terror at the sight of them. "Pick, this must be another dimension!"

After seeing Julia, it seemed to take Toothpick a second to process what JP had said. He pushed up his glasses and looked around. "Actually, this must be the breathable air Julia was talking about," he said, as if it were the most normal thing one could find on Mars.

Meanwhile, Cupcake had knocked Mars down to the ground in her customary way, nudging his face and neck. "Cupcake, Cupcake, great to see you, girl!" Mars said to her.

But there were more shrieks, too.

"The tardigrade is attacking Mars!"

"It's eating him!"

Caddie and Julia apparently were not having much luck getting through to the colonists. Then came another sound, this time a piercing one, cutting through the air.

"Everyone, cool it!" Julia yelled, a bright yellow whistle in her hand.

There was an immediate silence.

Julia gave a look of satisfaction. "And I thought a whistle wouldn't come in handy on Mars. Listen, colonists, that's Cupcake, and apparently she loves Mars. She is NOT eating him. Everyone calm down and finish your berries. Everything is under control. We are NOT being attacked by tardigrades."

At this point, Toothpick made his way to her.

"Nice device," he said. "Very law and order."

"I know." She grinned.

Mars got up from the ground, brushing off twigs and leaves.

"Welcome to Cloud Forest," he said to Toothpick and JP. He thought of his mother growing all those species for the tardigrades over the years. "Courtesy of my mom."

⌒

Everyone spent the next few minutes catching one another up on what had happened since they'd last spoken. The only silent one was Cupcake. After her reunion with Mars, she had dragged herself to the side of the clearing and lay down. Now her eyes looked dull and listless, and she was breathing unevenly.

"Cuppy, are you OK? Speak to me!" JP said.

But Cupcake just closed her eyes and curled into a ball.

"Maybe taking us through the portal sapped her energy," Toothpick said.

"Let's feed her," JP said. "Anyone got food?"

"I'll get some berries and nut porridge," said Axel, who had joined them.

"Nut porridge?" JP asked. "I can't tell if I'm intrigued or nauseous."

Axel shrugged. "To be honest, it's only slightly better than mud."

"I'll help you, Axel," Orion offered. "Cupcake's a big girl. She'll need a lot of berries."

While they went off to get food for Cupcake, everyone else assembled at one of the makeshift tables Orion had set up.

"We have to figure out how to get the adults back to our

dimension," Mars said. "There must be a way. I was on Alt Earth, and I got back. The adults can, too."

"Also, we have to transport four hundred and twenty kids from here back to Earth," Julia said. "Toothpick and JP came through the portal. So did Mars. How did you all do it?"

"It was Cupcake," Toothpick said. "We followed her into the elevator."

"Same," Mars said. Then, "Hey, where's Aurora?"

"Before you start freaking out," JP said, "we had to leave her behind because she was talking to her mom, and Cupcake was in a hurry."

"Her mom?" Mars repeated. "You mean Aurora and her mom could see each other?"

"Not exactly," Toothpick said. "Aurora talked and her mom could hear in the background. Like in her consciousness." He described the scene at the top of the Needle.

"When that portal is activated," Mars said, "all kinds of things seem to happen. Like we can travel in space, or even between dimensions."

"I bet if the portal was activated, we could send all the kids home," Caddie said.

"I bet we could communicate with the adults, too," Mars said, "like Aurora did with her mom, and Caddie did with me."

Caddie nodded. "Droney helped transmit the message. But it did work."

"So we do same thing. We tell the adults to break away,"

Mars said. "Like what Caddie told me when I was on Alt Earth."

"Harnessing the power of suggestion," Toothpick said. "Like group meditation. Very cool."

"That *is* way cool," JP said. "But here's the thing. Aurora used a ton of energy to get through to her mom. I heard her yelling at the top of her lungs. And didn't Caddie lose all her energy trying to get through Mars? I guess my question is, are we enough?"

"But there's more of us, right?" Mars said. "We *all* send a message. There's you, me, Toothpick, JP, and Julia. That's five. Plus Orion and Axel."

"Actually, there's a lot more," Toothpick said. He pointed to the kids in the clearing, who had resumed their game of tag. "We have four hundred and twenty."

"Toothpick's right!" Julia said excitedly. "All four hundred and twenty of us go through the portal, and we use our collective minds to tell the parents to break away. Yes!"

"But we haven't solved the most important problem," Toothpick said. "How do we activate the portal?"

Everyone's gaze fell on Cupcake, who was still curled up with her eyes closed.

"Do you think she's OK?" whispered JP.

"I'm not sure," Mars said. "Look, there's Orion and Axel."

By now, Orion and Axel had returned with a bag of berries and nuts. They poured it on a plate and brought it to Cupcake, who had still not opened her eyes.

"Poor Cupcake," JP said. "She's been epic."

"She's still a baby, isn't she?" Caddie asked.

"I'm going to see how she is," Mars said, and ran over to her. "Cupcake?"

By now the tardigrade had woken up. When she saw the food on a plate next to her, she started eating ravenously. Mars sat down next to her and stroked her head as she ate. She grunted at Mars and continued eating. After several minutes, Cupcake let out a burp.

"Better?" Mars asked.

Cupcake nudged him with her snout.

Mars hugged her. "I'll take that as a yes. Can you help the colonists back to Earth now?"

Cupcake sat up, her ten eyes fixed on him, and shook her head. She seemed sad.

"How do we activate the Needle?" Mars asked. "Like you did when we were in Seattle."

Cupcake kept shaking her head.

"I guess you can't talk to us like Tartuffe," Mars said. "That's OK." He stroked her head. "I just wish there was someone who could tell me about the reset."

Cupcake trembled. Mars turned around as shrieks of terror resumed, and the colonists ran behind the Needle in panic. Out of the canopy of trees emerged Tartuffe and Emi. Following behind them was Oliver Pruitt.

"Oh crud," Mars said. "What now?" Even as he said it, though, he couldn't help marveling a little. How did his dad always manage to get right back up?

"Can't get rid of me so soon, my son," Oliver Pruitt called out to him.

Then Tartuffe spoke, his words hanging crisp in the Martian air.

IT IS TIME TO RESET

42

RESET

As Mars got up from the forest floor, Cupcake ran to the elevator and threw her body in front of the doors. Tartuffe stood in front of her.

GET UP LITTLE ONE

YOU CANNOT STOP THE RESET

"Can someone tell us once and for all, what is the reset?" Mars demanded.

Tartuffe looked at Oliver Pruitt, who was standing in the back of the clearing.

OLIVER PRUITT WILL EXPLAIN IN HUMAN WORDS

All eyes turned to him in shock.

"Tartuffe is speaking!" shouted someone.

"Was that him?" someone else asked. Murmuring went through the crowd.

"Wait, you mean our fate rests in Pruitt's hands?" JP said, clearly more dismayed by that possibility.

"Let's hear what he has to say," Caddie said. "Mr. Pruitt, what does the power outage have to do with the reset?"

Everyone continued murmuring.

"Yes! We want to know!" someone called out.

"Start talking, Pruitt!" JP growled.

Oliver Pruitt saw the tired and impatient faces looking at him. He sighed. "You know about the power outage on Earth? How the power has gone out everywhere? No lights, no electricity anywhere around the globe?"

"That's what it is?" JP asked. "That's the reset?"

"That's only part of the reset, JP," Oliver Pruitt said. "Right now, the system is shut off. When Tartuffe shuts down the portal, the system will reset."

"What does that mean?" Mars asked. "What about the kids on Earth?"

"Nothing," Oliver said. "They continue as they did before. They've got a fantastic start with all their inventions so far. And the US has got a healthy election with two candidates. Life goes on marvelously for the kids. And here, the portal closes forever, power is restored on Earth, and the tardigrades get on their spaceship."

"Spaceship?" Julia exclaimed.

"Well, of course. How did you think we got here?" Oliver asked. He gestured at the woods behind him. "Behind those trees is a massive state-of-the-art tardigrade spacecraft. Remember, the tardigrades are light-years ahead of us. So is their spaceship! Large enough to house all the tardigrades and myself. You and your friends are welcome to join us."

"All of us?" Mars asked. "All four hundred and twenty?"

"Oh, that's too many, I'm afraid," Oliver said. "Most of them would stay here. I guess there is enough oxygen for now."

"For now?" Mars clenched his hands into fists. "Our food is going to run out in twenty-four hours. So you know what? Your offer stinks. You're closing the portal with four hundred twenty kids still stranded here with almost no resources. You're leaving it all behind, for what? A reset of Earth?"

"Mars, please calm down and think it through," Oliver Pruitt pleaded. "I'm not offering this lightly. You have no idea what the tardigrades have designed. It would be space travel beyond your wildest dreams. Don't you want to see what's out there? Don't you want to see it with me? I promise you, it will change your life and everything you know to be true."

"What about the adults?" Mars pressed. "Why can't they come back?"

Oliver paused. "Because their dimension will disappear as soon as the power comes back on."

"What?" There were cries of distress from everyone. "No!"

"No reset!"

"Stop them! We're not afraid of you!"

A few colonists ventured out from the behind the Needle and lay down on the ground. Slowly, more and more kids came and lay down until there were hundreds of kids barricading the way to the elevators. One of them started to chant, "No reset! No reset!"

The others joined in. Pretty soon, their chanting reached a fever pitch.

"No reset! No reset!"

Meanwhile Tartuffe and Emi observed the protest with disbelief.

WE CANNOT LEAVE WITHOUT SHUTTING DOWN THE PORTAL

Tartuffe turned to Oliver Pruitt.

THEY ARE YOUR HUMANS STOP THEM

Oliver Pruitt looked back helplessly, equally stunned.

"I'm afraid I can't control so many of them," he said. "And Cupcake is on their side."

Next to the kids, Cupcake bellowed loudly.

"No Reset! No Reset!"

Caddie ran up to stand next to Mars. "But we have a plan, Mr. Pruitt. And if you listen to us, we can solve everyone's problems."

"Open the portal and let all of us kids go home," Mars said.

"As we go through the portal, we'll send a telepathic message to the adults to break away from their dimension," Toothpick said. "It worked with Mars and Caddie. It might work with the adults and us. Four hundred and twenty of us could generate enough energy to reach their dimension."

"But . . ." Oliver said, looking from one person to another.

"There's no guarantee. You might go through the portal and find no one there. We've never sent that many people from this direction. And you won't be able to come back after the reset. You could be stranded, Mars!"

Caddie and Mars looked at each other as Toothpick, JP, Julia, Axel, Daisy, and Orion stood together in a half circle around them.

"We want our parents back," Mars said. "And we want to go back home. Right, everyone?"

There was a loud cheer.

"We're behind you, Mars and Caddie!" yelled someone.

"Yeah!"

"We're ready."

"No reset, no reset!"

Tartuffe stood considering amid the deafening voices. Then he spoke to Emi, grunting until she nodded.

MARS VERY WELL

ASSEMBLE YOUR HUMANS IN THE NEEDLE

"Awesome! Thank you!" Mars was ecstatic.

"Hooray! Way to go, Mars and Caddie!" Daisy yelled out.

For the next several minutes, there was a flurry of activity as Daisy counted everyone off. "Form a line by age group," she directed. "When I call your name, say 'here.'" Within minutes, she had organized an orderly procession of colonists.

"You are going to the top of the Needle," Toothpick explained to everyone.

"Will we all fit at the tippy top?" Lindsee asked, worried. She craned her neck to peer up at the structure.

"Don't worry, with the observation deck and lobby, it's bigger than you think," Toothpick said. "Now remember, as soon as the colors start to change, think of the adults in your lives. Parents, family, teachers, friends. Think of them hard and tell them to break away. If we all do it at the same time when the colors start to change, it might just work. We can bring the adults back home."

"Break away!" someone yelled.

"Right," Toothpick said. "Just like that. But not yet. Wait for the colors."

There was a swell of whispering and wishing and hoping, and then the kids went up the Needle, twenty-five at a time. Up and down went the elevator. Julia and Caddie gathered samples from the forest floor, and Orion and Axel took photos of the space buggies and hovercrafts on their phones.

"We'll build again on Earth, right, Axel?" Orion said. "Better ways to travel."

"Totally," Axel said. "Hovercrafts for the win!"

JP hugged Cupcake. "I'll see you again, girl. One of these days."

When the last elevator ride was ready to go up the Needle, JP, Julia, Caddie, and Toothpick entered first. When Mars and HELGA followed them, Tartuffe spoke.

NO ROBOT

Mars started. "I don't understand. Why can't HELGA come with us?"

NO NONLIVING ENTITIES ALLOWED THROUGH PORTAL

THIS IS A SAFETY FEATURE

"To stop from unwanted technology making its way in either direction," Oliver said. "Only humans, animals, and plants, I'm afraid. Anything else will get automatically destroyed."

Mars looked at HELGA. "I—I don't know what to say," he said, feeling sick to his stomach. "I'm sorry, HELGA. I don't want to leave you here."

HELGA WILL COME WITH US

Mars felt a burning in his throat. "HELGA is special," he told Tartuffe. "I'm glad you're taking them, but they deserve to be treated equally."

YOU HAVE MY WORD

"No worries, Mars," HELGA said cheerfully, and embraced him. "I am an adaptive robot. I will adapt to tardigrade life in outer space. It will give me new opportunities to learn and thrive. What could be better than that? I will give your father company, too. He is lacking in friendship and social graces."

"What?" Oliver said. "Er . . . I'm an inventor. We need to be loners."

"My social-emotional modules tell me differently. You will

need to upgrade your attitudes, Mr. Pruitt." HELGA gave Mars their customary U smile. "Mars, I bid you a fond farewell. Ad astra!"

As soon as HELGA had finished, Cupcake crept up to Mars and knocked him down with her nudging.

Mars smiled and hugged her. "Bye, Cuppy! I'm going to miss you so much." How would he ever manage not having her around? "Keep an eye on everyone, OK?" he added.

Cupcake nudged him as if to agree, and then darted behind the other tardigrades. To Mars's surprise, he saw that one of them was Muffin. Had she and the other tardigrades managed to swim over from Gale Island and pass through the portal, too? Muffin let out a bellow as if to say yes.

Meanwhile Tartuffe stepped forward.

IT IS TIME MARS

Mars walked inside the elevator and turned around to see Oliver Pruitt waving to him. In the morning light, the Martian sun seemed to make Oliver's red-and-gold space suit glow, as if he were surrounded by a halo. With his helmet off, he looked as handsome as ever, his hair swept back like a celebrity.

"You could come with us," Mars said suddenly. "You don't have to go with the tardigrades."

"And miss the adventure of a lifetime?" Oliver said lightly. Only careful listening revealed a shakiness in his voice as he spoke. "No, son, you go on. Go home to your mom. She deserves that. Break away, all of you. Break away!"

"Bye, Dad," Mars said. He felt his throat tighten. Could he run out and grab him? Pull him inside the elevator? They could be a family. They could have photographs on the mantel. Was there time to change his father's mind?

BE THE LIGHT MARS PATEL

The doors closed.

"Mars," Caddie whispered, squeezing his hand as the elevator began to rise.

"We're gonna do this, OK?" JP said.

"The power of suggestion," Toothpick said.

"And hoping for the best," Julia said.

"I love you guys," Mars said, trying not to weep. "I'll see you on the other side."

"The walls are changing!" Caddie said. "It's happening!"

The colors of the elevator began swirling into pinks, reds, and purples.

Everyone shouted in unison. The light was tremendous, everywhere, inside and outside. "Break away, break away, break away . . ."

Mars held Caddie's hand tightly as he closed his eyes and thought of his mom.

43
BE THE CHANGE

Mars opened his eyes to bright, fluorescent overhead lights and the sound of a bell ringing. He was standing in the hallway of H. G. Wells Middle School. The bell continued to ring, along with the familiar sound of lockers opening and banging shut, and kids everywhere, shouting and laughing, while down the hall, Ms. DeTemple, the English teacher, was talking to a student. It was all unbelievably back—students, teachers, lights, life.

"Yo, Earth to Mars," said a voice. It was Jonas, standing next to him. They were in front of their lockers. "Five days, I know, I know. You don't have to keep telling me."

"Five days?" Mars repeated.

"That's what you just said," Jonas said. "Until you went into that trance just now. But I know. I get it. Five days."

Mars felt a sudden, sickening dread that he had been wrong,

that he had not returned to normal life as he'd expected, but was stuck in some infinite time loop.

"Jonas, five days again?" he asked in despair. "*Now* who's missing?"

Jonas stared at him. "Huh? Nobody's missing. Five days until school gets out. Yesterday was six. Tomorrow's four. You're the one who's been counting down. Well, you and Aurora."

"Five days!" Aurora called out, walking up to them. "Then sixth grade is officially over!" She was wearing a slate-blue romper and Doc Martens, and her hair was up in a ponytail. A hairstyle first for Aurora. But there had been so many firsts for her that it was hard to keep track.

It took Mars a moment to register what Aurora had just said.

"Sixth grade?" he repeated. "But we were in seventh grade. And the kids were . . ."

"Seventh grade? That must have been some dream you had this morning," Aurora said, grinning. "In five days, school is done, then my mom and me are flying to Alaska. We're back-packing in Denali and visiting a hot spring. It's going to be epic!"

"Your mom? Isn't she . . . not home?" Mars asked.

"Of course she's not home," Aurora said. "She's in the office. We came to school together. She's getting ready for first-period announcements. But you know that already." She smiled. "I'm glad she decided to work here. At first I thought it would be weird having my mom as the school secretary, but I like seeing her around. And I always have a ride to school and back, and we have vacations at the same time."

"But . . ." Mars thought hard. "You both don't remember, do you?" he asked slowly. "The Space Needle? The power outage? Oliver Pruitt? The Colony?"

Jonas and Aurora looked at each other.

"Is this that podcast again, Mars?" Jonas asked. "What tale is Oliver Pruitt spinning now?"

"Come on, Mars," Aurora said. "We'll be late for English. See you in enrichment, Jonas. Mr. Q is back from his trip to the Galápagos. He has videos to share."

"Awesome. Catch you later, AG," Jonas said easily. "You, too, Mars. Whoops. Better take my pill. I almost forgot."

"Yeah, I know," Mars said. "Or it will be a Code Brown . . ." He stopped, bracing himself for the Code Red alarm that would tear through the school any moment.

But there was none. Only Jonas looking at him strangely. "You've got some weird humor, Mars." Then he gave him a friendly punch on the shoulder and sauntered off.

Just then, another figure bulldozed his way through, throwing Mars off balance. It was the Boof, sporting an enormous backpack. Mars opened his mouth, wondering if he should say what he'd always said.

But then the Boof turned around. He was wearing

tortoise-framed glasses. "Sorry, Mars," he called out. "Didn't mean to bump you." Then he continued down the hallway.

Surprised, Mars closed his mouth. In a daze, he followed Aurora to Ms. DeTemple's class. While they walked, Aurora chattered about the trip to Denali, the supplies they would need, how her mom wanted to do everything outdoors, with tents and backpacks. The whole time, Aurora's face was awash with happiness. Meanwhile, Mars found himself suspended between doubt and suspicion, wondering what could be waiting for him around the corner. Charging tardigrades? Mr. Q presiding over endless detention? His father in a space suit?

As they reached the door to English, Mars felt a buzz in his pocket. His phone! He pulled it out and saw a text flash on his screen.

JP

If u get this and u remember
come to the janitor closet asap

Mars felt a bolt of energy as the world came back to focus. "Um, Aurora, I'll be right back," he said. "You go in and sit down."

Aurora blinked. "OK, but hurry up. First period is starting soon."

Mars took the stairs two at a time and was at the janitor closet in seconds. He opened the closet and saw JP, Toothpick, and Caddie huddled inside. JP pulled Mars in and shut the door.

"Mars!" JP said. "Glad you're here!"

They made room for him next to the mops.

"*You* all remember, right?" Mars asked cautiously.

"Heck, yeah," JP said. "But as you noticed, no else does."

"None of the kids remember, none of the teachers," Caddie said. "My mom was on the way to a dental appointment when I called her."

"My mom wanted to know why I was calling her when I should be in class," Toothpick said.

"Mine, too," JP said. "My mom even mentioned last night's dinner when I called. Which sounded amazing to me. I love lasagna. Glad there's leftovers."

Mars listened to everyone and wished he'd had a chance to call his mom, too. It was all happening so fast. "Aurora and Jonas don't remember, and they were with us," he said.

"Why do you think we remember," JP asked, "when no one else does?"

Toothpick was scrolling through messages on his phone. "We're not the only ones. I just got a text from Julia."

When he said that, everyone pulled out their phones. The darkness of the closet was soon illuminated by their screens.

"I got a text from Daisy!" Caddie said.

"Axel and Orion, too!" Mars said. "A whole bunch of others."

"It's all the kids from the Colony!" Caddie said. "This is

a group text from Susie: 'Why does no one remember what happened?'"

Just then Mars got a video conferencing request from Julia. He accepted and was instantly connected to her along with Daisy, Axel, and Orion, so they were all on Mars's screen. He held up his phone for everyone in the closet to see.

"We're all back, but Earth is different," Julia said.

"Plus, we've gone back in time," Orion said. "It's May, and school is almost over. Except I fell back a grade."

"No," Toothpick said. "If I'm correct, we've returned to Day Zero. When the adults first went away. Which means we went back to sixth grade, but later in the year. It must be the effect of the portal."

"Also, maybe only the people who went through it remember," Julia said. "That would explain all the colonists remembering, but not anyone here."

"Or Aurora and Jonas," Mars said. "They stayed on the Earth side."

"When we went through," Toothpick said, "the portal must have merged the dimensions together with the kids and adults, and reset the clock. Literally."

"But that means we're back to the same problems, too," JP said. "The same rain, floods, and forest fires are heading our way. And the adults are gonna make the same awful mistakes. Earth is going to be unstable and who knows what will happen to us."

A somber silence struck the video call. For a few moments no one spoke.

On the screen Mars saw a text flash from his mom.

Ma

My 4pm class got canceled
Be home right after enrichment
I'll be back to make your favorite dinner

Mars took a moment to parse the words. His mom was teaching? And would be home to cook dinner? He thought of Aurora's happiness when she was talking about her mom working at H. G. Wells.

"No," Mars said to everyone. "It's *not* all the same. There are differences. Good differences. I think my mom is a professor. Aurora's mom is taking her on a vacation. We're in enrichment. Our lives are better."

"Mars is right," Caddie said. "If I was still going to boarding school, my mom and I would be picking out sheets or something. Instead, my parents said we're hiking this weekend."

"We're visiting the Space Needle," JP said.

"And it's not only that," Mars said. "*We're* different. We know a lot. So do the colonists. And Daisy and Caddie. You guys rebuilt a colony! With Julia, Orion, and Axel."

"We know sooo much," Daisy said. "Oodles!"

"I can build a tech hub with my eyes closed," said Orion.

"I can pilot a small aircraft," Axel said.

"I know all about the Northwest power grid," Toothpick said, "and solar energy."

"And I have a *lot* to share on the direction of AI," Julia said.

"I can run a free health clinic," JP said. "I can even do stitches."

"Don't you see?" Mars said. "We can infiltrate. We can enact change. Through research, social activism, and talking to our teachers, families, and communities. We can teach other kids, too. Who knows, maybe we can even start a new school. Better than Pruitt Prep!"

"Actually, there's no Pruitt Prep," Toothpick said. "I checked. Gale Island is now a wildlife sanctuary."

"See?" Mars said. "We'll change it up even more."

"Gandhi said, 'We need not wait to see what others do,'" Toothpick said. "In other words, we can be the change we want to see in the world."

"That's right, Pick," Mars said. "*We'll* be the change."

"We'll be the change!" Caddie agreed.

"We'll be the change!" said Orion and Axel at the same time.

"Brilliant!" Julia cried. "Let's organize. Daisy, can you send out a blast to the colonists?"

"Absolutely!" Daisy said. "We'll organize by age groups and assign tasks to everyone!"

"Hooray!" Caddie said. "We're going to spread new ideas. It's going to be better this time!"

"Let's hug it out, y'all," JP said.

"Virtual hugs for everyone!" Julia said.

When Mars, Caddie, JP, and Toothpick came out of the closet a few minutes later, they smiled at each other, buoyed by a sense of hopefulness.

"See you in detention!" JP called out.

"That would be enrichment," Toothpick corrected. "Check your schedule, JP."

"Score!" JP said as they walked down the sixth-grade hall. "I just hope they've upgraded the school lunch."

Mars and Caddie lingered a moment longer in front of the janitor closet. It seemed like so much had happened since the first Code Red rang through the halls. They had gone on a journey through time and space, and returned. Dimensions might shift and change, merge or pull apart. But Mars's friends had held him together, and when he'd traveled through the portal, he'd arrived with his mind and heart still intact. But did Caddie feel the same?

"Everyone's happier, and my mom's home. Did it all work out for you, too, Caddie?"

She smiled. "I think it's nice to have our life in front of us. To feel like we're in it again."

"Yeah," Mars said. He found he didn't have to say the rest of what he was thinking because in the quiet that followed, Caddie said, "You're right, Mars. It *is* all good."

The Inspirational Appearances of Mars Patel and His Friends

Port Elizabeth, WA—Sixth grader Mars Patel gave an impassioned speech in front of a packed arena on the importance of going green, as a part of the Rally For Positive Climate Change that he and several H. G. Wells Middle School students organized for the weekend.

"We can have clean air, clean water, and clean technology for generations," Mars told a cheering crowd as a part of his keynote speech, "but we have to work together. And we have to say NO to the adults when they try to screw things up!"

"We have to say NO to fossil fuels," Caddie Patchett said, "and YES to hiking with our families."

"We have to say NO to landfills," JP McGowan said, "and YES to real grass on the soccer fields! And organic meats and vegetables, people! Let's make a smaller carbon footprint and yummy home-cooked food!"

Student-body President Randall "Toothpick" Lee outlined a ten-step plan for expanded windmill and solar power, and met with local congresspeople after mounting pressure from students of all ages across Puget Sound, who are adamant that the time for change is NOW.

"I've never seen anything like it," commented honor society member Epica Hernandez. "I mean, I had my doubts about Mars Patel, but he's right, and in the end we all agree with him. It's time to listen to the kids. Make space for us. Because we have good ideas!"

Similar rallies are scheduled to take place across the world in key cities. Later this month, Mars, Caddie, JP, and Randall will be traveling to the White House for a special briefing with the president.

"If we start at the top," Mars said, "then we can only go higher."

For the young and old residents of Port Elizabeth, Mars and his friends are not only inspiring, but are showing us that change can happen, one rally at a time! ∎

Hello, podcast listeners! Joining me is my new cohost!
HELGA, please say hi to our listeners.

HELGA: Hello. I am a repurposed traveling robot,
here to make your podcast adventures more meaningful.

Oliver Pruitt: What's your favorite thing about space travel?

HELGA: I do not have favorites.

Oliver Pruitt: Er . . . pick one anyway. Our listeners would
like to know.

HELGA: OK, the view from the window. The same constant
void of darkness. Very pleasant. And you?

Oliver Pruitt: I love the speed, the thrill, the feel of
weightlessness, like you don't have a care in the world.

HELGA: Even so, you must care about your son.

Oliver Pruitt: Why, yes.

HELGA: That must explain why sometimes you are heard muttering to yourself, "Did I make the right choice?"

Oliver Pruitt: Yes, well . . . <cough> Space travel is the best.

HELGA: So true. And so are people. Including you.

Oliver Pruitt: Let's say it together, HELGA.

Oliver Pruitt and HELGA: To the stars!

300 Comments ⊗

staryoda   22 min ago
HELGA sounds cool

allie_j   20 min ago
just where are u guys u never say

JPplaysoccer   16 min ago
HELGA stay real! And watch ur back lol

lostinlondon   15 min ago
Now i've seen everything! Hurray for the dynamic duo!

axelizer   15 min ago
stay real HELGA OP is a bag of trix

caddiepatchett   11 min ago
so happy for u2!!

orion-awesome   10 min ago
peace out dynamic duo

toothpix   9 min ago
3 cheers for dynamic duo

daisy_does_good_deeds 8 min ago
awesome!!

thisismars   7 min ago
<3 u guys

HELGA_adaptive   1 min ago
I appreciate your support!

The universe is adaptive

So is love always

ACKNOWLEDGMENTS

It's been an amazing journey! Sometimes I think I might know Mars (the person and the planet) better than I know myself. Just kidding! There is still so much we don't know about the planets in our galaxy, including our own. It starts with our own personal responsibility to learn and respect one another. Writing the Mars Patel series has taught me to think about my own connections to others, to the spaces where I live, and what I can do to make our lives better.

I continue to be grateful to Benjamin Strouse, Chris Tarry, David Kreizman, and Jenny Turner Hall, who first conceived of these wonderful characters and their journey through time and space. Thank you to my team at Walker Books US: Susan Van Metre, Lindsay Warren, Maria Middleton, Phoebe Kosman, Anne Irza-Leggat, and the rest of the crew for lovingly supporting this project. Thank you so much to Marietta Zacker and Steven Malk for continuing to be formidable agents in my universe. And I will never get tired of looking at the gorgeous cover art that graces all the books thanks to Yuta Onoda. And finally, love always to my family! Thank you, Suresh, Keerthana, and Meera!

ABOUT THE AUTHOR

SHEELA CHARI is the author of *Finding Mighty*, a Junior Library Guild Selection and Children's Book Council Children's Choice Finalist, and *Vanished*, an APALA Children's Literature Award Honor Book, an Edgar Award nominee for best juvenile mystery, and a *Today* Book Club Selection. She has an MFA from New York University and teaches fiction writing at Mercy College. Sheela Chari lives with her family in New York.